Empty ME OUT

THE LIQUID SERIES - BOOK 1

S A HEALEY

EMPTY ME OUT

DEDICATION

This book is dedicated to my dear readers. A million thank-yous will never be enough to express my love and gratitude. You are the fuel to my passion.

ONE

MOST OF MY FRIENDS lived away at college, but not me. I'd heard all the stories of wild campus parties and dorms with co-ed showers. I knew I was in the minority, but that kind of college experience never appealed to me. How anyone managed to concentrate on their studies in that kind of environment, I'd never know. Yup, for me, the decision to commute to school these past few years while enjoying the benefits and comforts of living at home in Quincy, Massachusetts, was a-no brainer.

"Ughhh!" Bent over the bathroom sink—its edges lined with every styling product known to man—I cursed the mirrored medicine cabinet in an act of reflection rebellion. "Oh, come on. *Do* something!" I barked at my barely-there curls, extracting the last of the hot rollers failing to live up to their advertised promise of "flounce, bounce, and spring." After a last-ditch, upside-down do-flip and a generous dousing of hair-spray, I turned out the light and headed for the stairs. I wasn't about to let my limp locks flatten my spirits.

For the past several weeks, I'd been relishing the time catching up with my friends, most of whom I hadn't seen since the start of the fall semester. They were home from their respective college campuses, celebrating the winter holiday break and their temporary hiatus from lectures, homework, and exams. My best friend Calista and I had practically been joined at the hip, fitting in as much girl time as possible before she resumed dorm life out in the western part of the state.

"Hey, Kelsey, you gonna be ready anytime this century? I'd like to get there before we lose our reservation." Calista checked herself out in my front hall mirror, applying another coat of cherry-red lipstick while waiting for me to finish putting myself together upstairs. She and I had been inseparable since grade school. Through all of life's ups, downs, twists, and turns, we'd always gone through it together. She was the kind of friend every girl would be lucky to have, and I loved her to bits.

With a hopeful fluff of my one remaining curl, I leaned against the top banister, chuckling as I watched my friend twist from side to side in obvious admiration of her own reflection. "I'm coming, I'm coming. Keep your shirt on, okay?" Slowly, I made my way down the stairs, careful not to take a header in my new, too-high-to-be-functional, black platform heels. I was clearly not in my right mind when I bought the damned things.

"Wow, Kels! You are rocking those heels, hon. I told you they would accentuate those sexy long stems of yours!"

Grabbing me by the arm as I descended the last stair, she pulled me toward the front door. "Let's *go* already! We're gonna be late!"

"Hold it! Let me get my bearings. I feel like I'm just learning how to walk for the first time." I held my arms out to my sides to keep my balance in check. "Why in the world did I let you talk me into buying these…these…*stilts?*"

"Because you asked me to help you sex up your look, remember? You said you were tired of being single, right? So, let's get out there and watch the guys take notice!" Calista scanned me up and down approvingly. "You look gorgeous, by the way. You clean up well, girlfriend." I rolled my eyes in dramatic fashion, while secretly loving the compliment. I was never one to put much thought into my look. I'd had the same shoulder-length, straight brown hair since high school and rarely wore any makeup. I also normally dressed for comfort over style, sporting jeans, sweats, and T-shirts. But, after a year-long dry spell in the boyfriend department, I thought it was high-time to put some effort into my appearance. I figured it couldn't hurt, and Calista was more than happy to take on the challenge as my fashion and makeover consultant.

Stepping out the door and into the cold night air, a chill went straight through me, instantly making me regret my decision to wear a flimsy dress, and long for my sweats and UGGs. Suddenly recalling how icy the New England sidewalks often got in January, I began mumbling under my breath about the likelihood of my impractical footwear causing me to break my neck before the night was over. Calista pretended to ignore my quiet ranting, but as I snuck her a sideways glance, I could see the irritation on her face. I had to remind myself that we were out to have a night on the town—that it was supposed to be *fun*. My mood perked back up when I remembered where we were headed: to the latest restaurant hot spot in Boston's Back Bay. My mouth watered as I began to fantasize about the lobster pot pie I would soon devour.

A short time later, we arrived by cab, not wanting to deal with navigating the confusing one-way and often construction-laden streets with our own cars. As I exited the vehicle, my feet practically slipped out from under me, and I swiftly grabbed onto the door to keep from planting my fanny on the sidewalk. No one ever accused me of being graceful.

Calista exited without incident, no doubt, from her years of heel-wearing expertise. Joining me on the sidewalk, she hooked her arm through mine, knowing she'd probably have to help keep me vertical all night. With her laughing blue eyes, she chuckled at my clumsiness, shaking her head of long, wavy blond hair. I couldn't help but let out a giggle.

Entering the restaurant, we decided to grab a drink while waiting for our table, and we lucked into two empty bar stools side by side. Depositing ourselves there, we each ordered a glass of wine, flashing our IDs while the bartender poured merlot into crystal-stemmed glasses. Calista and I both turned 21 earlier this year, and it felt good to enjoy an adult beverage in an atmosphere devoid of sticky floors and beer bongs. With drinks in hand, we clinked our glasses in a toast to "girl power" and engaged in easy conversation.

As we savored our wine, laughing and reminiscing over our summer in Martha's Vineyard, our girl-bonding bubble broke with a ruckus from behind us. We turned to see a small, round table littered with beer bottles and shot glasses, surrounded by five rude, obnoxious guys hootin' and hollerin' and swearing like truck drivers. The other nearby patrons shot them disapproving looks, but I felt embarrassed for them, really.

Far as I could tell, the guys were all pretty lit, but one was clearly drunker than the rest as his hyena-like laugh and disheveled appearance indicated. Still, I couldn't help but notice how good-looking he was. Observing me gawking at him and his group of Neanderthals, he gave me a large, goofy smile.

"Seriously, could those dudes be any more annoying? How long do you think it'll take before they get thrown outta here?" Calista pondered.

"Hopefully sooner than later. I can't imagine a nice place like this putting up with that kind of crap," I said, trying to keep my eyes off the group and their shenanigans, but it was like rubbernecking a crash site—I couldn't help but watch. The *super* drunk guy was reaching for his beer while staring in my direction, proceeding to knock his bottle over and earning a few choice expletives from his newly soaked drinking compadres. He just continued to look at me, completely oblivious to his pissed off pals—that damned smile still plastered to his face.

Finally turning back toward the bar, I took another sip of my wine with a silent prayer for our table to be ready so we could get away from the train-wreck-in-progress. Apparently, my prayers wouldn't be answered anytime soon. With a tap on the shoulder, Calista leaned in and whispered, "Looks like you've got an admirer...and he's coming this way." Oh-oh.

I reluctantly turned around again and there he was, standing a little too close for comfort. "Hiiii there. Saw you checkin' me out. Name's Mark." Swaying a little on his feet, he stuck his hand out and waited for me to shake it, that goofball smile still in place.

Wow. This guy was full of himself. "I absolutely was not checking you out. Just simply noticing your state of drunkenness. Such a charming quality," I said with as much sarcasm as I could muster. Refusing to shake his hand, I left it hanging in midair.

He cackled loudly in my face, and his breath practically knocked me over. "Good God, could you go brush your teeth or something? You smell like a brewery," I spat.

"What? You got somethin' against *beeya?*" he slurred, seriously lacking in conversation skills. As he watched me with glassy eyes, I could see him struggling to stay focused.

"No, I don't have a problem with *beer.* But you might want to leave some of it for the other customers." I couldn't hold back my continued sarcasm.

Mark laughed again, and despite the eye-watering effect of his booze breath, I noticed he had beautiful teeth—a gorgeous set of straight, white choppers. "Heeey, you're fuckin funneeee," he said, taking me in from head to toe. "And sexy as hell toooo." Now feeling extremely self-conscious in my little black dress, I suddenly wished I could throw on a big, baggy sweatshirt.

"Alright, cool it, Lover Boy. Leave my friend in peace and let her enjoy her drink, okay?"

At those words, Mark abruptly turned toward Calista—as if he hadn't even noticed her until now. "Ooh heeey there." He stuck out his hand, the one I refused to shake just a moment ago. "I'm Mark."

After a brief hesitation, Calista relented, extending her hand to quickly give his a shake. "Hey, Mark. I'm Calista. Listen, we're trying to have a girls' night, so if you wouldn't mind leaving us to it—"

"—Soooo *Carla*, what's your friend's name?" Mark interrupted, turning to gesture in my general direction, limply flailing his right hand and stumbling slightly. The movement caused his longish black hair to fall forward, covering one of his light brown eyes. He lazily raked his hand through it, moving it off his face while giving him the appearance of having just rolled out of bed.

He was a hot mess.

"Uh, listen pal, you can't even get *my* name right, so why should I tell you hers? Not to mention, my friend is *not* into guys with drinking problems." Glancing down at her watch, Calista took longer than necessary to check the time, dropping a big, obvious hint that she wanted Mark to get lost.

He didn't.

"Heeey...I don't have a problem. Just havin' fun...knockin' back a few with the guys." He motioned toward me again with a floppy hand. "This chick was checkin' me out and..." Pausing in a lost train of thought, his expression morphed into one of deep concentration as he reached for the rest of his words. "I-I-I'd like to take her back to my place later for a nightcappp." He overemphasized the "p" in *nightcap*, resulting in a bit of spittle dribbling down his chin.

How lovely.

Somehow, I miraculously resisted the urge to throw my glass of wine in his face. "Did you just say *nightcap?* Who the hell says that—what are you, sixty?" The way he continued to ogle me made me uncomfortable, so I threw him a stern look. "I'm afraid I'll have to pass on your offer because you are clearly wasted and talking out of your ass. But don't worry, tomorrow you won't even remember me or this conversation."

"Ooohh, I'll remember you, babeeee. Never forget someone with a bod like that." And with a maneuver that was likely intended to be suave, he casually crossed one leg over the other while leaning onto the bar with his elbow, misjudging it entirely and instead, plowing right into me, nearly knocking me off my bar stool. My wine glass tipped into my chest, spilling its dark red contents down the front of my dress.

So far, I was having myself an *epic* night.

Suddenly, I felt Mark's body like dead weight on mine, his paws unintentionally groping me in places normally reserved for the bedroom as he sloppily tried to right himself back up. By the time he stood up straight on his own two feet, I had to readjust my dress into place, which was no easy feat considering how wet and sticky it was.

Distracted by my movements, Mark muttered, "You're sexy as hell."

"I think you covered that already, Casanova," Calista retorted on my behalf, frustration at the evening's turn of events apparent in her voice.

One of Mark's Neanderthal companions from the drinking circle made his way over in an obvious attempt to rescue his pathetic friend. "Mark, buddy, I think you've had enough, huh? Why don't we get outta here and let these lovely ladies enjoy their evening."

Upon closer inspection, this guy actually appeared sober, unlike the others. Perhaps he was the designated driver? Looking over at Calista and me, he shook his head apologetically. "Sorry about my friend. He had a few too many, but he's really not a bad guy. We're going to head out now so he doesn't bother you two anymore."

Sighing in relief, I smiled at him, grateful for being rescued. "Thanks for saving us, uh...I'm sorry, I don't know your name." When he offered *his* hand, I didn't hesitate to shake it.

"Brett Jones. No problem—happy to help out a couple of gorgeous ladies." With that, he winked specifically at Calista, causing her cheeks to flush.

Surprisingly quiet during my and Brett's exchange, I noticed Mark was looking a little green. "You okay?" I asked, because I wasn't completely heartless.

"Yeah...just a little dizzy. I'm fine." He sounded unconvincing.

"Want a glass of water or something?" When I turned to get the bartender's attention, Mark stopped me with a clammy hand on my shoulder.

"Nah…I'm good. Gonna go outside and get some air." His greenish hue now replaced with a pale gray look of death, he stood with one hand on the bar to hold himself up. His eyes closed for a moment—then suddenly flew back open, darting around the bar frantically, seeking out the nearest exit sign. When they landed on their target, Mark rushed through the bar—losing equilibrium and knocking into several tables along his flight path, until finally, he was gone.

"Well, I better go make sure he's alright," Brett said with some reluctance, his eyes still fixed on Calista. "Nice meeting you both." Waving a casual farewell, he turned on his heel and strode through the bar after Mark. The remaining three from the booze brigade quickly followed suit, making cat calls and whistling at us as they departed. *Classy.*

"Oh. My. God. Brett is so yummy!" Calista proclaimed, her gaze lingering on the exit long after Brett left. I couldn't argue with her; Brett certainly was a good-looking guy, with his sandy blond hair, crystal blue eyes and athletic build. And I could tell the attraction was mutual for him, the way he'd looked at Calista as though she were the only woman he'd ever laid eyes on. I, myself, preferred tall, dark, and lean. It did not go unnoticed by me that Mark happened to possess those physical traits. Too bad he was such a tool. My thoughts drifted to how sickly he looked when he left the bar, and I wondered if he was okay.

Snapping myself out of Mark la-la land, I turned to Calista. "Brett's a cutie, and I think he likes you, Cali," I said with a raise of the eyebrows. "He was checking you out like he wanted to rip that green velvet dress right off you!" I laughed.

"You really think so? Dammit, I knew I should've offered my number!" She sighed, kicking herself for missing out on her chance with Brett. Resolving not to dwell on it, she muttered, "Oh well, c'est la vie, right? Let's go find out what the hell is taking so long with our table." She took a peek at her watch. "Shit, our reservation was for over an hour ago!"

Now sitting in a damp, black silk dress reeking of merlot, I just wasn't in the mood for this kind of night out anymore. "Hey, would you be pissed if we didn't stay for dinner after all? I'm all sticky and gross, and maybe it's best if we just cut our losses and head home."

"Oh, come on, Kels, don't let that douche Mark ruin our night. *Please*." Clearly disappointed, I felt bad for Cali, but my mojo had left the building. I just wanted to go home, get comfy in my fleece PJs, and stuff my face with junk food.

"I'm sorry, Cali. I know I'm being a total buzzkill, but I'm just not into it anymore. Do you hate me?" My expression turned pleading.

"Ugh. Fine, we'll go, but can I at least chill with you at your house for a while? We can watch movies, or just hang out, or whatever."

Calista was the best friend ever.

"Of course you can hang out with me! We can eat Ben & Jerry's and talk about your future boyfriend Brett." With a wink, I hopped off my bar stool. "Thank you so much, Cali. I owe you one." I gave her a quick hug.

She returned the hug affectionately. "Damned straight, you owe me *big*—and you *will* repay the favor at a time and place of my choosing." With a mischievous smile, she retrieved her purse from the bar and headed for the exit. I quickly settled our tab—one measly glass of wine each—before following her out. As we grabbed our coats in the restaurant foyer, my mind wandered again to Mark, which frustrated me because I couldn't figure out why I was even thinking about him.

He was kind of a jerk.

Bundled up and ready to brave the winter night, Calista and I stepped outside. Pulling my phone out of my purse, I was about to call us a cab, when I noticed a male form slumped over to my right, hurling onto the sidewalk. Pedestrians tossed him disgusted looks as they passed by the vomitus display. I recognized immediately that the figure was Mark, and that his friends had seemingly abandoned him. *Nice friends.*

Cali and I exchanged the look of two mind readers: *We can't just leave him here.*

Unsure how he'd react to our presence in his current state of upheaval, I took a deep breath and approached him slowly. But being the graceless creature that I am, my heels made contact with a long, narrow patch of ice, sliding my feet in opposite directions, nearly sending me awkwardly into the splits. I finished off the move by landing on my ass, cheeks kissing the cold cement beneath. I heard Cali trying to stifle her laughter from behind me.

Mark looked up from the ground, no doubt curious who the klutz was, and when he saw that it was me, he rose to his feet. Wiping his mouth on the sleeve of his leather jacket, he unsteadily shuffled over, offering his hand to help me up.

I didn't leave him hanging this time.

When I put my hand in his, he somehow managed to pull me to my feet. I looked up, noticing how tall he was—easily a foot higher than my petite, five-foot-two-inch frame. "Thanks," I mumbled, embarrassed by my show of clumsiness.

With a sad smile, he sighed. "Sorry about bein' a dick." Now that he'd sobered somewhat, his douche-y attitude was gone, probably due to his recent purging episode. He seemed to consider something for a moment before continuing, "Maybe I could make it up to you some—" As an apparent wave of nausea cut him off, Mark leaned over, knees slightly bent, hands resting on his thighs, head hanging low.

Calista piped up on my behalf. "The only way to make it up to her is to let her forget this night ever happened." When I shot her an angry look for her rudeness, her expression turned regretful. "Sorry. That was a bit harsh. I get really bitchy when I'm hungry."

Mark chuckled weakly as he slowly straightened back up to look at me. Maybe Calista had a point, and we should all try to forget about this night and put it behind us. And I knew I shouldn't care about Mark's feelings in all this, especially after his offensive actions at the bar, but... He just looked so sad and alone out on the sidewalk, coming down off his booze-induced stupor, with nobody to help him. Before giving myself a chance to rethink things, I stuck out my hand to Mark. "We were never officially introduced. My name is Kelsey...Kelsey

O'Reilly." And then I shocked myself by adding, "And, yes, I'd like that...you making it up to me sometime."

As a wide smile replaced his sad expression, he took my hand, but instead of shaking it, he brought it up to his mouth, softly brushing his lips across my knuckles. "Nice to meet you, Kelsey O'Reilly." The gesture was sweet, so I tried not to dwell on the fact that he'd tossed his cookies out of the same mouth that just touched my hand.

Cali was looking at me like I had completely lost my mind, and maybe she was right. But I couldn't explain it. There was just something about Mark. I wasn't exactly sure what, but...*something*.

Then it dawned on me that he probably didn't have a way to get home. "Your friends leave you high and dry?" I asked in disbelief. I did not have a very high opinion of his friends right then. Mark, however, didn't seem the slightest bit pissed about it. "Yeah...I deserved it, though...you don't need to hear 'bout it."

"Okay, if you say so." I wasn't sure what he meant, and I didn't want to appear nosy, so I dropped it. "Well, you can't just stay out here all night alone, and I can tell you feel like shit, so let me call you a cab so you can get home in one piece." Pulling my phone back out, I made the call without waiting for his answer.

Looking a little green again, Mark ran his hands over his face before nodding. "Thanks, Kelsey. You're a sweetheart." When his cab pulled up a few minutes later, I stayed with him until he was safe inside. "You remember your address, right?" I asked innocently.

"Yeah...I remember." He looked a bit insulted. "I'm not *that* far gone." Waving me off, he closed the door to the cab, and I watched through the window as he slunk into the backseat. As the taxi pulled away from the curb, speeding off down the street and out of my line of vision, I just stood there, wondering where he lived, or how he was ever going to make things up to me...

We'd never even gotten around to exchanging numbers.

Cali walked over to me, draping her arm around my shoulders. "What a night, huh? Let's get out of here and see if we can salvage what's left of it." She had taken it upon herself to call us a cab while I'd dealt with Mark, and soon, we were on the road, headed back to my place.

TWO

FIVE DAYS LATER was lunch with my friends at our favorite café in Milton for a last hurrah of sorts—a time to cherish one final moment of bonding with my girlies before they headed back to college that weekend for the start of the spring semester. We were an eclectic bunch: Maia, a culinary arts major attending school in Rhode Island; Debra, a computer science enthusiast fine-tuning her skills in New Hampshire; and Calista, my overambitious best friend, who was knockin' 'em dead in Amherst, Massachusetts, with a double major in theatre arts and psychology. And then of course, there was me, the lone commuter and business major, attending university in Boston. Even though I'd never regretted my decision to live my college experience from home, a part of me had always envied my friends and their independence. And I was going to miss them terribly.

"Kels, you've got to promise to visit me this semester, okay?" Calista looked at me expectantly while chomping into her Monte Cristo sandwich.

Debra jumped in. "Ooohhh, I wanna tag along too! Cali always has a way of finding the best parties...the *best*." With a sip of mocha latte, she continued, "Remember that one last year at the frat house? Oh my God, I think I was drunk for three days straight!" She laughed boisterously.

I rolled my eyes. "This is exactly why I avoid you all like the plague when you're at school." I picked at my turkey club, removing the tomatoes. "I just end up playing nursemaid and cleaning up puke."

"Totally with you on that, Kels," Maia chimed in. "I'm so over the partying scene." Lifting her empty iced tea glass, she signaled the waitress for a refill. "Been there. Done that. Bought the T-shirt." She winked at me—it was nice having someone else on my side.

Calista shook her head exasperatedly as she swallowed another bite of her sandwich. "You only play nursemaid because you won't allow yourself to let loose." She gestured her hands toward me for emphasis. "If you'd just relax and not worry about things so much, you might actually surprise yourself by having fun." And to further entice me, she added, "There are so many hot guys I could introduce you to."

The prospect of meeting someone sounded tempting, but college parties weren't exactly the best places to meet the type of guys I'd be interested in. With a shrug, I offered a compromise. "I promise I'll think about it, okay?" Maybe I could suck it up for one weekend...after all, she was my best friend, and I hadn't paid her a visit at campus since sophomore year.

She smacked her hands down on the table in excitement. "That's my girl!" Obviously, she thought I would cave in, and...she was probably right.

Maia tucked a lock of curly red hair behind her ear as she glanced over at me. "You're a glutton for punishment, my friend." With a sympathetic smile and fork in hand, she stabbed at her Caesar salad.

"Don't I know it?" I replied, popping a French fry into my mouth. "Cali is still trying to corrupt me. She's persistent, I'll give her that."

"Aw, cut Cali some slack, would you people?" Debra defended. Focusing on me, she continued, "Kels, parties and out-of-control behavior are a rite of passage for college students." Deep in thought, her fingers played through her short, black, bobbed-cut hair. "Since you're always so cooped up at home, she just wants you to experience a little taste of that freedom and reckless abandon you've been missing out on."

"Wow. That's deep," I remarked, but immediately regretted my snark when Debra's face fell flat. "Look, I'm sorry. I get it...I do." I turned to Cali. "You're having the time of your life out there in Amherst, and I know you want to share it with me." My expression now sincere, I continued, "And I appreciate that, I really do....but to be honest, that whole scene...I find it very...overwhelming."

"Okay. Okay." Reaching across the table, Cali grabbed my hand. "I won't pressure you. You come visit only if it's what you want." After a deep inhale, she let out a long, drawn-out breath. "When I was younger, I guess I always imagined us doing the college thing together, you know? And yeah, I love attending school in Amherst and all the fun that goes along with it, but without you there...I don't know...it's not quite the same as I'd envisioned." Tears began to form in her eyes. "It's just that you're my best friend and...I miss you when I'm gone."

My eyes watered at hearing her words. "I miss you too." I gave her hand a squeeze.

"God, now you're making *me* cry!" Debra sniffled while digging through her purse for a tissue.

The three of us then simultaneously turned toward Maia and burst into a fit of giggles when we noticed the tears streaming down her face. "What? I just love you guys, okay?" She laughed at herself as she wiped her fingers across her wet cheeks.

"Well, aren't we just an emotional bunch." Smiling meaningfully at my friends, I threw some cash on the table to cover my portion of the check. After the others followed suit, we all rose to our feet, giving each other hugs of farewell.

As we approached the exit, I was rifling through my purse, looking for my car keys, when I collided with a man's broad chest. "Kelsey O'Reilly," I heard from above.

I lifted my chin to find Mark, the guy from the bar the other night, peering down at me. His smile was huge and white, perfect teeth gleaming. God, he looked good. The last time we saw each other, he was a little worse for wear, but today he looked like he'd walked straight out of a men's fashion catalog. In that pair of snug-fitting black jeans and gray V-neck wool sweater, I could really appreciate his masculine assets. Lean, yet muscular, his physique reminded me of a swimmer's build. Realizing my mouth was agape, I snapped it shut to feign nonchalance.

He touched my shoulder unexpectedly, giving me goose bumps. "Hey, I'm really glad I ran into you." Recalling our last encounter, he shook his head in embarrassment. "I was so stupid not to get your phone number last week." He let out an exasperated breath, blowing a tuft of black hair off his forehead. "I guess I wasn't exactly thinking clearly that night."

Surprising myself for being so forward, I replied, "Well, I could give it to you *now*." Then I paused for a moment. "Uh...if you want me to."

"Yeah. Of course I do." With an enthusiastic nod, he took his phone out of his back pocket. As I gave Mark my number, he quickly entered it in before returning his gaze to me. It was the first time I'd seen his eyes properly focused, and they were warm, friendly...the color of caramel. "I look forward to making it up to you," he said with a grin.

"Me too," I replied. Why did I suddenly have butterflies in my stomach?

"Well...I guess I'll talk to you soon, then." Did Mark seem nervous now, too, or was that my imagination?

He turned on his heel to notice Cali standing nearby. "Hi Calista. Nice to see you again," he said while beginning to maneuver through the crowd of customers waiting for tables. It impressed me that he remembered my best friend's name this time. Approaching the cashier, Mark ordered a coffee to go, before briefly glancing over his shoulder to catch me staring. When he flashed me another megawatt smile, I felt the fluttering in my belly accelerate.

Sensing two pairs of eyes burning holes into me, I turned to find Maia and Debra shooting me daggers, their glares making it clear they expected answers regarding my mystery man.

I quickly left the café, not wanting to get into it with them in front of an audience, but they were hot on my trail as I walked the half-block to my parked car.

"So, are you going to tell us about your gorgeous new *friend*, or do we have to beat it out of you?" Debra asked, standing with one hand on a hip, pretending to be offended at not hearing about Mark sooner. Maia looked more amused than anything. I noticed Cali exiting the café and headed toward us. She didn't look happy. I wondered if Mark had said anything to upset her. When she caught up to us, I feared she would spill the beans about how we came to know Mark, but she remained surprisingly mum. In no mood to rehash the gory details of that night, I breathed a sigh of relief.

After looking to Cali for confirmation that she was indeed going to keep quiet, I decided to buy myself some time with Debra and Maia. "I'll tell you...but not right now. It's a...*long* story."

Dissatisfied with my answer, they jumped to their own conclusions and screamed in unison, "Holy shit, you *like* him!"

THREE

THE NEXT DAY I rode *The T*—Boston's subway system—to the university bookstore to buy the textbooks and study materials I needed for the final semester. It was hard to believe that in a few short months, I'd officially earn the title of *College Graduate*. Just the thought made me giddy.

As I waited in line to pay for my things, the blaring *AH-OOO-GA* of my annoying, yet effective ring tone alerted me to an incoming call. Juggling my teetering tower of school supplies with one hand, I rummaged through my purse with the other, pulling the phone out just in time to catch the call before it went to voice mail.

"H-hello?" A quick glance at the caller ID revealed an unfamiliar number, so my answer was tentative.

"Hi. Kelsey? It's Mark."

Just the sound of him resurrected the butterflies in my belly. "Hi."

"I was wondering if by chance you were free today?"

At the hopeful tone in his voice, my heart rate picked up. "Well, I'm buying my school books right now, but I think I'm free later," I replied.

"Great! Can I take you to lunch?"

I checked my watch to notice it was already after noon. "Oh…I'm not sure…I still have to take *The T* home from Boston and get ready."

"I can come pick you up. What school are you at?"

"Bay Colony University."

"I'm actually not too far from you. I can be there in 20 minutes."

Panic set in at the thought of my grubby appearance. "I should really go home and change…"

"I'm sure you look gorgeous. I'd really like to see you. I'll meet you in twenty, okay?"

He thought I was *gorgeous?* How could I refuse him? "Um…okay."

"Awesome." I felt his smile over the phone. "See you then."

I hung up, made my way to the cashier, and paid for my stuff. Then I headed to the nearest ladies' room to scrutinize my reflection in the mirror. *Ugh—worse than I thought.* I wasn't wearing a drop of makeup, so I pinched my cheeks to give my complexion a rosier tint. There wasn't much I could do about my outfit: a ratty, bleach-stained pink T-shirt, black hoodie, distressed blue jeans, and gray UGGs. Normally, I wouldn't care how presentable I looked, but today was an exception. Mark had only ever laid eyes on me twice, and on both occasions, I'd been dressed nicely, with my face done. I wondered if he'd even recognize me in my *au naturale* state. Removing my ponytail holder, I let my poker-straight brown hair fall loose to my shoulders in hopes of upping my game. I didn't even have a brush with me, so I worked my fingers through it until satisfied. I wasn't thrilled, but it would have to do.

Once outside, I leaned against the building to wait, my heavy bag of school supplies at my feet. It occurred to me that I didn't tell Mark specifically where the bookstore was, so I hoped he'd be able to find me. Five minutes later, an old, abused, black four-door sedan pulled up to the curb, looking as though it had ridden more than its share of miles. Emerging from the vehicle, Mark made his way over, leaning down to retrieve my bag from the ground and carry it for me.

As he gazed down at me, a piece of his black hair hung lazily over one eye, and I held back the impulse to reach up and move it out of the way for him. His expression was cheerful. "Hi Kelsey. You ready?" he asked.

"Sure," I said, smiling up at him.

Following closely behind Mark, I took a deep, cleansing breath before exhaling slowly in an effort to calm my nerves. As I watched the man in front of me walking in fluid strides, it was near impossible to control my wandering eye, which seemed intent on observing his marvelous backside. I continued to take in the view in all its denim-clad glory until we arrived at his car.

As I reached for the passenger door handle, Mark gently shook his head in protest, letting me know he'd like to do the honors. I stood back, allowing him to open the door for me. He then waited to close it until I was comfortably settled inside with my seatbelt securely fastened. *Such a gentleman.*

Mark got in on the driver's side and turned to face me, flaunting a movie star smile before starting the car and pulling away from the curb. My heart was beating a mile a minute.

"You look beautiful," he said softly.

My face instantly turned beet red at the compliment. "Thank you. Although I wish I was dressed a little nicer."

"I think you look perfect just the way you are."

His words melted my insides. "You look pretty nice yourself," I said. Understatement of the year. Dressed casually in a tan Henley shirt under a weathered brown leather jacket, with dark blue jeans and brown loafers, he looked spectacular and I could hardly keep from staring.

"Do you like hamburgers?" he asked. "I know a great place on Beacon Street."

My mouth watered. "Beefy Burger?" It was my favorite burger joint.

"That's the one," he replied. "I take it you've eaten there before?"

"Yeah. Their food is awesome," I stated, growing more ravenous by the minute.

"Cool. Looks like we already have something in common," he grinned.

"Yup," I replied with a toothy smile.

As Mark continued to drive, I turned my head to the passenger window, watching the city's landscape whiz by as we settled into a comfortable silence. The rattle and hum of the car's mature engine was strangely soothing, reminding me of the old jalopy in which my dad used to drive Mom and me when I was little. Although a happy memory, it made me realize how much I still missed my dad after all these years...

Snapping myself back to the present, I turned away from the window to glance at Mark, taking the opportunity to examine his features. I studied his strong jaw and cheekbones, his straight and slightly prominent nose, and those radiant eyes of warm caramel. Shifting my gaze downward, I then focused on his hands, watching them as they navigated the steering. I noticed what appeared to be some light bruising across the knuckles of his right hand. I wondered what the story was behind it and wanted to ask, but it didn't seem to be the appropriate time.

~ ~ ~

When we arrived at Beefy Burger, Mark grabbed a miraculous metered parking spot right out front. Opening my car door, he took me by the hand as I got out. I was used to fending for myself on dates, so his chivalry was a welcome change of pace. He continued to hold my hand as we made our way inside the restaurant.

As we waited for an available table, I took in the atmosphere and aroma of the place. I chuckled to myself at the familiar plaques adorning the walls with beef-related ad slogans from years past and present, with "Where's the Beef?" still my all-time favorite. My stomach rumbled as I got a whiff of the sizzling patties from the kitchen. It smelled like heaven in here.

Soon, we were seated at a booth across from each other with our burgers in front of us. I tried to eat like a lady at first, taking small bites and chewing slowly. But the melt-in-your-mouth goodness won over before long, and I shamelessly scoffed down the rest of my deluxe bacon burger, unaware of the grease dripping down my chin.

"Hey you've got something there," Mark pointed.

My right hand flew up to touch my chin, feeling the slimy wetness. "Oh God." Reaching for my napkin, I said, "You must think I'm such a pig."

Mark grabbed my napkin. "Here, let me."

As he gently wiped my chin, our eyes locked. My heart pounded so hard and loud in my chest, I felt like I was listening to my own personal drum solo.

He pulled back and shook his head. "For the record, I don't think you're a pig. You're the farthest thing from it, in fact. I like that you have a good appetite and aren't afraid to get a little dirty." Then he blurted out, "I think it's really sexy, actually."

Blushing deeply, I looked down at the table, speechless.

An awkward silence.

"Kelsey, I'm sorry…the part about you being sexy—I wasn't thinking and it just sort of slipped out. I didn't mean to be so forward." Raking a hand through his hair, he moved that stubborn piece out of the way. "Here I am trying to make it up to you, and I'm probably just making you more uncomfortable."

My face was still hot, but I tried to ignore it. "It's okay." I took a big swig of soda.

Mark let out a breath. "No, it's not okay. Look—Kelsey, I owe you a huge apology for my behavior at the bar that night. I should never have come onto you like that. When I saw you, I thought you were so pretty and I wanted to talk to you, but nothing I said or did came out right because I was so shattered."

Still trying to wrap my head around the fact that he thought I was pretty, I replied, "I'm sure you weren't yourself that night."

"No, I wasn't. But that's still no excuse. I was a real asshole and I'm so sorry for the way I acted and for making such a wreck of your night out."

Unable to ignore the sincerity in his voice, I replied, "I accept your apology." Eyeing the rest of his burger, I wondered if he was going to finish it. "Besides, you've more than made it up to me by bringing me here."

He shook his head as if I'd said the most ridiculous thing in the world. "Oh, no. I've only just begun making it up to you."

I felt the corners of my mouth turn up but didn't want to seem overeager. "Oh, really? What do you mean?"

"Well, I'd like to spend some more time with you, for starters. Would you be okay with that?" he asked.

"Yes." I didn't even hesitate.

"I'm really enjoying your company and I don't want to bring you home yet. Do you want to catch a movie or something?" he asked.

"Okay," I said.

I wasn't ready to go home either.

FOUR

MARK TOOK ME to see a romantic comedy, which was ironic since I usually hated chick flicks. Horror films were more my speed, but I couldn't fault him for not knowing I didn't fit the stereotype of the average female moviegoer.

Meandering up and down the crowded theater aisles, we eventually scouted out two empty seats in the very last row. As the lights dimmed to signal the start of the coming attractions, we sat down, and I placed the bucket of popcorn Mark insisted on buying between my legs. Despite feeling completely stuffed from our Beefy Burger gorge-fest, I dug into the popcorn, more to occupy my nervous hands than anything. I tended to fidget.

When the coming attractions ended and the movie began, the theater grew completely dark, the only source of illumination the glow of the screen. Sitting in the blackened space in such close proximity to Mark, I experienced a heightened awareness of the senses. He reached over to grab a fistful of popcorn from the bucket between my thighs, and it made me a little crazy.

My body now felt tingly, like electricity connecting me to Mark in a current. I raised my hands from my lap, eager to touch Mark in some small way, but I couldn't find the nerve. Realizing how awkward I must have looked with my hands in the air, I began anxiously rubbing them together—the friction warming them almost to the point of sweating.

Breaking me free from my panic-driven tendency, Mark took one of my hands in his and held onto it gently. My eyes remained fixed ahead on the movie, but I didn't see any of it. I could concentrate on nothing other than the feel of his hand as it touched mine—how he rested my left palm on his right thigh while rubbing back and forth over my knuckles with his thumb. I could have been watching a cinematic masterpiece or a blank screen. I wouldn't have known the difference.

When the movie ended, we remained in our seats until the last of the moviegoers headed for the exits. Mark held my hand the entire time, and was still holding it. *I never wanted to leave this theater.*

Turning to face me, he asked, "So, what did you think?" Finally, he let go of my hand to reach for more popcorn in the bucket I was still straddling.

I answered quickly and truthfully, needing to distract myself from Mark's hand and its location between my legs.

"Well…it's not really my type of movie, to be honest," I replied with a sheepish grin. Not that I'd been able to pay enough attention to actually know if the movie was any good or not.

"What?!" he cried out in mock anger. "Why didn't you *say* something?!" With good humor, he tossed a piece of popcorn at me.

With a laugh, I caught the kernel and popped it into my mouth. "Sorry! I didn't have the heart to tell you."

"And I thought all girls liked romantic movies," Mark shrugged. "Well, just so I know for future reference, what kind of movies *do* you like?" he asked with a raised brow.

"Horror movies are my favorite," I replied enthusiastically. "I have a love-hate relationship with them, really. I love to watch them but hate the nightmares they give me. Silly, huh?"

"Nah. Not silly at all. I'm definitely going to have to watch one with you sometime," he winked.

Feeling bold, I asked, "Oh yeah? Is that a promise?"

With wide eyes, he answered, "Most definitely."

~ ~ ~

After we finally left the theater, Mark drove me back to my home in Quincy. When I told him where I lived, he happily informed me that he resided only one town over in Braintree. Knowing we were so close to each other was a pleasant surprise, and everything about the day seemed to be falling into perfect place. I couldn't remember the last time I enjoyed myself or anyone's company so much.

As we pulled into the driveway of the small, brick red, Cape Cod-style house in which I lived with my mom, I noticed her car wasn't there, which jogged my memory. She had made plans to go out after work with her book club friends. *And she wasn't due home for several hours.* "Did you want to come inside for a bit?" I asked, hoping to prolong the perfect day just a little more.

Mark appeared flattered by the invitation. "Sure. I'd like that."

We walked along the concrete pathway and up the few steps leading to my front door. Ever the gentleman, Mark insisted on carrying my bag of school supplies into the house even though I offered to do it myself. When we reached the door, I opened it and stood off to the side, allowing Mark to enter ahead of me. I watched from behind as he took a quick perusal of my home's interior from the front hall, unwilling to move in any further without my permission. "You have a nice home here," he said sincerely.

"Thanks. I like it…or at least I'd better, since I spend an inordinate amount of time here," I said, half laughing at my own lame remark. "Here, let me take your jacket," I proposed, to which he obliged, offering it to me after setting my bag of books down on a small wooden bench. It was the same leather jacket he was wearing when I found him heaving onto the sidewalk outside the bar that fateful night. As I lifted the jacket up to hang it on the coat rack, I passed it by my nose discreetly, inhaling the scent of leather and Mark, an intoxicating combination that reminded me of a campfire.

"I wouldn't have pegged you as someone who spent a lot of time at home," Mark stated matter-of-factly.

"No? Why is that?" I asked, spinning around to face him for clarification.

"Well, look at you," he said, waving his hand up and down before me as if I were on display. "You're smart and funny and sweet…and *beautiful.* Surely you have guys fighting for your attention on a regular basis."

I wanted to laugh out loud at the absurdity of his statement, but his expression told me how serious he really was. It did funny things to me knowing that's the way he viewed me. Shaking my head, I uttered, "No…not really. I don't date much."

"No boyfriend?" he asked, watching me intently.

"No. I mean, yeah…I used to…for a couple of years…but that's over now," I blabbered, not knowing why I felt compelled to divulge details of my dating history. *A simple "no" would have been sufficient.*

"I'm sorry it didn't work out," he said, a smile playing on his lips.

"You don't look very sorry," I chuckled softly.

"No. I guess I'm not." Stepping closer, his demeanor suddenly turned serious.

My heart turned frantic.

Mark continued moving in toward me until we were mere inches apart. My face burned hot and I lost the capacity to breathe. He peered down at me, his eyes boring into mine with an intensity that made me weak in the knees. The ever-present silky black hair strands that hung over his right eye became too much to bear. Seeming to have a mind of its own, my hand traveled up the side of his face, continuing until it reached his ebony wisps, then moved the pesky strands aside with a gentle sweep of the fingers. As I slowly lowered my hand away from his face, Mark grabbed onto it tightly, pulling it toward him swiftly, causing my body to press up against his. Leaning his head in toward mine, he was now so close, I could feel his warm breath in my face. I stared at his mouth, anticipating his next move. He continued moving in slow motion…getting closer…closer…his lips parting slightly. And then…

Mark's phone rang from inside the back pocket of his jeans, making us both jump a mile.

Fuck. My. Life.

"Shit!" Mark yelped, clearly startled and annoyed by the interruption. "I-I guess I should answer that." He pulled out his phone and barked, "What do you want?!" Then snapped, "Tonight? When?" His eyes shifted away from me nervously. "Alright…I'll be there as soon as I can." When he ended the call, I wondered who or what had him so flustered.

"Kelsey, I'm sorry, but I'm afraid I have to go." Hastily retrieving his jacket from the coat rack, he sure was in a hurry all of a sudden. Brushing by me quickly while reaching for the front door, he stopped himself, whirling back around and bounding over to where I still stood frozen in place—the same spot where the spell of our impending lip-locking episode was broken without warning.

He grabbed my face in his hands, catching me off-guard and I gasped. "When can I see you again?" he asked, his caramel irises searching my hazel orbs.

Barely able to form a coherent thought, I mumbled, "W-whenever you want."

"I'll call you tomorrow, okay?" he asked, releasing me and retreating backwards.

Struggling to get my breathing under control, I huffed, "Yeah…okay."

And then suddenly, Mark was out the door.

Remaining in the same spot, my feet glued to the floor, I brought my hands up to my cheeks, yearning to relive the feel of his warmth cradling my face. The effect Mark had on me was something I had never before experienced, not even in the two years I'd spent with my ex-boyfriend, whom I cared about deeply.

The feeling both terrified and exhilarated me.

Finally gaining my composure and mobility, I moved from my spot, taking off my black hoodie and hanging it up. Removing my UGGs, I placed them under the bench where my schoolbooks sat. As I headed into the kitchen, a stark realization hit me: *Mark had never made it any further into the house than the front hall.* The ridiculousness of it reduced me to a fit of giggles that nearly brought me to tears.

~ ~ ~

The following day, I busied myself while eagerly anticipating Mark's phone call. I couldn't wait to see him again—and hopefully get a do-over of our would-be first kiss. *Without the interruption.*

I spent the morning cleaning and organizing my room, a project long overdue. When the afternoon rolled around, Mom and I passed the hours watching *Seinfeld* reruns and looking at old photo albums together, reminiscing over the many good times we'd spent with my dad. The trip down memory lane was always a bittersweet experience, but we both strongly felt the importance of keeping his memory alive, no matter how much it hurt sometimes.

That evening for dinner, I made us a chicken cacciatore recipe I'd found online. It turned out surprisingly well, but I had a hard time forcing the meal down past the lump forming in my throat.

When night set in, I stayed up reading until eleven o'clock, finally giving in to exhaustion and going to bed. Disappointment hung over me like a dark cloud.

Mark's phone call never came.

FIVE

THE SPRING SEMESTER had been in full swing for a little over three weeks, and I was already burnt out. My business courses were a real killer, and I was struggling to keep up with the workload. As a result, I was spending more and more time holed up in my room surrounded by textbooks, flashcards, and piles of notes, trying to make heads or tails of it all.

I felt like a hermit, and I missed my friends something fierce. Dealing with a sense of isolation and loneliness was an unfortunate side-effect of my live-at-home college arrangement. When threatening to overwhelm me, I combated those feelings by staying connected to my friends in various ways. FaceTiming, texting, and good old-fashioned phone chats kept me from being an island unto myself. Spending as much time as possible with my mom even though she worked a lot helped too.

I also stayed occupied with favorite hobbies—or, in the case of scrapbooking, favorite obsessions—to keep my mind focused on something other than Mark. Remaining busy proved to be the most therapeutic way to move the energy of my thoughts away from his radio silence since our near-perfect date. *No phone call. No text message. Nada.* It absolutely pissed me off, but I sure as hell wasn't going to waste any more brain cells worrying about it. It didn't matter—I barely knew the guy anyway. *At least, that's what I kept telling myself.*

A knock at my bedroom door jolted me out of the doldrums. "Come on in," I said, flipping my opened *Principles of Marketing* textbook over and setting it face-down on the bed to mark my place. The door creaked as it swung open, revealing my mom still dressed in her business attire, fresh from the small, private law firm at which she was a paralegal. Entering my room, her heels clip-clopped across the hardwood floor. Her two-piece lavender pantsuit brought out the silver flecks dispersed throughout her short, dark hair. Hazel eyes resembling mine gazed upon me with affection as she sat down on the bed beside me, my phone in her hand.

"Oh, you poor baby. You've been working so hard," she remarked while observing the mess of books and papers strewn all over my yellow and white striped, down comforter. Leaning over, she kissed my forehead. "You look tired. Why don't you take a break, and I'll make you something to eat."

"Yeah, Mom, that would be great. Thanks," I said. She always seemed to know just what I needed, and I loved her for it.

Mom smiled warmly at me, happy to do her part in easing a little of my stress. "Grilled cheese and tomato soup sound good?"

"Perfect," I agreed, returning her smile.

Standing up to leave, she hesitated, remembering her other reason for the visit. "Here." Extending her hand to me, she continued, "You left your phone downstairs, and it's been ringing like crazy. Sounds like someone's trying to track you down." She placed the phone in my open palm before retreating downstairs to prepare my night-time snack.

I glanced down at the screen to notice three missed calls from Calista, plus her text message:

Where the hell are you?!! You need to call me ASAP!

Wondering what could be so urgent, I immediately dialed Cali's number. "Oh my God, Kelsey," she answered on the first ring. "I've been waiting *forever* for you to *call!*" Her shriek made me hold the phone away from my ear. I could hear a throng of loud voices coupled with the pulse of bump-n-grind music in the background.

"What's the matter? Are you okay?" I asked, suddenly panicking and hoping she wasn't in any kind of trouble. I glanced at my clock on the nightstand—just after 8:30 PM.

"I'm completely fine, Kels," she said, but the inflection in her voice was peculiar and hard to read. A long pause rang out as I waited for her to elaborate. Soon, the background noise grew muffled as faint sounds from another conversation came through the muted connection. Obviously, she was talking to someone and didn't want me to hear what was being said.

"What's going on, then?" I asked, feeling grumpy and wanting her to get to the point so I could eat my snack, which was probably stone cold.

"I need you to drive up here tonight. I miss you," she said with forced sincerity. *She was up to something.*

Still irritable and not up to making the three-hour drive so late in the day, I complained, "I can't, Cali. I've been studying all day and I'm exhausted."

"Oh, come on, Kels! I *really* want to see you," she begged.

"I'm really sorry, but I don't think so. Not tonight," I replied, drowsily eyeing my pillow.

Cali changed tactics, resorting to reel me in with guilt. "Pleeeease! You *owe* me one, remember?!" Oh, she was good.

Never one to renege on a promise, I relented, albeit half-heartedly. "Ughhhh. Alright. Alright. I'll come," I said with a dramatic groan. Rising from my mattress, I schlepped over to the full-length mirror on the backside of my bedroom door to assess my current appearance. *Good Lord...I was a horrid sight.*

"Yes!" At Cali's victorious squeal, I yanked the phone away from my ear yet again. "You'll have a great time, Kels! I swear!" she spouted, no doubt, hoping to improve my sour mood with her excitement.

"Where are you?" I asked, dreading the long, monotonous commute ahead.

"I'm at a frat party. Just call me when you get close, and I'll meet you at my dorm," she answered.

"Have you been drinking?" I queried suspiciously, hoping I wasn't going to have to play babysitter for the night.

"No. No. Well, yeah, just a little, but I'm fine...I promise," she blathered. She didn't sound intoxicated, but something was definitely *up*.

With great apprehension, I conceded. "Okay, I'll see you in a few hours, then."

"Thanks, Kels. You won't be sorry." Confident last words as Cali ended the call.

Despite my trepidation, I resigned myself to whatever fate awaited in Amherst. I paced about my room while searching for my duffel bag and a clean set of clothes. After packing everything I would need for my overnight stay, I headed for the door. With a moment's hesitation, I considered taking the time to primp for my visit but ultimately decided I was too tired to care. Taking one last glance around the room, I opted to deal with my bed-top clutter of books and study materials when I returned.

I flew down the stairs two at a time, on a mission to get on the road as soon as possible. The smell of tomato soup stopped me in my tracks, making me feel badly for neglecting the meal my mom took the time to prepare. Walking into the kitchen, I wrapped my arms around her from behind as she stood at the sink washing dishes. "Mom, I'm sorry it's so last minute, but I'm going to head to Amherst and spend the night at Cali's."

When Mom turned to face me, it forced me to release her. "Are you sure you want to go this late, honey? You won't get there until after midnight." I could see the concern etched into her features.

"Yeah, I'm sure. Cali says she needs me, so I think I should go," I replied.

"You're a good friend, you know that?" she said, with a kiss on my cheek. "Please just promise me you'll be careful and call me when you get there, okay?"

"I will, Mom. I promise." And I meant every word.

Squinting at the hall clock while rushing out the front door, the time, 8:50 PM, sent me into a sprint. When I reached the driveway, I threw my duffel bag into the backseat of my forest green, two-door coupe. It had just started to rain—a cold, icy, pelting stream that had the potential to make driving a challenge. *Just great.*

As I pulled out of the driveway, I heard the ping of a new text message. Retrieving my phone from its docking station, I hurriedly peeped at the screen, not wanting to take my eyes off the road.

Check out who's waiting to meet you!! O_O

Attached to Cali's text was a photo of some guy I didn't know. I pulled over to take a closer look without causing an accident. A grainy image revealed a moderately good-looking guy, at least, from what I could tell, but his double "thumbs-up" to the camera completely ruined any hope of me being interested. And now, the reason for my *all-important* visit to Amherst was abundantly clear: *I was being fixed up!*

Returning the phone to its cradle, I pulled my car back onto the road. I couldn't afford to waste anymore drive-time by texting Cali. The pavement was now slick, the visibility worsening, and my knuckles turned white as I tightened my grip on the steering wheel. I quietly recited a prayer, pleading for a safe arrival.

With the bad weather reducing my driving speed most of the way, I didn't arrive in Amherst until 12:35 AM. Although it was well past my bedtime, I knew from experience that the campus parties would still be thriving. I made a quick phone call to my mom to let her know I had arrived safely, then called Cali to let her know I was close by. *No answer.* Assuming she couldn't hear her phone ringing over the frat house racket, I sent a quick text, hoping she'd know enough to check for messages.

Almost there. Be at your dorm in 15.

A short time later, I arrived at McKinnley Hall—Cali's home away from home. Entering through the front door, I requested a visitor pass from the security desk. As the person in-charge called up to Cali's room, I momentarily panicked, fearing she wasn't back yet. The last thing I needed was to be left stranded with no pass and no place to stay. Fortunately, my worries were put to rest when Cali came bounding into the lobby from the stairwell. She looked radiant, dressed fashionably in a cropped, camel-hair sweater, skinny low-rise jeans, and brown suede boots. Her golden hair was up in a messy twist, with loose strands framing her face. I suddenly felt pretty damned homely.

"Kels! You made it!" she yelled, running towards me with outstretched arms. Picking me up in a large embrace, she lifted me off the floor, swinging me around like we were long lost lovers. I laughed out loud at her over-the-top display of affection.

"Hey, Cali. It's really good to see you," I said, realizing just how much I missed my best friend. My fears of her being plastered when I arrived, were luckily, unfounded. And come to think of it, when it came to partying, Cali always talked a good game, but I'd only actually seen her truly drunk on a few occasions. I supposed it was the free-spirited atmosphere of the college bashes that drew her in more than the alcohol. Being raised by strict, overbearing parents probably had a lot to do with it as well. After keeping her on such a tight leash all throughout high school, I was shocked they'd allowed her to attend college beyond a hop, skip, and a jump from their 24/7 supervision—never mind *live* at one. But true to form, they'd nixed her plans to move to an off-campus apartment this past fall, leaving her to round out her undergrad experience with the scant population of seniors still slumming it dormitory-style.

"It's so good to see you too, Kels! I've missed you tons," she replied. Signing me in as an approved guest for the night, she handed me a dorm visitor pass. She then took me by the arm and pulled me toward the stairwell.

"Wait a sec," I said, stopping short. "I forgot that I left my stuff in the car."

"What did you bring to change into—a sweatshirt and yoga pants?" I could tell Cali knew her guess was spot-on by the way she eyeballed my current get-up of warm-up suit and running shoes.

I rolled my eyes at her lack of subtlety. "Yeah...so what?"

"Well, we can't have you meeting Tracy dressed like that, now can we? Come on, I've got just the outfit for you upstairs..."

"Hold on just a minute, Cali. Did you just say *Tracy?*" Confusion over the purpose of my visit set in. I had assumed it was for an arranged rendezvous with Mr. Thumbs-Up, but maybe I'd misunderstood Cali's intentions. As relief washed over me, I felt my body begin to relax.

Not seeing my point, Cali replied, "Yes, his name is Tracy, and he is soooo nice, Kels. You'll love him. And he's super hot!" As she fanned herself, she stumbled backwards in a mock-fainting spell. My spine stiffened at the realization that I was indeed being set up. *And with a guy named Tracy.*

Cali was obviously hell-bent on seeing this thing through and I knew I had no hope of backing out. Eager to get the night over with, I turned to Cali and said dryly, "I guess you better get me ready, then."

We arrived at *Tracy's* frat house by 1:15 AM and would have gotten there sooner had I not been forced to wear a pair of black leather shoe-boots a size too small. Luckily, the straight-cut jeans Cali selected for me were flattering and comfortable. She completed my look with a leopard print cardigan over a black silk camisole. I had to admit, she knew how to play up my assets.

The party was still going strong as we walked up the steps to the over-sized Victorian-style house with chipping white paint. Passing through the door and into the red-plastic-cup-holding sea of bodies, the stench of cheap beer made me throw up a little in my mouth. *I* found the techno music pumping through the sound system to be deafening, but Cali, raising her arms above her head, started swaying her hips to the beat. She was clearly in her element.

I followed her through the crowd into another room with disco lights and the most archaic DJ setup I'd ever seen—a makeshift turntable connected to a CD player—at which the DJ dude tried his best impression of David Guetta but wasn't quite pulling it off. When Cali spotted him, she shrieked excitedly, pointing to me as if I was a prize he had just won. Right then I knew that Tracy was our music man. Giving me the once-over, he inspected me from top to bottom before lifting his hands off the turntable with an approving, enthusiastic...*thumbs-up.*

Apparently, it was his signature move.

When Cali shoved me in front of Tracy, he smiled, offering his hand for an introduction. I zeroed in on his nicotine-stained teeth, unable to stop comparing them to Mark's gorgeous, pearly-whites. This guy was cute in his own way, sporting a crew cut and soft, rounded facial features that gave him a boyish look. Had I never met Mark, maybe I would have even found Tracy attractive.

"It's nice to finally meet you. I'm Tracy," he said, with a firm handshake.

"I'm Kelsey. It's nice to meet you too," I responded courteously.

"Can I get you a beer?" he asked, gesturing toward a keg in the corner of the room.

With a shrug, I answered, "Sure. Why not." *May as well try to blend in.*

While Tracy went to pour me a cup of piss-warm beer, Cali came up behind me and whispered in my ear, "Isn't he totally adorable?"

Poor Cali. Her heart was in the right place. "Sure. He's cute," I answered truthfully, but without much enthusiasm.

"I just *knew* you would like him. He's perfect for you!" she declared proudly.

Shaking my head, I resolved to clear up any misunderstanding. "No, that's not what I meant. Yes, he's cute and all, but I'm not interested in dating him, or anything," I stated firmly.

Her brows knit together in disappointment. "Oh, come on, Kels! You haven't even given him a chance yet."

Just then, Tracy returned with my beer. I thanked him politely, but upon first sip, had to rein in my gag reflex. Without taking his eyes off me, Mr. DJ went back to his station to pop in a new CD. With animated eyebrows, he said, "This one's for you."

As the familiar, bouncy bass line of Drake's "Hotline Bling" reverberated throughout the space, I couldn't help but shimmy my shoulders—involuntarily—to the drum of the beat. It was my favorite song, and whenever it came on, I had a hard time controlling my need to bust a move. Setting my beer down on the floor, one quick look at Cali and her evil smile told me all I needed to know: She had arranged the whole thing.

Not known for my sense of rhythm, seeing me dance was comparable to watching *Seinfeld's* Elaine Benes boogie at her holiday office party. But a quarter of the way into Drake's song, I had found my groove—clapping, gyrating, and twisting like my life depended on it. I knew I probably looked ridiculous, but I was having too much fun to care. Cali joined me, taking me by the hand and twirling me around the room like we were two ballroom dancers.

As soon as Cali's hand left mine, I felt another pair of mitts land on my hips from behind. I tilted my head back to find Tracy peering at me over my shoulder. His expression was serious, focused on perfecting his dance moves. Spinning around to see what he was up to, I nearly doubled over in hysterics. *He was just as bad of a dancer as I was!* He was a good sport about it, though, and with an awkward mix of off-rhythm bends, jumps, and turns, we danced to the rest of the song together. Then when the next song came on, we danced to that one too. And the next several songs after that. I had to admit I was having a great time.

Completely drenched in sweat and wiped out from my turn as a disco diva, I headed for outdoors to cool off. When I checked on Cali to make sure she was okay, I found her canoodling in a corner with a very handsome campus jock.

With his hand on the small of my back, Tracy guided me as I made my way out. It was drizzling, but it felt so good, I didn't really care about getting wet. Sitting down on the front steps, I lifted my face to the sky, basking in the cool mist falling down on me. When Tracy sat next to me, he reached over and grabbed my hand.

Oh no.

I needed to set him straight before I led him on any further. Turning to face him, I spoke directly. "Tracy, I had a great time with you tonight, but—"

"Don't tell me. You have a boyfriend, right?" As he asked the question, he placed my hand back in my lap.

"No. Not exactly," I said, searching for the right words to let him down gently. "I'm sorry, but I'm just not interested in dating anyone right now."

"Hey, that's cool. No worries," he said. I could tell the smile he tried was his most convincing, but he still looked a little defeated.

I never enjoyed handing out rejection, but I just didn't want to start something I had no intention of finishing. "I'm sorry," I repeated, awkwardly looking down at my lap.

"No. Don't be," he said, leaning over with a playful shoulder nudge. "It was really cool meeting you regardless." A hearty laugh escaped him as he continued, "Besides, it's not every day I find someone who can keep up with my dance moves."

"Next time I pay Cali a visit, I'll have to challenge you to a dance-off," I joked.

"You've got yourself a deal," Tracy replied, grabbing my hand again to shake it and seal the deal. Perhaps this was a new friendship-in-the-making.

With the pressure now off us both, I enjoyed conversing with Tracy for a little while longer as we waited for the party to wrap up. When Cali came out to find us, we both gave Tracy a friendly, good-bye hug before heading back to McKinnley Hall for a few precious hours of much-needed sleep.

Cali was quiet as we changed into our PJs and put ourselves to bed. I tucked myself into the bottom bunk belonging to her roommate Jenna, who had gone home for the weekend. When I heard Cali sigh heavily from the top bunk, I asked, "Are you gonna tell me what's wrong, or what?"

"I don't understand you, that's all," she replied flatly.

Her statement baffled me. "What don't you understand?"

"Here you have a great guy who obviously likes you, and you can't even be bothered." Her tone was cold.

"Cali, it's not like I was rude to him. I enjoyed meeting him and we had fun, and I agree...he's a nice guy, but..."

"...But he's not Mark," she finished.

Of course, Cali had just stated the obvious, but I was in denial. "Mark has nothing to do with it," I insisted.

"Don't give me that shit, Kels. I listened to you whine about him over the phone for days when you didn't hear from him." With a loud exhale, she added, "Admit it...you still like him."

She could read me like a damned book.

"Maybe I thought I liked him for five minutes, but..." With a deep breath, I recalled my last conversation with Mark. "But he never called me, so...I'm over it."

"Yeah, sure you are," Cali huffed.

"For God's sakes Cali, we went out *one* time! It's not like we were even dating or anything. He's clearly not interested in me, so I've moved on," I persisted, trying to mask my anger.

"Okay, if you *really* don't think it's a big deal, then I'm relieved," Cali replied. "Because that day at the café...I told him to stay away from you."

My face burned hot as her words sank in. "Why would you do that?" I gasped.

"Kels, I know his type. You don't need to waste your time with a loser like that."

I found her assessment of his character completely *off* the *Mark*. How could she make such sweeping assumptions when she didn't know him any better than I did? With that thought, I replied, "He's not a loser, Cali." Then I wondered why I would defend the honor of a guy who couldn't even give me the time of day.

"Okay, maybe he's not a loser, but he's not right for you. A guy like that will only bring you down, trust me." Leaning over the side of the top bunk, she gave me a level look that said, *"I speak from experience."*

"It doesn't matter anyway because I haven't heard from him in weeks...you obviously got your wish," I said. Deep down, I knew Cali wasn't the reason for Mark's lack of contact, but I felt the need to direct the blame at someone other than me.

Cali climbed down from her bunk to crawl into bed with me, wrapping her arms around my middle and laying her head on my chest. "I'm sorry, Kels. I just want you to be happy, that's all. You deserve a guy who will treat you like a queen."

I brushed the hair out of her face so I could look into her eyes. "*He* made me feel like a queen—even if it was just for one day," I finally admitted. With that, I rolled over and drifted off into a deep sleep.

The next morning, I dragged myself out of bed at 9 AM, trying not to disturb Cali as I quickly gathered up my things to head out. She was still in the bottom bunk, curled up in a ball and snoring softly. Leaning over, I gave her a quick peck on the cheek before trudging to the door to let myself out. As I opened it, she whispered softly from behind me, "Love you, Kels. Call me when you get home."

Turning back around, I whispered, "I will. Go back to sleep. Love you too," and blew her a kiss as I left.

~ ~ ~

With light traffic this time, I made it back to Quincy in less than three hours, but fatigue weighed heavily upon me as I pulled onto my street. Remembering that my mom would be putting in extra hours at the law firm and not home until evening, I looked forward to having the house to myself. I planned to spend most of the afternoon napping and vegging out on the sofa. As I neared the house, my eyes widened in shock upon seeing a certain over-sized, beat-up, black sedan sitting in my driveway.

My heart began to race.

As I pulled my car into the driveway behind his jalopy, Mark got out, leaning against his driver's side door to wait for me. For a fleeting moment, excitement bubbled up in my belly. But that was quickly replaced with the anger I'd been harboring for weeks. Shutting off the car, I sat silently for a minute to collect my thoughts. But the more I thought, the *angrier* I became until I reached my boiling point. I rubbed my palms back and forth on my thighs, hoping to soothe my fuming mindset. This guy had some nerve showing up after all this time, and I refused to give him the satisfaction of an outward emotional reaction. Inhaling deeply, I decided my best strategy was to feign indifference. With a long, calming exhale, I got out of my car and approached Mark slowly, my best blank expression in place.

"Hey," he said softly, carefully gauging my disposition.

"What's up?" I asked casually, avoiding eye contact.

Mark ran his hands through his hair, which had grown longer since the last time I saw him. It was a good look for him. "I'm sorry I haven't called," he said.

"How long have you been here?" I asked, ignoring his apology.

"Since about ten o'clock this morning," he replied matter-of-factly, as if it were completely normal behavior to stalk someone in front of their house for hours.

"Why are you here?" I asked, my eyes drawn to the large hole in the leg of his jeans.

"I wanted to apologize to you," he said.

"Don't worry about it," I spat. "It's no big deal," I finished, lying through my teeth.

"Oh." He looked down at the pavement. "Is that really how you feel?" Reaching out as if to touch me, it seemed he had a change of heart as his hand went right back down to his side.

Backing away, I shook my head. "It doesn't matter, does it?" Finally, I looked up into his light brown eyes. "I didn't hear from you. End of story. It's done."

"I don't want it to be the end." At that, he took a step toward me.

Anger coursed through my veins as I spoke. "Well, you should have thought about that before—"

He wouldn't let me finish. "—I know, and I'm sorry about that. I really am. It's just that I...had to go out of town unexpectedly."

"Out of town? You mean for school?" I was genuinely confused.

"No." His voice grew quiet as he looked down at his sneakers, his feet now nervously tapping.

"Well, for what, then?" Nothing was making any sense.

"I can't really tell you that right now," he replied.

"You *can't* tell me or you *won't?*"

With another step forward, Mark reached out both hands to grasp my upper arms. Turning me around, he backed me up against the hood of my car. "I have some shit that I'm dealing with right now, Kelsey," he revealed. "But I'm working through it, and it's going to be fine." Lifting my chin with his index finger, he forced me to look up at him.

I struggled to remain unaffected, but my body had its own ideas. As my skin prickled with his touch, I desperately wanted to feel more. When Mark's finger retreated from under my chin, I brazenly grabbed it, opening his hand and interlocking my fingers with his. Moving in closer, he leaned his forehead against mine. Our breathing became labored even though we were standing perfectly still.

"I thought about you a lot while I was away," he whispered, bringing his other hand up to gently stroke my cheek with the backs of his fingers.

"Then why didn't you—"

I couldn't finish the thought.

Because suddenly, Mark's lips had come crashing down on mine.

SIX

THE MOMENT OUR mouths met, I was lost, moaning deeply—instantly—upon contact.

His lips were incredibly soft, the press of his tongue driving me mad as it slinked out to mesh with mine. I thrust my fingers into his hair, tangling them up in that silky mass of black strands. When a long wisp escaped my grasp, sweeping over my face to tickle my nose, it drove me even crazier. My fingers tightened their grip and tugged, which seemed to egg Mark on, making him grab the back of my head with both hands to crush our faces together.

As his body bumped against mine, I instinctively arched my back, itching to get closer. The weight of his body overcame me, forcing me to lie back on the hood of my car. Mark groaned as he intensified the kiss, scraping my bottom lip with his teeth. I whimpered into his mouth and pulled at his hair even harder. His hands left the back of my head to skim down my sides and land on my hips. He began fiddling with the bottom of my jacket, as if contemplating what to do next. Then with one hand still on my hip, the other traveled up my torso until it reached the zipper and he gave it a tug. As he slowly pulled it down, the chill of winter air hit me when my jacket fell open, bringing me out of the confines of my lust-filled mind.

"Mark, stop," I heaved into his mouth, panting heavily.

He immediately froze, breaking the kiss and fixing me with a hooded stare—eyes still smoldering. Then, squeezing them shut, he lifted himself off me, bringing his hands to his head to rake his fingers forcefully through his hair. Peeling his eyes back open, he looked at me again—a familiar warmth now present in his gaze. "God, Kelsey. I'm sorry."

Hoisting up from the hood of my car, I zipped my jacket with fumbling fingers. My legs felt like rubber and my whole body still trembled. My chest rose and fell rapidly as I fought to regulate my breathing. *It was the best damn kiss I'd ever had in my life.*

Continuing to compose myself, I snickered, imagining the show we must have given the neighbors. "No, don't be sorry," I said. Taking a few steps forward, I gave Mark a gentle, reassuring squeeze on the arm. "I just needed us to slow down, that's all."

A look of relief spread across his face as his shoulders visibly relaxed. "I guess I got a little carried away."

Embarrassment became evident in my reddening complexion as I accepted blame for my own lack of self-control. "Yeah, I think we both did," I concurred.

Straightening his back and puffing out his chest, Mark held his hands up in surrender. "I'll be on my best behavior from now on."

I chuckled at his animated posture, wanting to make light of the situation. "I'm gonna hold you to it," I pledged.

~ ~ ~

Silence fell upon us as we remained standing in the driveway, awkwardly watching each other. I lifted my winter-chilled hands and placed them on my face, hoping to soothe the burning sensation of my flushed cheeks. Mark shoved his hands into the pockets of his faded jeans and nervously jingled his car keys. I wracked my brain trying to come up with a conversation piece, but my mind was somewhere else. My head still swam in the vivid memory of his toe-curling kiss, and I just wanted to play it over and over again like a favorite scene from a movie. I wondered if Mark was feeling the same.

Removing his hands from his pockets, he opened his mouth as if to speak, but instead, let out a full-bodied yawn, stretching his arms high above his head while linking his hands together with his fingers. The movement caused his leather jacket to rise up from his waist just enough for me to catch a glimpse of his toned stomach. My eyes grew large as I gaped at his exposed flesh.

I needed to get a hold of myself.

Mark yawned again, bigger this time, setting off a chain reaction that triggered my own open-mouthed spectacle. I had forgotten just how exhausted I was.

"You look about as tired as I feel," Mark observed.

With an arched brow, I teasingly replied, "Is that your way of telling me I look like shit?"

He shook his head vigorously. "No. Not at all. You couldn't look like shit if you tried."

Maybe it was the fatigue making me punchy, but his comment struck me as funny and I snorted. "You wouldn't say that if you saw me first thing in the morning."

"Well, maybe if you play your cards right—" he halted that thought immediately, catching himself before his own foot wound up in his mouth.

Another awkward silence.

Mark smacked himself in the forehead repeatedly. "I don't know what the hell's wrong with me, Kelsey. I can't seem to keep myself from saying stupid shit around you."

I knew what his problem was because I'd seen it before: a classic case of diarrhea of the mouth. I, myself, had fallen victim to the affliction on many an occasion. Nervous excitement usually caused it, resulting in the absence of a speech filter. I found Mark's lack of vocal decorum strangely amusing. In fact, I thought it was kind of adorable.

"It's alright. No harm done," I said.

He scrubbed his hands through his hair roughly, obviously angry with himself. "I'm such an asshole," he muttered. His hair was sticking up every which way, resembling that of a mad scientist. I bit the side of my cheek hard to keep myself from laughing at how crazy he looked.

Mark reached out and took my hand. "Look, I need you to know that I'm not trying to get you into bed. That's not what this is about."

Looking down at our joined hands, I spoke in barely a whisper, "What *is* this about?"

"I...don't know," Mark answered frankly. Placing his other palm on top of my hand, he enclosed it between both of his. "There's just something about you. I think about you all the time."

His admission turned me into a puddle of goo on the spot. Tipping my head up to search his face, I was met with his beaming smile. I became distracted by his mouth, which got me thinking about that kiss again. As if on cue, Mark's eyes left mine, shifting their focus to my mouth. His lips parted ever-so-slightly as his head tilted in closer to mine. Wanting to close the distance, I leaned in, preparing myself for another mind-blowing make-out session.

Grappling with my extreme fatigue, I could feel a yawn coming on and I willed it to subside so it wouldn't ruin the moment. But the yawn won out, my lips expanding into a full-blown, gaping, open-mouthed display of unladylike proportions. I slinked backwards in horror, praying I didn't assault him with foul breath. Mortified, I covered my face with my hands, not wanting to witness Mark's reaction. Anticipating his disgust, I hesitantly peeked through webbed fingers. Bent over at the waist, his hands on his thighs, his face hidden from view, I could see his shoulders vigorously shaking.

He was laughing at me. "What's so funny?" I asked. Of course, I already knew the answer.

"*You* are. Come here," he said, grabbing my arm and pulling me into his chest. I inhaled the scent of rawhide as his leather clad arms wrapped around me in a bear hug. I could feel Mark planting tender kisses on the top of my head. "I should get going. It seems like you could use some sleep," he murmured softly into my hair.

Thankful for his sense of humor, I mumbled into his chest, "I *am* pretty beat."

"Well then, you should definitely rest." Grabbing my face in his hands, he gave me a quick peck on the lips before turning to stride over to his car. While opening the driver's side door, he asked, "Can I call you?"

With a nod, I replied. "Yes, but are you actually *going to call* this time?"

"I promise," he said, marking an "X" over his heart.

He got into his car and started the engine. I observed him through the windshield as he worked the gear shift, putting it into reverse. I continued to watch him as he backed out of my driveway, skillfully maneuvering around my car, which had been parked behind his. As he sped off down the street and out of sight, I hoped I would hear from him soon.

Turning away from the street, I sauntered over to my car to retrieve my duffel bag from the back seat. As my feet treaded the pavement, one of my sneakers made contact with a flat, shiny object, propelling it forward. The faint clanging sound it made upon landing got my attention. Looking down, I saw what appeared to be a collector's coin. I bent over and picked it up, curious as to how it got there. Inspecting the bronze medallion, I turned it over and over in my hand, hoping to discover its monetary value, but it had no numbers—no, what this coin had was an inscription:

Pain is necessary. Suffering is optional.

SEVEN

THAT NIGHT I PACED the living room like a wild animal. It was 11:45 PM and my mom still hadn't come home from work, nor was she answering her phone. None of her friends had any idea where she was. I was beyond panicked. My gut told me she was out with a man. *Having a one-night stand.*

Ever since my dad had died, Mom vowed never to fall in love again. She'd said that nobody could ever take his place. At times, however, I knew she was lonely and the pain was almost too much. So, to soothe the hurt, she sought the comfort of a warm body, her way of trying to forget. The problem was that ultimately, it made her feel worse. And I was the one left to pick up the pieces.

The thought of my mom offering herself up to a virtual stranger nauseated me. She didn't deserve to be treated like some cheap floozy, but sometimes I wondered if subconsciously, she did it to punish herself. She had always misdirected the blame for my dad's death, taking the brunt of the responsibility. And I understood it because for a long time, I blamed myself too. But I was finally able to make my peace with it, allowing myself to let go of all the guilt so I could move on with my life. It was clear my mom had yet to reach that same critical juncture.

I continued to pace—my fuzzy pink slippers making soft scuffing sounds as they passed across the floor. *Back and forth. Back and forth.* My only reprieve came from pausing at the window every now and then to peek through the lace curtain, hoping to spot Mom's car in the driveway. With each passing minute, I became more frantic, my mind whirling with worst case scenarios. *She could be with some lunatic. He could be hurting her.*

Finally, at 12:50 AM, she walked through the door. One look was all it took for my heart to sink into the pit of my stomach. With matted hair, blotchy complexion, and lipstick smeared across her face, I could tell that she had been crying. Keeping her head down to avoid my glare as she shuffled into the living room, her look of self-reproach confirmed my suspicions.

If the cheap cologne emanating from her wasn't clue enough, her ill-fitted ivory silk blouse, misbuttoned and untucked from her gray wool skirt, gave it away. She moved about the living room, determined not to make direct eye contact, while I stood there fuming, arms folded across my chest.

Busying herself by straightening up some scrapbooking materials I had left out on the coffee table, her body language told me to just let it go, but I knew I couldn't allow myself to gloss over it. This was a clear case of role reversal. I was the hard-ass parent ready to hand out punishment to my child, the one who'd just broken curfew and crawled home with her tail between her legs—you know, my mom.

"Why didn't you return my calls? Do you have any idea how *worried* I was?!" I huffed, slapping my arms at my sides in exasperation.

"Please, Kelsey. I don't need this right now. It's been a long day," she said while organizing the mess into tidy, symmetric piles.

Her disregard for my concern infuriated me. "Who was the lucky guy *this* time?" I cut right to the chase.

"Kelsey, I'm warning you…"

"Did he at least buy you dinner first?"

Taken aback by the interrogation, she said, "That's none of your business, Kelsey. I am a grown woman in case you've forgotten."

"Oh, thanks for clearing that up for me. Is *that* how grown women act? Is it *really?*" I spouted, realizing too late that I sounded like an insensitive tyrant.

That pushed her to the limit. Before I could apologize, she responded with fury, pounding her fists on the coffee table, which made me flinch. Dragging both arms in a swift, sweeping motion, she demolished her organized stacks, scattering the debris across the room and onto the floor. "Don't you *dare* talk to me like that! I am your *mother!*" she screeched.

I mentally berated myself for spewing such blatant disrespect. "I know, Mom. I shouldn't have said that. I'm sorry." Lowering my voice to a hushed whisper, I hoped to calm her down. Approaching her, I reached my arms out for an apologetic embrace, but she angrily swatted them away, conveying her wish to be left alone.

Reluctantly, I decided to give Mom her space. Turning to take my leave, I intended to head upstairs for the night, but as I passed the living room threshold into the hallway, the howl of a muffled cry broke out from behind me. I spun around and found my mom slumped into a heap on the floor. Her hands trembled as they masked her face.

I rushed back to her side. "Mom?"

She thrust her hand in my direction, palm face-out in a "stop" gesture. "Please…don't." Rising to her knees, she lifted her face to the ceiling, tears flowing like rivers down her cheeks, staining the collar of her blouse. "Just go," she finally said, her voice barely audible.

I was desperate to make things right. "Mom, please?" I begged.

"I said *GO!*" she yelled, clenching her fists at her sides.

I left the room without uttering another word.

Hurt and anger consumed me as I ascended the stairs to my bedroom. My own tears had begun to flow, and I furiously swiped the wetness away while the urge to scream threatened to overtake me. My mom's heart was aching. I knew it with a certainty that only I—her daughter, her blood—could understand. But sometimes she failed to recognize I had my own cross to bear.

It was almost 1:30 AM when I crawled into bed. Too wound up to sleep, I grabbed my phone from the nightstand, longing to talk to someone. I scrolled through my history of received calls, hoping to locate Mark's number. Once I found it, I stared at the screen, weighing my options. My index finger hovered over the number, knowing that one push would be all it took. With eyes closed and a deep breath…I decided to go for it.

A husky female voice answered on the third ring. "Hello?"

Right then, I regretted my decision. "Um. Is Mark there?"

"Who the hell is *this?*" she asked. *Bitch.*

"It's Kelsey. I'm a friend of Mark's. Is he there?"

"He's indisposed at the moment," she snickered, and it sounded evil.

I suddenly felt like vomiting. "Well, could you just tell him I called?"

"Yeah. I'll be *sure* to pass your message along," she replied sarcastically.

Ending the call, I threw my phone across the room, cracking the faceplate as it collided with the wall. *"FUUUUUCK!!!!"* I buried my face into my pillow and bawled like a baby.

Sleep eluded me that night.

~ ~ ~

As I peeled myself out of bed the following morning, I knew it was going to be a shitty day. My feet felt like bricks as they dragged across the floor, hauling my lifeless body into the bathroom for a shower. I stood under the steady, hard stream of water, basking in its near-scalding heat while my thoughts drifted to my mom…and to Mark. When I finished washing away the grime of the previous day, I wrapped myself in a fluffy white towel and made my way to the sink to brush my teeth. The mirror above it was fogged from steam so I wiped it clean with the palm of my hand. Leaning forward, I took a critical, up-close assessment of the damage from my insomnia, wincing at the sight of deep, dark bags under my eyes. Knowing that no amount of concealer would mask them, I resigned myself to spending the day looking like the walking dead.

After quickly brushing my teeth, I returned to my room to hunt for my most comfortable pair of jeans and a pull-over hoodie. I shot a glance at the clock on my nightstand to realize I was cutting it close on time. Getting dressed with record speed, I grabbed my backpack and headed downstairs without even bothering to blow-dry my hair. The smell of coffee lured me into the kitchen, rendering me defenseless against my craving for a caffeine fix. Mom was sitting at the breakfast bar with a steaming mug in her hand, already dressed for the office.

As I passed her on my way to the coffee maker, she didn't acknowledge me. I poured the piping hot liquid into a stainless-steel travel mug bearing my university's logo. She continued to sit in silence when I turned to face her. Leaning my backside against the counter, I murmured softly, "Morning, Mom," then took my first sip of liquid gold.

Awakening from her reverie, Mom tore her attention away from the mug in her hands. "Oh...hi, sweetheart." Her voice was a dull monotone, her eyes half-open.

"You working late tonight?" I asked.

Returning her focus to her mug, she placed it down on the counter to blankly stare at it. "Probably. I left some money for pizza on the counter so you won't have to cook dinner."

Enough of the small talk. I crossed the kitchen to stand before my mom and wait for a sign. With a gradual lift of her head, she gazed up at me with sad, sleep-deprived eyes. Finally, we exchanged a look of mutual regret over what had transpired the previous night. Broaching the subject delicately, I placed a hand on her shoulder in comfort and understanding. "I miss him too. Every day," I said, blinking back tears.

She reached back for her shoulder, placing her hand on top of mine. I found the warmth of it reassuring. We remained that way for several minutes, consoling each other without words. The 10th anniversary of my dad's death was drawing near, and it was a day that would prove to be excruciatingly difficult for both of us.

Mom took her hand away to wipe the tears that had sprung from her heavily lidded hazel eyes. Glancing down at her mascara-coated fingertips, she broke a smile. "Well, that's gonna give the lawyers something to talk about," she joked. Standing from her stool, she reached for a napkin, then dabbed at the black goop pooling under her eyes, doing her best to remove the mess without smudging it. Peeking at her reflection in the microwave, she asked, "Honey, shouldn't you be getting to school?"

"Ugh. Do I *have* to?" I asked in a fake whiny voice that made Mom laugh. The welcome sound was music to my ears.

"School's important and I'd hate for you to miss it on my account. So, off you go!" she said, playfully pushing me out of the kitchen. *This* was the mom I knew and loved.

I grabbed my navy-blue ski jacket from the coat rack in the hallway and Mom followed behind, grabbing her beige pea coat and brown velvet hat. Finally ready to face the day, we exchanged smiles and headed out the door. It had begun to rain, so I put my hood up while I walked her to her car, waiting as she got in and started the ignition. Backing out of the driveway, she'd almost made it to the street before screeching to a halt. Rolling down her window, she poked her head out and said, "Kelsey, I'm so sorry about last night. I wasn't very considerate of your feelings."

I approached the window and bent down so that we were eye-level. "I'm sorry too. I should never have disrespected you like that."

Mom shook her head in argument. "You had every right to be angry. I was feeling sorry for myself, and I sometimes forget that you're hurting too."

"We're gonna be okay, Mom. You know that don't you?" I asked.

"Yes...deep down, I think I do. It's just been a long road trying to get there."

"We just have to remember to lean on each other. Please don't shut me out anymore, okay?" I asked, fighting the tears that threatened to return.

"I promise."

"Good." I leaned in and gave her a kiss on the forehead.

"I love you, Kelsey."

"I love you too, Mom."

~ ~ ~

Somehow, I managed to muddle through my first few classes without falling asleep. While crossing Huntington Avenue *en route* to my Business Communication and Protocol class, I stepped into a rain-filled pothole, completely soaking one shoe and a good portion of my pant leg. I didn't want to draw attention to myself, so I continued on, seemingly unscathed, accompanied by the melody of my squish-squashing sneaker.

The rainy, cold dreariness of the morning matched my mood, adding to my case of the Monday blues, which seemed to be contagious, as indicated by the clusters of soggy students schlepping about campus with faces of stone. We were all just trying to make it through the day.

Entering the classroom, I sat at my usual desk, and since I was a few minutes early, I decided to check for messages. Retrieving my busted-up, yet functional phone from my backpack, I turned it on to find a voice mail from Mark, which I promptly deleted. I had also received two texts. Squinting, I tried to decipher the words through the large crack in the screen. One was from my mom, telling me that she loved me, and the other was from Mark:

Hi gorgeous.

What an asshole. My pissed-off fingers fired back a quick response:

Leave me alone.

Immediately, he texted back:

What?

To which I typed:

I want you to lose my number.

Finally, he replied:

You're mad? I don't understand.

I shut off my phone, refusing to partake in his little game. *I would not be played for a fool.*

EIGHT

L ATE THAT AFTERNOON, I rode *The T* home from Bay Colony University, relieved to finally have my grueling day of classes behind me. The subway car had filled beyond capacity with passengers crammed in like sardines, forced to spend their commute pressed up against the bodies of total strangers. Thankful for having scored one of the last available seats, I felt the tension of the day leave my body as I slouched forward with my backpack clutched to my chest. With my phone in my lap and earbuds firmly in place, I tuned out the inconsequential babble of the surrounding commuters, allowing the music to transport me to a happier place. As I absorbed the uplifting lyrics to U2's "Beautiful Day," I started to gain a new perspective on the events of the last 24 hours.

The jostling of the train relaxed me, causing my lids to droop, until I closed my eyes completely, sending my mind into a thoughtful state. As I pondered what transpired the previous night, my chest tightened at the recollection of the heartbreaking confrontation with my mom. But I rationalized that as agonizing as it was, a pivotal turning point in our relationship had been reached as a result. As hope filled my heart, I grew optimistic, encouraged by Mom's willingness to bare her feelings and work toward eventually freeing herself from the self-inflicted prison she'd been living in for the last ten years. When my eyes fluttered back open, I outwardly smiled, imagining a brighter future for her. A few nearby passengers shot me curious glances, but I didn't care.

My smile quickly faded as Mark began to weasel his way into my subconscious. I hated myself for letting him get under my skin. But a part of me was grateful for having learned the truth about him before he had the potential to truly devastate me. For all I knew, he had a limitless supply of female callers, and I'd be damned if I was going to be added to the inventory. Deciding he didn't deserve any more of my time…or my tears, I resolved never to think of him again. *It was for the best.*

~ ~ ~

When *The T* reached my stop in Quincy, I blended in with the rest of the herd exiting the station. Fortunately, I lived just a few short blocks away, which was a relief to my tired feet. The rain had finally stopped, the sun now poking out from behind the clouds to erase the bleakness of the day. As I walked home, I turned my face up to the sky, seeking the warmth of the rays to thaw my chilled skin.

I picked up the pace as I neared my house, eager to get a relaxing evening underway. As soon as I walked through the door, I flung my backpack off my shoulders, exhaling an exaggerated *AAAHHH* as it landed on the floor with a thud. My jacket came off next, followed by my rain-soaked sneakers and socks. When I was done, I stood perfectly still in the front hall, taking a moment to absorb the silent tranquility of my surroundings. *It was soooo good to be home.*

With wet socks in hand, I plodded over to the small laundry room off the kitchen, tossing them into the washing machine along with a pile of dirty clothes that had been abandoned in a wicker basket on the floor. I took off my still-damp jeans—*compliments of the puddle incident*—and added them to the wash as well.

Wearing just my hoodie and panties, I padded into the kitchen, my bare feet slapping against the cold linoleum floor. On a mission to appease my rumbling stomach, I fetched some cheese spread and a can of soda out of the fridge, and a box of crackers off the counter. Once I got a knife out of the silverware drawer, I set everything down at the breakfast bar, planted my behind on one of the red vinyl-padded stools and commenced Session Pig-Out. Having barely eaten all day, the cheese-n-cracker combination never tasted so divine.

A good hour passed in quiet solitude as I polished off half a box of crackers and an entire can of cheese spread. Leafing through a celebrity tabloid magazine my mom had left out, I shook my head in amusement at her morbid fascination with such mindless gossip. But that didn't stop me from becoming engrossed in an article analyzing the latest iteration of "Bennifer." Soon, I was in full zone-out mode, completely satiated and relaxed, when an unexpected chiming of the doorbell made me leap out of my skin. *Who the hell could that be?*

Caught off-guard by the piercing interruption, I clutched my chest on my way to the front door, willing my racing heart to settle down. Opening the door just a crack, I peered through the narrow gap. At the sight of Mark's eyes looking back at me, I clutched my chest even tighter. *"Go away,"* I snapped. Grabbing the door with both hands, I forcefully swung it back shut. However, Mark's shoe in the jamb prevented it from slamming completely in his face. *Dammit.*

"Kelsey, wait…" he pleaded.

With a snarl, I pushed the door harder against his intruding foot. "Don't you get it? I don't *want* to see *you!*"

His brows drew together. "Why?"

"Because you're an asshole," I blurted.

"Please. I just want to talk to you. Can I come in?"

"No."

"Just five minutes. That's all I ask. Then if you still want me to leave, I'll go."

"Alright, *fine.* But just five minutes." Although I did concede, my decision to let him in was quite reluctant.

Passing through the doorway, Mark suddenly stopped short, his eyes bugged out in astonishment as they traveled down my bare legs. *"Damn,"* he murmured under his breath.

"What?"

He appeared flabbergasted as he struggled to use articulate speech. "Your um…thighs…uh…" he stammered, his perusal fighting a losing battle to behave as it shifted from my face to what I had going on below the waist.

My eyes widened in horror as the realization of my state of undress struck me like a two-by-four. Frantically pulling at the bottom of my hoodie, I chanted, *"OH GOD!* Shit! Shit! *SHIT!"* I stretched the fabric as far down as it would go in a feeble attempt to cover myself.

Mark simply continued to gawk. "I take it you weren't expecting company," he speculated.

"Would you stop…*looking at me?!*" I shrieked.

"Uh…yeah. Of course. Sorry." He covered his eyes with one hand.

"I'm going to put on some pants. Do *not* follow me," I demanded.

"I promise I'll stay right here," Mark called out.

As I turned to stomp up the stairs, I pretended not to see him peeking through his fingers to catch a glimpse of my hindquarters.

I flew into my room, flinging myself onto the bed and covering my face with my pillow. "Just kill me now," I groaned into the cotton-filled casing, wishing I could fade away into oblivion. Afraid that Mark would come looking for me if I stalled too much longer, I tossed the pillow to the side, bounding off my bed toward the closet. Snatching a pair of black yoga pants from the top shelf, I headed for the bathroom, hopping as I pulled them on along the way. I brushed my teeth and put up my hair, securing the limp brown pieces with a silver alligator clip. Determined not to let embarrassment override my intentions, I marched back down the stairs with my head held high. *He was history.*

Approaching Mark with newfound tenacity, I took his hand and pulled him into the living room. Waving my other hand toward the floral-print loveseat, I said, "Sit."

Mark sat down on one end and leaned to the side, resting on his elbow. He combed his hair off his forehead while waiting for me to join him. Sitting on the opposite end, I angled my body toward him. "Look, Mark, I don't know what you're trying to pull, but I'm not interested in your games."

"I'm really trying to understand, Kelsey, but I just don't—"

"—Oh, *come on!*" I interrupted with a loud slap on my thighs. "How stupid do you think I am?!"

"Can you please just tell me why you're so upset?" He placed his palm on my knee. When I shifted away in protest, his hand fell to the cushion.

Drained from the back-n-forth jabbering, I laid everything out on the table. "Mark, I don't understand you. Why can't you just leave me alone? You've obviously got other girls to occupy your time..."

A crease formed between Mark's brows as his eyes flicked to mine. *"Girls?"*

I stroked my thumb and index finger under my chin in mock contemplation. "Well, let's see...there's that *lovely* girl who answered your phone when I called. I'm sure she was keep-ing you pretty busy."

"Lena?"

I cringed at her name. *She could rot in hell.* "I don't care what her name is. As a matter of fact, I'd appreciate it if you'd spare me the details of your little tryst."

"Jesus, Kelsey. Is that what this is about? I was never with her."

Jumping up from the loveseat, I paced circles around the living room. *"Bullshit!* She made it pretty clear that you two were…*entertaining* each other."

Mark shook his head, adamantly denying my claim. "No! Lena is a friend of Brett's."

"Brett?" I asked, recalling the name.

"He's my roommate."

"If she's with Brett, then why was she answering *your* phone?" I asked, but it sounded more like an accusation—I was still so wary of the whole situation.

"I have no idea."

"And you really expect me to believe you?" *Wary as hell.*

"Yes…because it's the truth."

Dizzy from walking in circles, I faced away from Mark, stopping at the wall opposite where he sat. Bracing myself, I placed my hands flat on the daisy-print wallpaper, dropping my head down between my shoulders. I spoke into my chest, my words a muffled tirade. "See Mark, that's the whole prob-lem in a nutshell: I don't know *what* to believe. First, you don't call me for weeks. Then you're kissing me and telling me that you can't stop thinking about me. Next thing I know, I'm talking to some chick on the other end of your phone. My head is spinning, and I think it's all just too much for me."

Taking a deep breath, I was about to continue my rant, when suddenly, Mark's hands were on my shoulders. He spun me around, pressing me up against the wall, his forearms on either side of me. "I'm not gonna lie to you." His face was now dangerously close to mine as he spoke, and the blood beneath my cheeks caught fire. "I've had my share of meaningless hook-ups, and I'm not proud of it," he admitted.

I pushed at his chest in an attempt to escape the harsh reality of his words, but I was no match for his hard body. Unfazed by my objections, Mark continued, "But since I met you, I haven't been with anyone else. You're the only one I want."

I didn't see that one coming.

With a hard swallow, I croaked, "Oh."

He bent his head down, imploring me to look at him. Peeking up through my lashes, I met his seductive gaze. His mouth swept down to lightly kiss the top of my nose. When his lips hovered there, waiting for my acquiescence, I grabbed a fistful of his maroon fleece pull-over jacket, and drew him in the rest of the way.

We attacked each other's mouths hungrily, and when Mark plunged his tongue inside, I dug my nails into his chest through the protective layer of fleece. Our tongues meshed and stroked in perfect synchronization, and when Mark drew back, I whimpered in protest. But all was forgiven when his lips grazed my neck, trailing wet kisses from my jawline down to my collarbone and back up again. *Oh God.* When his mouth moved to my earlobe, he took it between his teeth, bearing down just enough to drive me completely insane.

Mark's breath was hot in my ear as he whispered, "Only you, Kelsey."

I was a goner.

NINE

I BOLT STRAIGHT OUT *of bed, awakened by the sounds of her garbled screams. I rush downstairs—my pink, frilly nightgown flapping around my ankles as I run. My bare feet smack loudly on the floor as I dart down the hall, through the kitchen, and to the basement door, following the terrifying sounds coming from behind it. The hinges squeak as I push against the oak paneling.*

"Kelsey, s-s-stay upstairs…d-don't come down here," Mom chokes out between sobs. She is hyperventilating. Her voice sounds distorted.

I ignore her warning. A feeling of dread washes over me. I know something is terribly wrong. I grab onto the rail and move down the stairs, each wooden plank creaking under my weight. Mom comes into view as I near the bottom. She's crouched over something, but I can't make out what it is in the dim light. Her body shakes with convulsions as she makes strange, animalistic howling sounds.

My eyes quickly adjust, everything coming into sharp focus as I reach the basement floor. I freeze at the sight before me: trouser-clad legs and black, wing-tipped oxfords jutting out from under Mom's hovering form.

"I hate you, Frankie! Do you hear me? You SONOFABITCH!!" she gags out, pounding on his chest with her fists.

"Daddy?"

As I stand by his feet, Mom snaps her head back at me so fast, it almost appears inhuman. She wails a desperate plea. "Kelsey…OH GOD…please go back upstairs. PLEASE!"

"What's wrong, Daddy? Are you sick?" I ask, taking a step closer.

Mom clutches my arm forcefully, digging her fingernails into my bicep. "Go upstairs NOW!" she yells.

"No!" I cry. "I wanna see Daddy!" I tear my arm out from Mom's grasp as I forge ahead, her nails puncturing my skin.

I drop down by Daddy's head, and my knees slide apart in the slickness on the floor. Placing my hands down on the concrete, I feel around the pool of wetness with my fingers. My eyes flick to his, imploring them to look back at me. They remain wide open and unmoving—expressionless and staring ahead at nothing. His head is all messed up and there's blood trickling out the side of it. My mind gradually puts the pieces of my new reality together. I lift up my hands, holding my palms in front of my face. They're saturated with his blood. I can hear my mom vomiting on the floor behind me.

"No, Daddy! NOOOOO!!!" I scream.

~ ~ ~

Tears streamed down my face as I sat up in bed, my hand pressed tightly to my chest. I could feel an erratic heartbeat hammering against my ribcage. It had been a long time since the terror of that night haunted me in my dreams. Nausea rippled through me as I pulled back the comforter, swinging my legs over the side of the bed. A quick glance at the clock on my nightstand revealed that it was 4:45 AM. Knowing I'd never be able to get back to sleep, I decided to go downstairs and put on a pot of coffee.

My palms were slick with sweat, making it hard to get a firm grip on the railing as I descended the stairs. My vision was blurred from tears, causing me to blindly fumble the rest of the way down. Once in the kitchen, I started to gag and ran to the sink. Dry heaves wracked my body as I held my head over the stainless-steel basin. When the waves subsided, I turned on the faucet to rinse out my mouth and pat my face down with cold water. Feeling marginally better, I started a pot of coffee and sat at the breakfast bar to wait for it to finish brewing.

"Can't sleep?" my mom asked, her voice quivering as she entered the kitchen.

I tried to be strong for her benefit, but just one look at her made me fall to pieces. I collapsed into a fit of sobs, my head down on the counter. "Why'd he leave us, Mom? Didn't we make him happy?" I panted, my lips moving against the cold granite.

Mom rushed to my side and began stroking my hair. I felt like her frightened little girl all over again—the distraught, confused, eleven-year-old child who had just lost her father to his own psychosis. "He wasn't well, Kelsey. I think he tried really hard to get a handle on it, but he just couldn't do it," she soothed.

Her words felt like a new revelation to me. Lifting my head from the counter, I scanned Mom's face for more answers. Red-rimmed eyes bore into mine, tears that had pooled in them now spilling over, flowing down her cheeks like currents. With a deep inhale, she tried to gain some composure before she continued, "He became so withdrawn toward the end, and I didn't know what to do for him. I should have tried harder, Kelsey. I should have helped him. I'm so sorry."

Abruptly, I rose from my stool, letting it fall to the floor, throwing my arms around Mom's neck and enveloping her in a tight embrace. "*No,* Mom. It's *not* your fault. You have to stop blaming yourself," I whispered gently into her hair.

Locking her arms behind me and squeezing tight, she replied, "I love you, Kelsey. I wish your father could see you right now. He'd be so proud of you."

I pulled back to look up into her glassy eyes. "He would?" I asked, wiping away fresh tears as they fell.

She nodded in earnest. "He loved you so much, Kelsey. He always told me how special he thought you were."

A smile broke through all the grief as I grabbed Mom's hands, bringing them up to my lips to plant a soft kiss on each one. "Thank you, Mom. I know he loved you too," I said, releasing her hands and bending down to pick up the fallen bar stool.

Mom went to the coffee pot to pour the fresh brew into two large, ceramic mugs. "Yes, he did," she replied. "And I loved him right back…very much." Carrying the mugs back over to the breakfast bar, she set one down in front of me while finishing her thought, "I just wish that it could have been enough."

~ ~ ~

I watched the Boston skyline unfold in the window opposite me as the subway car traveled its route toward campus. My head bobbed and weaved as it fought to stay upright. There was no way I was going to make it through school without catching some Zs.

The ping coming from my backpack snapped me out of my semi-conscious state. I pulled my phone out of the front compartment to decipher the text message partially camouflaged by the disfigured faceplate. *I needed to get a new phone, pronto.*

Thinking of you today. How you holding up, hun?

My eyes welled up at the sight of Cali's thoughtfulness. Struggling not to break down right there on *The T,* I tried in vain to stop the tremors in my fingers as I typed my response.

I'm ok. Can't believe he's been gone 10 years.

Cali fired back:

How's your mom? She working late tonight?

I tapped:

Yeah. I don't think she can handle being home today.

Her reply:

You need me to come stay with you?

The selfish part of me wanted to take her up on her offer, but the reasonable part overruled it.

No. I don't want you to miss your classes.

A typical Cali response:

Screw the classes!

She always knew how to cheer me up, even on my darkest days.

Cali, I love you. But, seriously, I'm fine.

Just then, my phone's outburst of *AH-OOO-GA* ended our texting session.

"Yes, Cali?" I chuckled as I answered the call. *God, it felt good to laugh.*

"You *sure* you don't need me to come visit?" she asked.

"Yes, I'm sure. I'll be okay. *Really.*" I tried my best to sound convincing.

"Alright, but call me if you change your mind," she offered.

"I will. Thanks for always being there for me."

"Love you, Kels."

"Love you too." With that, I hit, "end."

~ ~ ~

As much as I tried to shake off my exhaustion, it was a losing battle, and I dozed off during most of my lectures. Fellow students in my Business Ethics class were treated to the hog-calling symphony of my snores. I even managed to drool a little on my desk, much to everyone's amusement. My reputation as a model student was going down the drain fast.

When I burst through the doors of the Wheelock Academic Building after finishing my last class, I saw Mark standing at the bottom of the concrete steps waiting for me. My heart started banging around in my chest at the sight of him. We had seen each other several times over the last few weeks, but I was never happier to lay eyes on him than right here, right now, at this moment. Being with him would allow me to get through the day without completely losing my shit.

I bounded down the stairs as quickly as my feet would carry me to jump into his outstretched arms. "What are you doing here? Aren't you supposed to be at school?" I nuzzled my question into his neck.

"My last class got cancelled, so I thought I'd give you a ride home before I head out with the guys tonight," he said, leaning down to graze my lips with his.

Collapsing against his chest, my body sagged with disappointment. "I'm not going to see you tonight?" I spoke against the side of his mouth as I posed the dreaded question.

"Brett got courtside seats to tonight's Celtics game. All the guys are going," he explained. He fixed me with a warm stare as he tucked my hair behind my ear. "But I promise, tomorrow I'm all yours."

Under normal conditions, I would have welcomed a night to myself. But these weren't normal circumstances...*not by a long shot*. The thought of spending the night in my empty house was almost unbearable. Suddenly feeling very alone, I began to unravel. I swung around to head in the direction of Mark's car, hiding the fact that my eyes were laced with tears.

Mark gained on me in a matter of seconds. "Kelsey, what's wrong?" he asked, blocking my path.

Looking down at my hands, I grappled to keep the water-works at bay. "It's nothing. I'm just having a bad day," I said, fingering the fringe of my charcoal, cable-knit scarf.

He reached out and cupped my face in his hands. "You're crying."

"I'm *not*," I said, struggling to maintain control over my emotions. But my efforts were futile and a single tear escaped, slipping past my cheek to dawdle at the end of my chin.

Mark wiped the tear away with the pad of his thumb. "Please talk to me, Kelsey," he urged.

I was done talking. I just wanted to feel something…*any-thing* other than the hollowness in my gut. I clutched the front pockets of Mark's leather jacket and pulled him to me almost forcefully. Moving my hands upward, I locked them behind his head, tugging it down to mine. I kissed him aggressively, slipping my tongue inside and taking what I needed from his mouth. I had little experience with the art of seduction, but the way Mark's mouth and body responded to mine confirmed his willingness and ability to satisfy my desperate need for relief.

Breaking the kiss, I locked eyes with his, which were shim-mering in a soft shade of gold. We exchanged a look of mutual longing. "Take me back to your place. I want you to make me feel good. *Please*," I begged.

TEN

THE RIDE TO HIS apartment seemed endless, giving me too much time to second-guess myself. To keep my objective in sight, I applied visualization techniques, imagining the pleasure that would come from Mark's lips as they delivered their drugging kisses…his hands caressing my bare skin…the warmth of his body connecting with mine. But despite my steadfast determination, the anguish still lurked behind it, threatening to crack my resolve. As it persisted, refusing to stay hidden regardless of my efforts to barricade it into the utmost recesses of my soul, memories of the suicide marred my mind, seeping through my protective walls like a noxious gas.

"You're quiet," Mark commented as he drove, watching me closely out of the corner of his eye.

"I'm sorry. I guess I'm not quite myself today," I admitted, staring down at my lap. Tears welled up again and I speedily fluttered my lids to keep them from making landfall.

"Did something happen at school?" he asked, concern evident in his voice.

I shook my head while turning to look out the passenger window. "No, nothing like that."

"Are you sure you don't want to talk about it?"

"Yes," I replied, my tone adamant.

Because all I'd done for the past ten years was talk about it. I was sick of talking…sick of analyzing…sick of reliving it…sick of the screaming in my head replaying over and over like a song stuck on repeat. "I don't want to talk. I–I just…I want…" I floundered, unable to get the words out.

Mark spoke reassuringly, sensing my unease. "It's okay, Kelsey," he said.

Summoning my courage, I spat out the words, my throat burning as they dislodged like foreign objects. "I just want… *you.*" My voice was low and gravelly. "I want to *feel* you. *All* of you," I clarified, leaving no room for misinterpretation.

Mark's jaw slackened as my words sunk in. "God, Kelsey," he said, taking one hand off the steering wheel to place it on my leg above the knee. A fiery sensation spread through my limbs, warming me instantly.

Mark continued to drive one-handed, leaving the other one free to stroke my thigh. As he alternated between rubbing back and forth and drawing invisible patterns with his fingers, bullets of lust ricocheted throughout my body. It was all I could do to keep from combusting right there in the passenger seat.

By the time we arrived at Mark's place, the air had grown thick with anticipation. He led me up the stairs to the beige, aluminum-sided, triple-decker home that boasted ornate, stained-glass windows and a rooftop deck. As we held hands, we both pretended not to notice that our palms had gotten sweaty. When we reached the door to his third-story apartment, Mark fumbled his keys anxiously, taking several attempts to get us inside. The implications of what we were about to do hovered over us like a lead balloon. *Things would never be the same.*

We barely made it in the door before Mark pressed me up against it, crushing his lips to mine, seeking immediate entry with his tongue. I parted my lips, meeting his tongue thrust for thrust as I moaned my inner longing. Without breaking the kiss, Mark swiftly removed my scarf. Quickly moving on, he clutched the zipper to my ski jacket, forcefully jerking it down. As it opened, he pushed it off my shoulders to let it fall to the floor at my feet. Reaching out with surprisingly nimble fingers, I helped Mark shed the leather barrier of his jacket in kind.

Tearing his mouth from mine, Mark leaned over, resting his forehead against my shoulder. Both panting heavily now, we'd grown too breathless to speak. I brought my hands up to the back of his head, combing my fingers through his dark hair, reveling in its softness. As Mark slowly straightened himself up, my arms fell down by my sides. Taking a step back, he offered me his hand.

Despite my libido being kicked into overdrive, I was experiencing a mounting sense of apprehension. Deciding to ignore it, I accepted his hand, letting him lead the way down the corridor to his bedroom. Upon entering, it surprised me to discover a room devoid of any furniture—just a single mattress and box spring, fitted with a black flannel sheet. It looked lonely and out of place situated smack-dab in the middle of the scuffed-up hardwood floor. It immediately piqued my curiosity, but I figured it probably wasn't the best time for a game of *20 Questions*.

Turning around to face Mark, I noticed he'd wasted no time in removing his T-shirt. I gawked shamelessly at his taut abdomen, feeling my mouth go dry in the process. As I stood there and awkwardly fidgeted with the ends of my hair, Mark swaggered on over, his eyes piercing mine. His gaze grew more seductive as it followed a leisurely path from my eyes down to the hem of my sweatshirt. Grabbing both of my wrists, he raised my arms over my head. Understanding what was about to happen next, I held them there while Mark pulled my sweatshirt overhead, removing it and tossing it onto the floor by the foot of the bed.

Hooking a finger under my bra strap, he pulled it down off my shoulder. He swept my hair to the side, bringing his mouth to my bare skin to kiss, lick and bite his way up to the nape of my neck. "So sexy," he breathed into my hair.

"Mmmmmm," was all I could manage for a reply.

Placing his hands on my hips, my breath hitched when I felt his fingers skimming along the low rise of my jeans. He nudged me gently, backing me up until I felt the edge of the mattress behind my knees. Pushing me down on the bed, he crawled over me, settling in with his knees between my legs, his arms supporting his weight on either side of my torso. He bent down to place a single kiss on my stomach. Rising back up again, he stared down at me with hooded eyes. "Are you sure this is what you want?" he asked, tugging at the button to his jeans.

That was the million-dollar question.

I opened my mouth to say, "Yes," but nothing came out. Instead, the affirmation hung in limbo, taunting me with its threat of refusal. I tried again, but still, nothing. My mouth opened and snapped shut repeatedly as I lay there warring with myself.

Is this what you want?

The question replicated itself over and over in my head like a mantra.

I squeezed my eyes shut. *This could not be happening.* I was so certain this was what I wanted…what I *needed.* In my effort to mask all the pain, I managed to avoid the brutal truth that had been staring me right in the face: I wanted to use sex as a coping mechanism…

Just like my mom.

Facing the music, I opened my eyes. Mark watched me intently, the expression in his gaze morphing from desire to utmost concern. I was at a loss for words, but my hesitation spoke volumes. A slow smile spread across his face as he leaned in close, swooping down and planting a tender kiss on my forehead.

He rose from the bed, and before I could process anything, he was back again, propped up next to me with my sweatshirt in hand. Without a word, I took it and pulled it down over my head. His eyes never left mine, and all that warmth behind them...it suddenly made me fall apart at the seams. I couldn't understand why he was being so sweet, and I didn't feel worthy. My hands flew to my face in embarrassment and shame as I began to cry.

"It's okay, baby," he said as he stroked my hair.

The term of endearment shook me to the core, and I launched myself into his arms, locking my own arms around his neck as I sobbed into his shoulder. He kissed the top of my head over and over while rubbing circles on my back with his palm. "Kelsey," he whispered into my hair. "Kelsey...Kelsey..." he echoed, each time conveying the depths of his compassion.

Mark gently rocked me back and forth as I continued to ride out my crying jag. Once the wailing finally tapered off, he pulled away slowly, looking as if he wanted to say something. Reaching up, he brushed away my tears with the pads of his thumbs while cradling my face in his hands.

"Oh, Mark. I—I'm s-so sorry," I gurgled through shallow breaths.

"*Shhhh*...don't be," he said, sweeping one thumb gently across my lower lip, his eyes scanning mine. "Kelsey, I don't know what's going on with you, but I want you to know that I'm here for you in any way that you need."

I nodded my head in understanding, unable to speak through the lump in my throat. Suddenly, I felt a shift in the atmosphere…and my grief? It was gone. When I looked at Mark again, I could tell by his expression that he felt it too. Something had definitely changed between us.

"I love you."

ELEVEN

I WATCHED WITH BOTH horror and rapt fascination as Mark visibly recoiled, his head jerking back, his facial muscles twitching in an obvious adverse reaction to my declaration of affection.

He rubbed at the sides of his face repeatedly before scratching vigorously along his jaw line—my words affecting him like an allergen. For a moment, I thought he may actually break out in hives.

The confession had sprung from my lips without warning, erupting like a geyser through the rawness in my throat. Mark stared at me, dumbfounded, as we sat huddled in his bed, absorbing the aftershocks. Those three "little" words made their escape without consideration of the consequences, said in a moment of impulse and emotional overload. I wanted to scoop them up and shove them back into my mouth while admonishing them for their prematurity. But it was too late. *The damage was already done.*

Plotting his escape, Mark lifted himself from the bed, his eyes scanning the floor for his T-shirt. Spotting the crumpled heap of black fabric, he treaded over to the spot by the door where he had left it. Picking it up, he threw it on over his head, and the static made his hair stand on end. Running his hands through his hair, he cleared his throat to break the silence that had grown increasingly uncomfortable. "I'm going to get us a couple of sodas. I'll be right back," he said, fleeing the room like he couldn't get out of it fast enough.

I stared at the doorway, shaking my head in self-condemnation. "Real smooth, Kelsey," I mumbled aloud.

Sitting cross-legged in the middle of the bed, I chewed on my nails, wondering how I was going to get myself out of this mess. It was universally known that nothing could send a man running for the hills faster than a profession of love made too soon. At that thought, panic set in, causing beads of sweat to break out along my hair line. I tapped into my ability to problem-solve, figuring I could handle the situation one of two ways: *One*—tell him it was a mistake. Or, *two*—pretend it never happened.

Option two, it was.

I scooted to the edge of the bed to dangle my legs over the side. My body felt limp as the aftereffects of the day's emotional drainage hit me full force. Deciding to spare Mark from any further demonstrations of instability, I pushed up from the bed with wobbly arms and walked out of the room, intending to ask him to take me home.

As I reached the end of the narrow corridor, the sound of Mark's agitated voice snapped me to attention. Rounding the corner of the kitchen, I spotted him leaning against the butcher-block center island, his back to me. His right hand raked continuously through his hair while the left one held a phone to his ear. The inflection in his voice indicated he was in the middle of a heated discussion.

"Look, today's just not gonna work for me," he announced into the phone, his pitch loud and firm.

I didn't feel right intruding on his private conversation, so I turned on my heel, planning to make my retreat. However, the sudden mention of my name rendered me stock-still.

"Don't bring Kelsey into it. This has *nothing* to do with her," he warned, the shrillness in his tone sending shivers down my spine.

My already palpitating heart banged harder against my chest. I swiveled back in Mark's direction, unable to resist the urge to eavesdrop. Mark was growing tenser, shaking his head while running a palm up and down his face. "I'm sorry, but it's *not* gonna happen. Get someone else to do it," he ordered.

I watched as Mark peeled his hand from his face, forming a fist as he brought it down by his side. Turning his head slightly, he revealed a profile that was red hot with anger. "I don't give a *FUCK!*" At that, he brought up his fist, slamming it down hard on the island countertop and making me gasp.

Mark spun around, his eyes wild with rage. Immediately, they softened when they saw the fear in mine. He came out from behind the island, shutting his phone off as he strode to where I stood open-mouthed under the threshold. He reached out, making me flinch automatically, as I was so stunned by the outburst I'd just witnessed. "Shit, I'm sorry. I didn't mean to scare you," he said, pulling his hand back.

I felt myself relax as I watched the anger drain from Mark's features. "Is everything okay?" I asked, now emboldened to take a step closer.

Taking my movement as encouragement, he reached for me again, skimming his fingers along my outer arms. "Yeah, it will be," he responded.

"I've never seen you angry like that before. It scared me," I admitted, peeking up at him through my lashes.

He grabbed my face and lifted it up, forcing me to look at him dead-on. "Kelsey, I would *never* do anything to hurt you. *Ever*," he emphasized.

The passion in his words ignited a fire in my belly, and I dared to look down, placing my focus on Mark's lips. The need to kiss him became overwhelming. I stretched up onto my tiptoes, wrapping my arms around his neck. Sweeping my mouth across his, I took my time to savor the moment. Mark's lips parted as they grazed mine tenderly, matching my rhythm— his breath bathing my face in its warmth.

Mark pushed gently against my hips, breaking the kiss. He wore a serious expression as his eyes bore into mine. "Kelsey, there's something I need to tell you—"

Before he could continue, the door flew open, smacking against the wall as his roommate Brett bounded into the apartment. "Mark, you almost ready to go, buddy? The game's gonna start soon," he called out.

Clamping his mouth shut, Mark exhaled through his nose, obviously displeased with the interruption. Forcing a grin, he took my hand and led me out of the kitchen.

We entered the living room where Brett stood sorting through his mail. "Brett, I want you to meet someone," Mark said, pulling me in the direction of his friend.

Brett turned to face me, his eyes lacing with recognition. "Hey, I remember you! Kelsey, right?" he asked, tossing the envelopes onto the coffee table.

"Yup, that's right. Your memory is very impressive," I teased.

He came up by my side and put an arm around me in a half-hug. "Yeah, well, I'm sure it's a hell of a lot better than Mark's was that night," he joked.

My eyes flicked to Mark, and upon seeing his complexion pink with embarrassment, my protective nature kicked in. "Hey, we've all been there at one time or another," I rebuked.

"Point taken," Brett said, pulling off his red baseball cap and tossing it onto the table next to the stack of mail. My attention immediately landed on his severe case of hat-hair.

"That bad?" Brett asked, scratching at his sandy blond mop.

"Afraid so," I replied, stifling a giggle.

"Alright, I think that's my cue to jump in the shower," he said with a wink.

Mark grabbed my hand and laced our fingers together. "Brett, about the game—"

"—Oh no, you don't," I interjected. *"Please,* go out with your friends. Have a *great* time. I'm about ready to crash anyway," I insisted.

"You sure?" he asked, scanning my face for approval.

My eyes crinkled as I smiled, aiming to put his mind at ease. "Yes, I'm sure. I think I just want to go home."

~ ~ ~

Later that night, I tossed and turned, unable to fall asleep despite being overtired. I desperately wanted to call Mark, but I didn't want to come off as too needy, especially given that I had already dropped the L-Bomb on him earlier. The house had grown eerily quiet, making me acutely aware of being alone. Feeling terribly sorry for myself, I whispered into the darkness, "I wish you were here, Dad."

Needing a distraction, I got out of bed and slid into my fuzzy pink slippers. I schlepped over to my desk and turned on the small lamp that sat atop it. Eyeing the textbook that had been left out from my last study session, I pulled out my chair and sat down. It seemed as good a time as any to brush up on my business acumen.

I became heavily engrossed in the subject matter, quickly filling the pages of my three-ring binder as I took copious amounts of notes. When I finally came up for air, my eyes widened in surprise when they noted the time on the clock—nearly

10 PM. I pushed back from my chair, ready to call it quits for the night.

Heading into the bathroom to wash-up and brush my teeth, I was in the middle of my second gargling cycle when I thought I heard the chiming of the doorbell. Suspending my oral hygiene efforts, I listened for the sound to repeat. Just when I'd surmised that my mind was playing tricks on me, the sound came again, replaying over and over and over, grating on my nerves like a siren.

"I'm coming! I'm coming!" I yelled, flying down the stairs in a mad dash to stop the incessant noise.

As soon as I opened the door, Cali barreled into me, latching herself onto my terrycloth robe. I hugged her back, bringing all of my emotions back to the surface. I cried into the collar of her winter-white, baby-doll coat. Cali pulled back while clutching my hands, holding me at arm's length while she assessed my bedraggled look. "You didn't think I'd let you spend the night alone, did you? Let's go upstairs and pick out a kick-ass outfit. We're going out," she asserted.

Mark

Going to the game tonight was a mistake. The temptation was everywhere and I wasn't strong enough. Brett couldn't deal with me when I was like this, so he sent me home in a cab. I couldn't say that I blamed him.

I must have dialed Kelsey's number a hundred times in the past hour, but she wasn't answering her phone. *Fuck.* I really needed to talk to her. My resistance was fading fast.

A knock at the door made me break out in a cold sweat. *I'm* the one that requested *her* presence, but it was my clouded judgment doing all the talking.

"Are you in there, sweetie?" she asked through the door. The sound of her voice made my stomach turn. Maybe if I ignored her, she'd go away. *Who was I kidding?* That was never going to happen.

"If you don't let me in, I'll go find someone else who wants it," she hissed.

In an eleventh-hour effort to save myself, I called Kelsey one last time. *Shit.* No answer. Where the fuck was she?

My legs moved of their own accord, propelling me to my destiny. I opened the door and saw her standing there, looking like she'd been dragged around by her ankles. The hauntingly familiar stench oozing from her pores made me want to both run away screaming and breathe it in as if it were my only source of oxygen.

Whooshing through the doorway, she sashayed into the living room. Making herself comfortable on the brown futon couch, she waited for me to follow. A voice in my head was screaming at me to get the fuck out of there. But deep down I knew I could never say, "No."

She patted the seat next to her. "You coming, or what?"

"Yeah," I replied. "I'm coming, Lena."

TWELVE

Mark

SUNLIGHT STREAMED into my bedroom through the slats in the window blinds, the rays searing through my lids like lasers. I opened my eyes begrudgingly, trying to remember what day it was. *Shit.* My mind was drawing a blank. It was obvious that I had passed out, but for how long?

Standing up, I staggered around the room, wearing only my black silk boxers and white cotton socks. The walls closed in on me, the floor, slanting unevenly under my feet. My stomach twisted in knots as bile rose up in my throat. I held my mouth and ran toward the corridor.

I flung open the bathroom door, sinking to my knees in front of the toilet. My body retaliated against its abuse, and I threw up violently. When I was finished hefting, I slid onto my stomach to hug the porcelain bowl like it was my best friend.

The concept of time was lost to me. Minutes, hours, or days could have passed while I laid there like a slug. When the room finally stopped spinning, I peeled myself up off the floor. I caught my reflection in the mirror above the sink. The person looking back at me was weak. He was a worthless prick.

I went into the kitchen to grab a bottle of vodka from on top of the fridge. I unscrewed the cap and brought the bottle to my mouth. The liquid burned like acid. It numbed my throat and settled my queasy stomach.

Taking the bottle back with me to my room, I downed another swig and sat on the bed. Out of the corner of my eye, I spotted my phone on the floor. I leaned over and picked it up, afraid of what I might find. When I looked at the screen, sheer panic coursed through my veins.

Kelsey.

How was I going to explain all this to her?

I put the phone up to my ear, bracing myself for her voicemail messages.

9:15 AM

Hey, Mark. It's Kelsey. I'm so sorry I didn't call you back last night. I was out with Cali and I left my cell phone at home by accident. Is everything alright? Call me when you can.

2:35 PM

Mark, it's Kelsey again. I waited for you after school. I hope nothing's wrong. When you get a minute, give me a call, okay?

5:05 PM

Did I do something to upset you? Call me. Please.

The concern in her voice tore me up inside. *Fuck.* I should never have started anything with her. She deserved better than me.

I stared at the phone in my hand. I took the easy way out and sent her a text:

Sorry I didn't call. Not feeling well. Talk to you tomorrow.

Lifting the bottle back to my lips, I flooded myself with more poison. Why couldn't I get my shit together? I didn't want to be like this. I *tried* not to be like this. Unfortunately, my willpower was a spineless jellyfish.

My vision clouded with tears, and I wiped my eyes with the back of my hand, hating myself for being such a pussy. Falling back onto my soft flannel sheet, I closed my eyes and prayed for sleep.

~ ~ ~

"Wake up, Prince Charming."

Lena's raspy voice penetrated right through me, waking me from my catatonia. I looked around, confused and discombobulated. Her silhouette stood in the doorway, blocking my escape route. She moved out of the shadows of the corridor and into the light of my room. "Time for you to take care of *your* end of the bargain," she seethed.

Propping myself up on my elbows, I narrowed my eyes at her. "Now's not a good time, Lena," I deadpanned.

Lena slithered toward me and sat on the edge of the bed. "You know how this works, sweetie," she said as she patted my leg.

I sat up and grabbed her hand. "Don't fucking touch me," I warned.

"Oooh, so sensitive," she chided.

My eyes cut to her haggard face. It was caked in makeup, which did nothing to cover up her years of hard living. She looked so much older than her 29 years, and I almost felt sorry for her. *Almost.* "Just tell me what you want me to do," I said.

With a forced, tight-lipped smile, she said, "Now, that's a good boy."

THIRTEEN

Kelsey

SITTING AT MY DESK, I leaned forward, my elbows propped on its edge. Supporting my head with my hands, I looked down absently at my open textbook, struggling to pay attention to the words, begging them to take on meaning. But they stared back at me blankly, refusing to enlighten me with their significance. My phone rested on the corner of my desk, connected to its charging cord. I obsessively checked it every few minutes to make sure it was fully charged and working properly.

It had been almost a week since I had last spoken to Mark, and each day that passed made my heart hurt a little more. All my calls went straight to his voice mail, and after leaving him several desperate messages, I finally ceased my phone stalking. His evasion was slowly eating away at my core, the fear of rejection looming large in my mind. I regretted telling Mark that I loved him. It was a blunder of epic proportions, and now I had no choice but to suffer the consequences.

How had I allowed myself to become so wrapped up in him? It was an overt contradiction to my usual practices in self-preservation. I had always been meticulous in my cautionary approach to life and relationships. I prided myself on it, in fact. Yet Mark, with his intoxicating kisses, fiery stares, and an aura shrouded in mystery, managed to chisel his way into my heart. I was drawn to him like a moth to a flame. I could feel myself singeing in the fire, but I was powerless to stop it. The point of no return had already been reached. A part of me wished I had never laid eyes on him. My life would have gone on, business as usual, uninterrupted and comfortable. And I would have been none the wiser.

But meeting him changed everything.

Pushing back from my desk, I stood and stretched my arms out in front of me, rolling my head from side to side, working out the kinks in my neck and shoulders. I walked over to the window and stared out at the sun-filled sky, dazzling and vibrant, without a cloud in sight. From somewhere down below, a beam of light shot up and temporarily blinded me, making me shield my eyes from the onslaught of intense brilliance. My gaze dropped down to the driveway, seeking out the culprit.

Cupping both hands over my eyes, I zeroed in on my car's rear view mirror reflecting the sun's rays back at me.

This was a sign.

Backing away from the window, I scanned the room for my car keys, which were on the nightstand. I grabbed them, shoving them into the front pocket of my jeans. My feet moved with a new sense of purpose, reenergized and unwavering as they propelled me down the stairs and out the door.

As I got in the car and sat behind the steering wheel, an uncomfortable feeling curled in my stomach. *Maybe this was a bad idea.* What was I going to say to him? Taking a deep breath, I reeled myself back in, refocusing on the task at hand. I was done playing the role of scorned lover. Mark's unforeseen withdrawal from my life required an explanation. And I was going to demand one. He owed me that much.

~ ~ ~

Driving with urgency, my lead foot controlled the speed, and I arrived at Mark's apartment in Braintree less than ten minutes later—which had to be some kind of record. My heart rate spiked to an all-time high when I saw Mark's black sedan parked out front. *He was home.* Parking across the street, I took a moment to collect myself, then, with a hard swallow, I stepped out of the car to head toward the triple-decker.

Flinging open the main door, I went inside and began my ascent to the third floor, each step bringing me closer to the moment of truth. The staircase seemed to go on forever, and my legs felt like wet noodles as their strength depleted. When

I finally reached the door to Mark's apartment, I realized that my whole body was trembling. I was scared shitless.

Summoning what little courage I had left, I knocked on the door and waited. I knocked again and waited some more. I could hear movement from inside the apartment, but nobody answered the door. This time, I *pounded hard*, using the bottom of my fists. The sound of sliding metal garnered my full attention—the lock unlatching.

"Oh, hey there Kelsey," Brett said as he peered around the door.

"Hey, Brett. I need to see Mark," I asserted while thrusting the door forward with my hand.

Brett pushed back against my palm, denying me entrance. "He's tied up right now. How about you come back tomorrow?" he offered lamely.

I stood my ground, unflustered by his refusal to cooperate. "Let me in, Brett."

His expression turned sympathetic. "Kelsey, I'm sorry, but Mark doesn't want to see you right now."

My skin burned feverishly hot as anger rippled throughout my body. "I'd like to hear him tell me that himself. *OR DOESN'T HE HAVE THE BALLS?!*" I yelled, loud enough so that Mark might hear me from inside.

Brett studied me for a moment before stepping back, shaking his moppy blond head in resignation. "Alright, Kelsey. You win."

Pure instinct directed my movements as I pushed through the door, making a beeline for Mark's bedroom. When I got there, I stood in the doorway, gaping in utter disbelief. Mark was sitting on his bed next to a woman, her hand resting on his leg. Their shoulders were touching. My heart plummeted, settling heavily in my gut. I choked back a sob.

Mark's head snapped up, his eyes landing on mine. Neither of us said a word as we stared at each other, stunned. The woman stood up from the bed and lit a cigarette. She strutted to the window with her black leather skirt swishing noisily against her untoned thighs. She bent over and blew smoke out the open screen, revealing the dark roots at the top of her bleach blond hair. She angled her head toward me in acknowledgement, her lips curved with arrogance as she spoke. "So, you must be Kelsey."

I recognized her voice immediately. She was that bitch I had spoken to on the phone. *Lena.* My eyes moistened with hurt and confusion. Mark had deceived me, and I felt like a complete fool. The need to leave overtook me.

My eyes cut back to Mark. "You're a *liar.*" I barely choked the words out before I turned and fled the room.

"Kelsey, wait!" Mark hollered after me.

I ran.

Barreling down the corridor and out the door, I raced down the stairs, fighting back the tears that were brimming in my eyes. I'd just made it to the street when I felt something pull at my sweatshirt. Mark had a wad of the blue cotton in his hand, immobilizing me.

"Kelsey," Mark pleaded.

"Let go of me!" I screamed.

Instead of loosening his grip, he pulled me flush against him. "It's not what you think," he insisted, his breath hot in my face. The stench of bourbon washed over me, making my nostrils flare and my eyes burn.

"You're drunk," I spat, disgusted.

He released me, his eyes darting to the ground in shame and remorse. "Yes…a little. I'm sorry."

"Your apologies don't mean anything anymore, Mark."

He kept his head to the ground, his dark hair fallen like a veil over his eyes. "Then you should probably go."

His words bit into me, infecting me with their venom. My voice hardened in response, "Yes. *Of course.* I wouldn't want you to keep Lena waiting." And with that parting shot, I crossed the street to my car.

My fingers fumbled around my key ring, searching blindly for the automatic unlock button. I pulled it out of my pocket and tried to focus, but it was blurred from the wetness that obscured my vision. Thanks to Mark, I had become a dispenser for the tears that wouldn't stop coming. I squeezed them back and refused to let them fall. I felt used and unwanted, like a piece of leathery steak that had been chewed up and spit out.

As I stood facing my car, I caught Mark's reflection in the passenger side window. Before I could protest, his arms suddenly enveloped me from behind. "Did you mean it when you said you loved me?" he heaved into my hair.

I shook my head vigorously as I tried to wriggle free from his hold. "No."

"I don't believe you," he said, his arms tightening around my waist.

I sagged against him, emotionally and physically deflated. "Why are you doing this to me?"

"I never wanted her, Kelsey. I don't..."

"I-I can't deal with this. Please, just let me go."

His hands moved from around my waist. He grabbed my shoulders and spun me around forcefully, making me dizzy. "I can't!" he yelled. He dug his hands into my upper arms, shaking me. His caramel orbs pierced me with their intensity. The whites of his eyes were red and raw and filled with emotion. "God knows I've tried! I know I don't deserve you. But...I'm just so fucking miserable without you."

My eyes stung and I could no longer hold back the tears. "But you're sleeping with *her*. She was in your room…on your bed."

Mark shook me again, harder this time. "No! I swear to you, Kelsey. I never laid a hand on her. Ever."

My head was swimming with confusion and uncertainty. "I don't understand any of this, Mark! I feel like I'm going fucking crazy."

Mark broke hold and took a step back. He dragged both hands through his hair, the muscles in his biceps flexing beneath the short sleeves of his pale-yellow crew shirt. He released a shaky breath. "I want to tell you," he said, his eyes glistening with moisture. "I want to tell you *everything*. I'm just so fucking scared of what you'll think of me," he admitted.

I wrapped my arms across myself, hugging my stomach in self-consolation. Protectiveness rose from within me, and I narrowed my eyes at Mark in distrust. "You know what? I don't think I want to know. *I'm done.* Goodbye, Mark." I unlocked the car and opened the door.

Mark snatched my hand away from the door handle and pulled it back, forcing my body to angle toward his. His face was pained, despair flitting across his features. "Kelsey, please. Don't give up on me."

I jerked free and got in the car, slamming the door for full effect. I started the engine and peeled away from the curb, my tires screeching angrily against the concrete. Glancing in the rear-view mirror, I watched as Mark's motionless form gradually faded from my line of vision.

FOURTEEN

Mark

WATCHING KELSEY DRIVE away annihilated me. A low rumble erupted from my throat as anger and self-loathing consumed me. I trudged back across the street toward my apartment. The sound of the pavement scratching under my boots echoed loudly against my skull. My head soon became too heavy to carry, weighed down by my fears and insecurities. I let my chin fall to my chest as I began the torturous climb to the third floor.

I hauled my ass through the door, shouting Lena's name. When she didn't respond, I ambled into the kitchen, snatching up the half-empty bottle of bourbon I had left out on the counter. Lifting the bottle to my lips, I funneled the contents through my esophagus into my stomach. My head whirled with each movement, my pupils shifting in and out of focus. When my body swayed, I grasped the edge of the countertop to keep from falling over. I wanted to feel numb, to become devoid of sensation and emotion. But the bourbon wasn't enough.

"Where the *FUUUCK* are you, Leeena?" I slurred as I wandered through the apartment in search of her. The walls rippled in waves on either side of me as I staggered down the corridor and into my bedroom. She sat on the floor with a small hand mirror placed between her pale bare legs, her leather skirt bunched up around her waist to reveal a small patch of her red lace panties. Repulsed by the sight, I wanted to look away. But she possessed what I needed, what my body hungered for so desperately. Everything hurt so badly, and all I wanted was to forget.

Lena looked over her shoulder, watching me rock back and forth on my heels behind her. She smiled wide and invitingly, her bleached teeth flashing like a neon sign. "Let me make it better, sweetie," she whispered.

Circling around her, I sat down on the dust-coated hardwood floor, my eyes ravenous as they fixated on the lines of white powder displayed enticingly in front of me. Lena offered me a rolled-up dollar bill, which I accepted without hesitation. I licked my lips in anticipation, leaning forward and taking it all in.

~ ~ ~

The next morning arrived unwelcomely. My head pounded as I rolled over onto my stomach, smooshing my face into the pillow. I flogged the mattress with restless arms, trying to get comfortable. They landed loudly, smacking against something fleshy, and I was suddenly wide awake.

"Cut the shit," Lena said, her gaze heavy-lidded.

I blinked once, then again. Maybe I was still high. Or drunk. Or seeing things. It was the only viable explanation. I pressed my fists into my eyes, unwilling to accept the alternative.

"And stop hogging the sheet. I'm freezing," she growled, yanking the black flannel away from my body.

I slowly lowered my hands, daring to take in the vastness of peroxide-treated snarls that engulfed my mattress. To make matters worse, red lace panties and a matching push-up bra were the only scraps of material clinging to Lena's pale form. My stomach twisted at the sight of it.

Shifting to the farthest corner of my bed, I slumped my shoulders in despair, eyes glued to my lap. Navy and white striped cotton boxers were the only fibers separating me from total nudity. The realization of what had likely transpired became too much to handle. I got up and tore down the hall to the bathroom.

Clutching the sink, I waited for my stomach to rid itself of whatever shit I had fed it, but the queasiness only got worse with no signs of dissipating. I dropped to the floor, tucking my knees up and hugging them to my chest, banging my head back against the wall in rapid succession until I saw stars. Tears gathered in the corners of my eyes, but I wouldn't allow myself to cry. I didn't deserve the emotional release. I had no one to blame for this mess but myself.

Not knowing what else to do, I got back up and pushed my boxers down from my hips, shaking out of them before lugging myself into the shower. I turned the nozzle and then stood motionless, vaguely cognizant of the now vulnerable spot on the back of my head that throbbed beneath the warm spray. I watched the water swirl around the bottom of the tub, trying to wade past the murkiness of my mind to something solid I could grab on to.

I stayed in the shower until the water ran cold, snapping my brain into action. The fog lifted and all recollection of last night's events came flooding back. I remembered...*everything*. Suddenly, I was overcome with such relief and emotion that I finally let myself have the release I'd been craving.

I didn't sleep with her.

Optimism and excitement churned inside of me as I turned off the shower and grabbed a towel from the rack. I dried my-self in a hurry before wrapping the towel around my waist and padding back out to the corridor. I headed toward my bed-room to fetch some clothes. *Then it hit me.* Lena was still here.

Rage swiftly permeated my excitement as I rushed into my room. The resonant boom of the slamming door caused Lena's eyes to spring open. They widened as I stalked over to the bed and yanked at the sheet she was tangled in. "What the fuck, Mark?!" she howled, sliding across the bed as I towed her along. "Have you lost your mind?!"

"I'm done Lena. Do you hear me? *No more.* You need to go."

One corner of her mouth turned up, an arrogant smirk on full display. "What's the matter, sweetie? Your little girlfriend doesn't approve?" she hissed.

I grabbed her skirt and tank top from the floor and threw them at her, my nostrils flaring. "This is *my* room, and *you* are not welcome here! Not now…not ever!"

She swung her legs over the side of the bed and shimmied into her skirt. "*Your* room? In case you forgot, this is Brett's apartment, sweetheart. He's doing you a favor by letting you stay here," she commented dryly.

Temper blazing, I could feel the veins in my neck jutting out. "Leave. *Now.* I am not going to ask you again," I threatened.

Rising from the bed, Lena pulled on her white tank top, its neckline bulging with red laced cleavage. "Okay, have it your way. But you'll be begging for more later," she boasted.

"I will never beg you for *anything* ever again. You can count on it," I scowled. Retrieving a shoe box from the top shelf of my closet, I barked, "And take this shit with you." Lena puffed out a sharp exhale when I shoved the box into her chest. "I'm not doing your dirty work for you anymore." And that was a promise.

Lena was unconvinced. "Mmmm hmmm. If you say so." With an evil smile, she slowly left the room.

Letting my towel fall from my waist, I pulled a T-shirt and a pair of black denim jeans from the closet floor. I couldn't find a pair of clean boxers, so I resigned myself to going commando for the day. Marching out of my room, I headed toward the kitchen, a new man on a mission.

I opened cabinets, rummaged through drawers, and cleaned out the fridge, gathering every last container of booze I could find. As I cracked open cans and unscrewed bottle tops, I prayed for infinite sobriety. Two at a time, I held the bottles and cans over the sink, tipping them upside-down and emptying them out. *I was reborn.*

"What the fuck are you doing?" A male voice filled the space behind me.

I spun around to find Brett standing with his arms crossed over his chest as he eyed me with disdain. *This was it. I couldn't turn back now.* "I'm done with this shit, Brett. It's killing me."

Brett threw his head back and chuckled. "I know what this is about. Just give Kelsey what she's been begging for, so you can get your head out of your dick and focus on your job," he rebuked.

"Shut up, Brett. It's not like that with her. She's important to me," I defended.

"I don't buy this high and mighty bullshit for one second," he said. Approaching me from the side, he clapped me on my left shoulder. "You are what you are, Mark. It isn't gonna change because some slut got her claws into you."

Without a second thought, my right fist connected to Brett's jaw in a sucker punch. He slumped to the floor like a ragdoll, shielding himself with his forearms. "Jesus Christ, Mark!" he screamed like a little girl.

I leaned over his cowering form with my fist still raised, anger oozing from every fiber of my being. "You say anything like that about Kelsey again, and I will knock your fucking teeth out, you got that?"

"Okay. I get it. Sorry, man." Rubbing his jaw, Brett slowly sat back up. "Just don't let this girl come between you and your job," he ordered.

Backing up to the center island, I loosened my fist, then grabbed my car keys from the countertop behind me. As I turned to leave, I spoke with conviction, "Oh, didn't Lena tell you? *I quit.*"

~ ~ ~

I couldn't pinpoint the exact moment I fell in love with her. It happened so fast, I didn't even see it coming. My heart, once cold and hardened, warmed and swelled just from being around her. She deserved better than what I had given her. And it killed me to know how much I had hurt her. But the thought of never seeing Kelsey again made me realize just how much I *needed* her. She made me want to change and be a better man. A man *I* could be proud of. A man who could be happy and make *her* happy.

I just hoped it wasn't too late.

Kelsey's last class of the day would be over at any minute. Double parking my car on Huntington Avenue, I got out, my muscles twitching with anticipation as I strode toward our usual meeting spot. I was nervous as shit.

Sensing her presence, I looked to the top of the cement steps and saw her. Talking and laughing with classmates, she didn't notice me right away. Worn loosely today, her hair fell like silk around her shoulders. *So beautiful.* Suddenly, she froze, as if sensing my presence too. She turned slowly, head cocked in puzzlement as her wide, hazel eyes found mine. I wondered if she may try to run, but she stood as still as stone. My feet climbed the steps before my brain could register their movements, my eyes never leaving Kelsey's as our bodies closed the gap.

In that moment, nothing else mattered except her. Making her understand. Making her *mine.*

When I got to the top of the steps, I noticed Kelsey's lips quivering. I reached out to brush my thumb across them. "Kelsey," I whispered.

FIFTEEN

Kelsey

WITH A TREMBLING hand, I grabbed Mark's wrist, wrenching him away from touching me. I shook my head, tamping down the rising emotions, but it was impossible to keep them there. The feelings of betrayal were a force to be reckoned with, surging to the surface and gushing all over.

"*Don't,*" I choked out. "I can't do this."

"Kelsey, *please*. Just let me explain." Mark wore the expression of pure anguish.

I could no longer stand to look at him. In an abrupt retreat, I rushed down the stairs, breaking into a jog when I hit the sidewalk. Mark stayed hot on my trail. "Kelsey…just listen to me." He tried to grab my hand, but I shook him off.

Stopping short, I whipped back around, pushing at Mark in a blind rage. "Why are you even here?!?! You ignored my calls. You didn't want me in your apartment. You made me feel like a fucking inconvenience!" My hands landed hard on his chest. "And worst of all, you *LIED* to me!" I screamed, anger bursting from deep within my throat.

Taking a step back, I lowered my hands, fingers curling into fists at my sides. I could literally feel my heart shattering, the pain of the shards sending tears down my cheeks as my chest rapidly rose and fell. "Why…can't you…just…let me *be?*" I fought to get the words out. It hurt just to *breathe*.

Mark wouldn't relent. Grabbing my face, he held it hard in his hands. His caramel eyes flamed with intensity as they found mine. Hot, minty breath washed over me as he spoke. "Because, Kelsey…I love you."

I sucked in a jagged breath as his announcement knocked me for a loop. More than anything, I wanted to buy into its sincerity. But the weight of what I knew…what I had *seen* with my own eyes…made thoughts of Lena in Mark's bedroom take precedence over his words of grandeur.

The sight of them together and how it felt continued to flash before me in living, breathing color. "But you were with Lena," I sniffed. "You've been avoiding me." I wiped my nose on the sleeve of my gray fleece hoodie.

"Kelsey, I know I haven't made it easy for you to trust me. I totally fucked up, and I'm sorry." I saw the regret clearly imprinted on his features as he spoke. "But I need you to believe me when I tell you that I was never *with* Lena. *Ever.* You're the one I want, Kelsey. Just you. Always you."

I searched his face—for truth, for clarity—now unable to look away. The ache in my chest subsided as his declaration slowly healed the cracks in my heart. "You love me?" I asked, tears rushing out like a waterfall.

Tentatively, Mark leaned in closer. When I didn't object, he tilted his head, nuzzling my face with his nose as he whispered, "I think I've loved you since the very first time I saw you." At that, he let out a soft humorless laugh, laced with bitterness, regret, and self-loathing. "I was so wasted and made such a colossal fuck up of that night. But I knew…you were something special."

Closing my eyes, I reveled in his words and his touch. Before I could reopen them, I felt the warmth of his mouth, the wetness of his tongue as it caressed my bottom lip. Coaxing. Begging. Welcoming him in, I parted my lips while meeting his tongue with mine. I reached my arms around his waist, sliding my hands up and under his leather jacket and T-shirt to rest my palms on the heated flesh of his bare back. We moved our mouths together feverishly while pressing our bodies flush up against one another. Mark pulled back slightly, tugging my bottom lip along as he gently bore down. A groan fled my throat, my mouth ablaze from his kisses. Fisting his hands in my hair, he pulled it to reveal my neck to him before descending upon my sensitive skin. He traveled a wet path up to my ear and whispered, "I love you." To drive that sentiment home, he took my earlobe between his teeth.

College students buzzed all around us as we stood making out on the busy sidewalk, but I didn't care. I was too caught up in the moment to worry about our public display of affection. I could have stood there kissing Mark forever, and it still wouldn't have been enough.

In his absence, my longing had only grown.

Mark kissed his way up to my jaw before reclaiming my mouth. "I love you," he repeated, and my heart beat faster.

"*Mark*," I sighed against his lips. My voice was choppy as the rest of the words broke free. "I-I love you," I murmured through ragged breaths. This time the words were spoken without regret. They were the truth…and they felt *right*.

Mark slowed down his movements, gradually pulling back and breaking his spell over me. Running his hands over my shoulders and down my arms, he grasped my fingers. With a gentle squeeze of my hand, he said, "Let me take you home. There's so much I need to tell you."

~ ~ ~

When Mark turned down my street, the sight of my mom's hatchback in the driveway surprised me as my house came into view. Pulling up behind her car, he put his into park. With the engine still running, he faced me. "I don't have to come in, if now's not a good time."

"No. It's okay. Mom probably just decided to come home from work early."

Mark shut the car off and stepped out, quickly circling around to my side to open my door. He took my hand as I got out and didn't let go as we walked up the paved pathway to the front door of my house. His fingertips caressed mine as I led him inside, sending shivers up and down my spine.

Following the sounds of the TV, I pulled Mark in the direction of the living room, where I intended to finally introduce him to my mom. But as soon as we entered, I winced. Curled up on the sofa with an afghan draped across her legs, her complexion was blotchy and tear streaked. On the end table beside her sat a box of tissues, several already used and discarded on the floor in crumpled up balls.

She looked…*broken*.

Immediately, I rushed to her side. "Mom, what happened?"

She stared straight ahead, her eyes clouded with torment. "I visited his grave today." Her jaw quivered as she spoke, her tone hoarse.

I swallowed past the lump in my own throat, determined to hold myself together in front of Mark. He had seen enough of my emotional outbursts to last a lifetime. Kneeling on the floor in front of Mom, I tried to get her to look at me, but she refused to meet my gaze, opting instead to stare at her lap. *So vulnerable—like a child.* She was breaking my heart. With a comforting hand on her knee, I suggested, "Mom, maybe you should go lie down in bed for a little while. You look exhausted." I proceeded to pick the damp tissues up from the floor.

She was quiet for a moment before breathing out heavily through her nose. Managing a weak smile, she peeled the afghan away from her body. "I guess a nap couldn't hurt. Thanks, honey." When her eyes finally met mine, she reached out, stroking the side of my face with her fingertips.

I was all too familiar with Mom's pain. Ten years hadn't lessened the immense feeling of loss we both felt every day. But instead of getting easier, as I'd hoped, her inability to cope with the loss seemed to only intensify in recent weeks. A part of me wondered if she'd ever find the strength to dig herself out of this ongoing depression. "I'll bring you up some tea," I offered.

Mom rose from the sofa and folded the afghan, gently placing it over the armrest. "That sounds great, sweetheart. What would I ever do without you?"

"Mom, I am always here, whenever you need me. Don't ever forget it," I reassured. My eyes followed her as she left the room to head upstairs.

Suddenly, it occurred to me that Mark was no longer there. I walked to the front door and opened it, peering out at the driveway. His car was gone.

As I closed the door, I heard my mom's voice calling down to me from upstairs. "Kelsey, have you seen my sleeping pills?!"

SIXTEEN

Mark

FUCK. I HADN'T MEANT to seal those pills. I had only slipped away to the upstairs bathroom to give Kelsey and her mom some privacy. But the bottle was prominently displayed on the edge of the sink, right there for the taking. I was powerless to resist.

I drove like a bat out of hell, flooring the gas pedal in a frantic attempt to distance myself from the scene of the crime. So many times, I had promised myself I wouldn't become this person—a man whose compulsion for a quick fix overruled all else. Yet, here I was, sabotaging the best thing I had going for me, all in the name of a good mindfuck.

A loser, a coward, lower than low.

And now, I could officially add *thief* to my growing list of deficiencies.

I blew through a red light, veering sharply NASCAR-style onto the expressway. I must have broken every traffic law in the book as I exceeded the speed limit, darted across lanes, and weaved around slower-moving vehicles and God-knows-what-else. The adrenaline coursing through my veins only spurred on my recklessness. It wasn't until I nearly hit the bumper of the car in front of me that I realized the danger I posed to myself and others.

Getting off at the nearest exit ramp, I pulled into a supermarket parking lot, sliding into the last free spot within the cluster of vehicles parked by the front entrance. I hoped to remain inconspicuous as I tried to figure out what the hell I was going to do.

I took the bottle of pills out of the front pocket of my jacket and stared at it. Twisting off the cap, I dumped a handful of little blue tablets into my palm. I just wanted to take the edge off, to ease the tightness in my chest…to stop the tremors that were rippling through my body.

All I needed was a handful. *Just this once. Then I'd stop.*

A voice from deep down inside of me knew better: *Liar.*

Plopping the pills back into the bottle, I screwed the cap back on, giving it a toss onto the passenger seat. I leaned forward to rest my forehead against the steering wheel. My eyes shifted back over to the bottle next to me. I wanted to take those pills. My body longed for them. The constant ache, dull at first, grew and grew, intensifying into sharp pangs of need. I was losing control. Temptation surrounded me in a heavy and ominous fog, bearing down on my resistance.

Reaching for the bottle, I held it between my thumb and forefinger. I rotated my wrist in one direction, then the other, listening to the pills rattle against the plastic. Conflicting voices echoed in my mind, one telling me to take the damn pills, the other screaming to throw them out the window.

Fuck it.

With a pop of the plastic cap, I poured the tablets directly into my mouth. My eyes darted around the car, searching for something with which to wash them down. *Shit.* Nothing. When my phone vibrated in the back pocket of my jeans, I nearly choked. My heart started racing in a panic. *What if they were on to me?* I shifted my weight forward so I could pull the phone out with one hand while spitting the pills out into the other.

I didn't even check the screen—I knew who this was. "Hey," I answered.

"Mark, is something wrong? You left without saying good-bye." The genuine concern in Kelsey's voice nearly killed me.

"I just wanted to give you and your mom some privacy," I explained. "It didn't seem like the best time for me to be there."

"Yeah…I guess that makes sense. Sorry about my mom, by the way. She's been having a bit of a hard time lately."

"No need to apologize, Kelsey. I'll meet her properly when the time is right," I assured.

"Thanks," she said. Then, sighing softly into the phone, she asked, "Mark?"

"Yeah?" I responded, fearing a possible accusation.

"Are you sure you're alright? You don't sound so good."

"Yes. I'm fine," I lied.

"Okay, then. And Mark?" she asked.

"Yes?"

"I love you," she said sweetly.

"I love you too, Kelsey. So fucking much," I reciprocated, forcing away the tears.

"I'll talk to you tomorrow, then?" she asked tentatively.

"Sure thing. Goodbye, baby."

The moment I pressed "end," the phone dropped into my lap. I studied the wet, sticky pills in my palm. *I had to find a way to stay clean.* Kelsey was everything to me. *I couldn't lose her.* Fear washed over me, pouring down and drenching my perseverance.

My recovery was going to be grueling. And I couldn't do it alone.

~ ~ ~

Pebbles crunched under my boots as I walked up the dirt path leading to the bungalow-style cottage on Whitman's Pond. The dilapidated structure looked like a swift wind would reduce it to a pile of sticks. Heart now in my throat, I stopped at the front door, which was half-hanging off its hinges. It seemed like a million years ago when I'd called this place home.

"Ma? Dad? You here?" I hollered as I pushed through the door.

"Mark, is that you?" Ma called out from the back of the house.

I ran my fingers through my hair repeatedly as I waited for her to grace me with her presence. I knew she wasn't going to make this easy. "I need your help," I explained, hoping that would get her attention. I was anxious to get this over with.

Ma appeared in the doorway to the small living room in which I was nervously shuffling my feet in place. "I should have known you weren't here for a social visit," she said.

Shoving my hands deep inside my pockets, I looked down at the worn, braided carpet. The smugness in her tone made my skin crawl. Despite the fact that I towered over my mother, she always managed to make me feel very small. "I'm sorry I haven't come around much," I groveled.

"Much? How about *never?*" she snapped. "Your father and I haven't seen you in nearly two months."

She was right and I knew I didn't have a leg to stand on. "I'm sorry, Ma. Things have been…difficult."

"You clean?" she asked.

"I am today," I answered.

With a dramatic exhale, she lowered herself into a lime green recliner. Rocking back and forth in it, she eyed me with visible criticism. "I'm not giving you any money," she informed.

I dropped into the sunken sofa across from her, poised for debate. "That's not why I'm here." Swallowing hard, I continued, "I was actually wondering if I could move back in with you and Dad. It would just be temporary, of course…until I can get back on my feet."

Her face turned grim and emotionless. "You know the rules, Mark," she rebutted.

"I know, Ma, but I really need your help. I can't do this on my own," I pleaded.

The chair stopped as she planted her feet flat on the floor. Folding her hands in her lap, Ma squeezed them together in a tense display of self-restraint. "Your father and I have done all we can to help you. We've given you so many chances, and all we got in return were lies and heartache."

Out of desperation, I countered, "Where's Dad? Maybe if I talk to him, he'll—"

She held up her hand to cut me off. "Your father is still at work. He's under enough pressure with the business losing money. He doesn't need your problems on top of it."

"Please, Ma, I'm begging you to just give me one more chance. I'm ready this time. I'll do anything."

A flicker of hope spread across Ma's features. "Will you go back to New York and finish rehab?"

The thought of leaving Kelsey for twelve weeks was just too much. "I can't do that, Ma. I'll do *anything* else, I swear. Twelve-step programs. Psychiatric therapy. *Anything*. I promise."

Shaking her head, she frowned with disappointment. "I'm sorry, Mark. I'm afraid there's nothing I can do for you." Pushing up from the recliner, she turned to take her leave. "I'm sure you can see yourself out."

At that, Ma left me standing there...and didn't look back.

~ ~ ~

Parked in front of the apartment now, I'd sat in the car for hours, unable to move. Although it was late, the lights still illuminated the third story windows. There was no mistaking the danger awaiting me if I went inside. I would be comfortably numb and back on Brett and Lena's payroll in a nanosecond—hell, I *wanted* to be comfortably numb. I wanted it so badly, it hurt. But if I gave in, I would never *stop* wanting it. It was always too much, yet never enough.

My phone rested in the palm of my hand. I wanted to call Kelsey, to hear her voice. I wanted her to tell me that everything would be okay. I just needed one goddamned person to believe in me. I needed *her* to believe in me.

Hesitating for just one more moment, my finger finally landed firmly on Kelsey's number. Picking up on the third ring, she whispered, "H-Hello? Mark, is that you?" audibly half-asleep and discombobulated.

At the sound of her voice, the tears began to fall. Overcome with emotion, I just couldn't form any words.

"Mark, are you there? Are you okay?" Her tone suddenly became alert.

"Kelsey…" was all I could manage.

"God, Mark, I *knew* something was wrong. What happened?"

"Please…*please help me.*"

SEVENTEEN

Kelsey

IT HAD BEGUN to rain heavily, a torrential downpour that could prove hazardous for someone in Mark's fragile state. He had called nearly two hours ago, and I was sick with worry. My heart clenched as I remembered the sheer desperation in his voice. Watching the clock like a hawk, I paced my room, mentally tallying the passing minutes as I waited. I dialed his phone repeatedly, each call going unanswered. Finally, at nearly 3 AM, the telltale rattling of a faulty muffler tipped me off to his arrival. Peeking out my bedroom window, I heaved out a long breath, relieved to see his car in the driveway. I padded quietly down the stairs so I wouldn't wake my mom.

Upon opening the door, I froze, riveted to the threshold as my eyes took in a bedraggled Mark. He stood on my front step, shaking uncontrollably, soaked to the bone as the rain ran over him in sheets. His skin was dreadfully pale, accentuated by the dark hair plastered to his face. He shoved both hands through the tangled mess, moving it out of his eyes to reveal the deep circles underneath. This was not the handsome, put-together man of my dreams I had come to know. A ghastly, frightful clone had taken his place.

Recovering from my state of shock, I ushered him through the doorway and into the front hall. I peeled off his jacket, hanging it on the coat rack to dry. Leading him over to the wooden bench, I pushed him down by the shoulders, encouraging him to sit. He landed heavily, slumping forward with his elbows braced on his thighs, head in his hands. His breathing was measured and deliberate. Crouching down in front of him, I pulled off his boots and socks. Silently, he dragged his head back up to look at me. His saturated hair had flopped down over his eyes again, the droplets falling and running down his face. I rose up to a high kneel, reaching to slick back his hair with my fingers.

And that's when I noticed it.

His light brown eyes, normally warm and beautiful, were clouded now—*his pupils unnaturally dilated.*

Embarrassment and guilt swam across Mark's face as he read the look of horror on mine. "I don't want to be like this," he rasped. He sucked in air through his teeth, as if in physical pain, then continued, "I *want* to stop…but I don't fucking *know how*."

I held his face tightly, struggling to grasp what he was saying. "Stop what, Mark? I don't understand."

He gestured toward his sopping wet leather jacket, which was forming small rain puddles on the floor. "In my pocket. Right side," he mumbled.

Immediately, I stood, taking two big steps over to the coat rack. Sticking my hand inside the right pocket, I felt around until my fingers made contact with something plastic. I wrapped my hand around the small container and pulled it out. Holding the bottle up to my face, my eyes widened as they read the prescription label—my mother's contact information printed in clear, bold text.

My eyebrows drew together in confusion. "How did you get this?"

Mark quickly averted his gaze from mine. "I stole it, Kelsey," he confessed. "Please…tell your mom I'm sorry."

"Why would you do that?" I replied in bemusement.

"I just…I couldn't stop myself. I wanted them, Kelsey. I…I needed them."

The weight of the bottle was practically nonexistent as it sat in my hand. It felt light. *Too light.* "This…this is almost empty, Mark." Suddenly panic stricken, my voice pitched higher and rang out, "Did you…*take* them?"

He squeezed his eyes shut as they moistened. I could tell he was trying really hard not to cry in front of me. "I'm s-so s-sorry," he sputtered.

Maybe I should have been angry, but all I could feel was empathy. Lowering my hands, I placed them gently on his thighs, my palms rubbing up and down in a soothing gesture. Peering up into his tortured face, everything suddenly just…clicked—so many bits of evidence that had always been there, but I hadn't quite connected. Like pictures projected in a slide show, it all flashed before me in a timeline: *The night at the bar. His unexpected trip out of town. The medallion left in the driveway. His acquaintance with Lena.* Yes, it all finally made sense.

"Oh, Mark," I said, stunned.

"Are you gonna leave me?" he choked out.

The fear in his voice broke my heart into a million pieces, and I threw myself at him. "I'm not going anywhere. I promise." I hugged him as tight as I could.

He hugged me back just as fiercely, clutching at me and burying his face in my neck. "I need you," he said quietly.

I pressed my face into his soaked hair, touching my lips to the side of his head. "We need each other," I whispered.

That sent Mark over the edge. Tears came in torrents—once they started, he couldn't stop them. His whole body shook as he completely lost it in my arms. He sobbed so hard, he could barely breathe. Tears sprang to my eyes as his misery ripped me apart. Stroking his hair and rubbing his back, I soothed, "*Shhh.* It's okay. Everything's okay." As I comforted and reassured him, I vowed to myself that I would do every-thing in my power to help him.

When Mark's sobs subsided, I pried myself out of his arms to push to my feet. Holding out my hand, I softly commanded, "Come with me."

Without a word, Mark stood from the bench and took my hand. I tugged him along, bringing him up the stairs to my bedroom. Sitting on the edge of the bed, I motioned to the spot beside me. Taking my cue, he sat next to me, awaiting further instruction. Reaching for the hem of his damp T-shirt, as I pulled it up, Mark helped me get it all the way off by im-mediately lifting his arms. My gaze drifted to his jeans, and, as if reading my mind, he unbuttoned and unzipped the fly. I stood up, leaning over him to gently push him down onto his back. When I grabbed the bottom of each pant leg with a tug, Mark lifted his hips from the mattress so I could pull his jeans all the way down and off.

Joining him on the bed again, I crawled up to the pillow and patted it, indicating that Mark should scoot back and get comfortable. He complied without hesitation. Grabbing the edge of the yellow and white striped comforter, I pulled it up, wrapping it around the both of us. "Sleep now," I instructed, and then kissed his shoulder.

Mark rolled onto his side to face the wall, his body still trembling. I wasn't sure if the tremors were a side effect from the narcotics, or if he was still chilled from the rain. I slid over to press against him, draping an arm around his waist. Burrow-ing in as close as possible, my body instinctively molded to the curve of his back and thighs, the soft flannel of my pajamas rubbing against his bare skin. I lay there, the little spoon holding the big spoon, listening to Mark's breathing even out as he drifted into sleep.

~ ~ ~

As expected, Mark woke up feeling like roadkill. He sat up and groaned, clutching his head in his hands. He moved to the edge of the bed and dropped his legs over the side. Pretending to be asleep, I rolled over and faced away from him so he could have a moment to collect himself. I listened as he blew out a deep lungful of air. "Shit," he muttered under his breath.

The sudden slamming of the front door echoed from downstairs. I held my breath, wondering what my mom might have heard. Moments later, the faint sounds of her car starting and pulling out of the driveway spread a sense of relief through me. *Dodged that bullet.* I wasn't sure how I would have explained a near-naked man being in my bed. Craning my neck to peer over my shoulder, I found Mark facing me, his mouth curved up in a crooked grin.

"Close one, huh?" he joked.

"I guess you could say that," I responded, turning full around to push up into a sitting position.

"Listen, about last night—" he began.

"It's okay," I said. Reaching out and touching his hand, I asked, "How are you feeling?"

"Honestly? Like shit," he replied, letting out a small chuckle.

"What can I do to help? Can I make you something to eat?" I offered.

"Thanks, but I don't think I can stomach anything right now," he admitted. "I could use a shower, though. Would that be okay?"

"Yeah, of course," I warmly replied.

Mark pushed himself up from the bed and headed to the bathroom. Falling back onto my pillow, I mentally played back the last 24 hours as I waited for him to shower. *What a difference a day makes,* I thought with mixed emotions.

The abrasive sound of my telltale ringtone broke me out of my reverie. Twisting to the side, I reached over to grab my phone from the nightstand. The name *Cali* flashed across the screen. "Hey," I answered.

"Spring break, chica!" she bellowed.

I rolled my eyes, knowing that my week of *fun* had already been planned for me. "It's not here *yet,*" I laughed.

"It's right around the corner, Kels. Just wait 'til you see what I've got lined up for us. It'll be *legendary!*"

Giggling at her over-the-top enthusiasm, I reminded her, "That's what you say every year."

"And have I ever steered you wrong?" she asked.

Not wanting to disappoint her, I replied, "No, I guess not."

"That's what I'm talking about!" she screamed.

"Jeez, who put extra sugar on your cornflakes this morning?" I teased.

"Oh, come on! Can't a girl get excited to see her best friend and have a little fun?" Her tone sounded mockingly hurt.

My eyes snapped to the doorway, catching Mark, fresh from his shower in nothing but a towel. "Uh…sure…" I trailed off.

"Kels…*HELLO?* Are you even listening to me?"

"Uh huh…sure I am. Listen, Cali, I need to go. Can I call you later?"

"Yeah, I guess so. What's going on with you?" she asked.

I wasn't in the mood for the Cali riot act, so I decided that a little white lie was in order. "Nothing. Just really tired. I think I'm going to skip classes today and crash." Mark walked over to the bed, and stood there, intently watching me.

"You? Skip classes? What's this world coming to?" Cali mused.

My conversation skills went out the window as my eyes roamed over Mark's damp skin. "Um…yeah. Gotta go. Bye." I ended the call before giving Cali a chance to object.

With a smile, I placed my phone on the bed and stood up to greet him. "Feeling better?" He looked like his old self again.

"Yeah, much better. Thank you."

Looking down at his towel, I said, "Your clothes are probably dry by now, if you want to get dressed."

Mark took a step closer. "Kelsey, can I ask you something first?"

"Yeah?" I replied.

He reached out, stroking the side of my cheek with the back of his hand. "Why are you so good to me?"

His question caught me off-guard and it made me feel sad for him. I closed in on the small space between us until our chests touched. Placing my hand over his heart, I felt it beating hard and fast under my palm. Looking directly into his eyes, I answered, "Because in here…underneath it all, is the man I fell in love with."

His features were overcome by unabashed emotion as he wrapped himself tightly around me. "I love you so much," he blurted, his voice nearly cracking.

I pulled back to cup his jaw in my hand. "Mark, we're going to get through this, okay? *Together.*"

With a nod, he leaned in and kissed the corner of my mouth. His wet hair swept down, brushing against my nose. *He smelled so good.* His lips found mine again, and this time, he kissed me deeply, passionately, his hands twisting in my hair. Electricity shot through me as my entire body responded. His chest, wet and warm against mine, drove me to insanity. Mark drew back ever-so-slightly to gaze into my eyes as he declared softly against my lips, "God, I want you."

EIGHTEEN

Mark

MY ENTIRE BODY grew heavy and deliciously lethargic as I held Kelsey in my arms. Despite being stone cold sober, I had never before experienced such a complete state of euphoria. As my eyes skimmed over her beautifully naked body, I wished for this moment to be a dream, one that I would never awake from. But I knew that as soon as we uncoiled our limbs and made the bed, reality would rear its ugly head once again.

Kelsey peeled her face from my chest, her hazel eyes wide and doe-like as she gazed up at me. "Well, *that* was unexpected," she uttered, referring to our spur-of-the-moment tango beneath the sheets.

I stiffened, scared that maybe I had come on too strong. The last thing I wanted was for my own overwhelming desires to coerce her into something she wasn't yet ready for. "Was *it*…are *you*…okay?" I whispered, pressing my face into her hair. When she didn't respond right away, my chest panged. "I should have stopped myself, Kelsey. I'm so sorry. I just wanted you so much and I thought you wanted me and…"

"Please don't talk like that," Kelsey interjected, her hands moving up to cup my face. "We just shared something truly special. So please don't act like it was a mistake."

"I love you, baby," I replied with a relieved sigh, clutching her fiercely before guilt moved in to dampen the mood. "I just wish I could give you the world. But all I seem to be good at is fucking everything up."

"Mark," she soothed. "You still have your whole life in front of you. One day you will go on to achieve great things. But *this*…you and me…it's the only world I need. The other stuff is just icing on the cake."

I smiled, resting my chin on top of her head. "You make everything sound so simple."

"It's really not that complicated, Mark. You have the power to create your own destiny. You just need to decide what you want and how badly you want it."

"I know I want *you*," I admitted, kissing the top of her head.

"Well, you've already *got* me, silly," she giggled.

I trailed my fingertips lightly down her sides, savoring the softness of her skin. "You're the best thing that's ever happened to me," I whispered.

Moments later, we made love a second time, and then again in our dreams as we drifted off in a tangled embrace.

~ ~ ~

During the course of the next week, I made a half-assed attempt to work my way back into the good graces of my professors at the community college, but it was difficult to keep my head in the game. My thoughts continually shifted, running the full gamut of conflicting emotions: *elation* over Kelsey's presence in my life, *guilt* over the free time she'd sacrificed for me, *frustration* over a body that continued to reject being straight and sober, *more guilt* over being pathetically stuck in a "next high" frame of mind, *sadness* over parents who didn't seem to give a fuck about me, *self-pity* over no longer having a place to call home, and yet *even more guilt* over Kelsey's commitment to helping me when I probably wasn't worth it.

An endless sadistic cycle.

As I sat in philosophy class, I could feel Mrs. Willis's eyes searing into me, but I pretended not to notice. It was the same look I got from all my professors. I'd coined it The 3D Look: *Disapproval, Disappointment, and Disdain.* At the end of class, I bolted toward the exit, hoping to make a quick getaway, when I heard a voice call out, "Mr. Hudson, may I have a word with you?"

Sucking in a deep breath, I mentally prepared myself for an awkward confrontation. I turned to face Mrs. Willis, sitting behind her desk, peering at me over her bifocals. "I know I've had a few absences recently—" I began to grovel.

Pushing back in her chair, she stood, the ear-bleeding sound of metal across tile interrupting me. She braced her hands on the edge of the desk. "A few absences would be understandable, Mr. Hudson," she sneered. "But I haven't seen you in my class in weeks."

Clearing my throat, I tried to defend myself. "I've been dealing with some…personal issues."

"And yet you've made no effort to contact me in order to explain your situation or to try to work something out. You've missed an important oral presentation as well as a midterm." Removing her glasses, she pinched the bridge of her nose mid-rant. "Give me one good reason why I shouldn't fail you."

I scoured my brain for a convincing answer but came up empty. With a humble shrug, I settled for honesty. "I can't really think of one. I probably deserve to fail."

With a sigh, Mrs. Willis came around the desk to approach me. Her plaid skirt resembled a kilt, only longer. I tried to ease my growing tension by imagining her playing the bagpipes. "Mr. Hudson…*Mark*. It just so happens that I'm in a generous mood today. I'm going to give you one more chance."

"*Thank you*, Mrs. Willis." Feeling like a huge weight had been lifted, I couldn't help but sling an overzealous arm around her shoulders. "I won't let you down," I promised.

She pulled away from my awkward, accidental side-hug, face contorted in discomfort. "Don't thank me just yet. You've got a lot of work ahead of you. And I expect perfect attendance for the rest of the semester. Understood?"

"Yes, Mrs. Willis."

"Good. Now, if you'll excuse me, I've got some papers to grade."

~ ~ ~

Kelsey and I had settled into an after-school routine of studying at my apartment. It would have been pure heaven if not for the fact that we still had to deal with Brett and Lena. They seemed to find my quest for living the straight and narrow life funny, parading their drug use in front of me intentionally to goad me. Thankfully, Kelsey's continued love and support empowered me to fight off the constant temptation. Another challenge before me was knowing that if I didn't rejoin the ranks of the illegally employed soon, it was only a matter of time before I'd have to find somewhere else to live. *Not that this place ever felt like home to begin with.*

With the start of Spring Break approaching, I also knew Kelsey would be leaving me in a couple of days. She'd repeatedly offered to cancel her plans, but I couldn't let her run her whole schedule around me and my fucked-up life. Instead of dwelling on how much I was going to miss her, I wanted to cherish this time with her.

Taking a well-deserved break from our current study session, we rummaged through the kitchen cabinets to look for sustenance. Kelsey hit the jackpot, turning to proudly display a box of chocolate chip cookies in her hands. I promptly snatched it away, hopping up onto the center island to rip open the box and hungrily dig in.

"Hey, don't be greedy!" Kelsey protested.

"If you want 'em, come and get 'em," I taunted, holding the box in the air.

Blowing her hair out of her face in simulated frustration, she replied, "Fine."

At that, Kelsey walked over to the island, turned around, and backed herself up to the edge. Reaching behind her, she placed her hands flat on the countertop to try and hoist herself up next to me. But she was vertically challenged, which made the task impossible. I watched with amusement as her cute little denim-covered ass continually stopped just short of reaching the top. Placing the box of cookies beside me, I crossed my arms at my chest, unable to hold back my laughter as I continued to observe her failed attempts.

"Need some help there?" Yeah—I sounded smug.

With a look over her shoulder at me, she rolled her eyes. "Gee, *ya think?*" she asked, annoyance in her voice thrown in for dramatic effect. She waited for me to offer her a hand, but I didn't budge an inch. Gusts of laughter burst from deep in my chest.

She banged her hands on the countertop in a desperate plea. "Help me up already!"

Still laughing, I brought my hand up to my head in a salute. "Yes, ma'am!" At that, I hopped down to grab her waist with both hands, hoisting her effortlessly onto the island in under three seconds. Then, just as easily, I hopped back up to sit beside her.

"Show-off," she teased.

Poking her in the side, I teased right back. "I do what I can, Short-stuff."

"You did *not* just call me Short-stuff!" she shouted, raising her fists in a threatening gesture.

"Oh, you think you can take me? I'd like to see you try," I taunted.

Rising to the challenge, she lunged, playfully pounding me in the chest. "You like talking shit?" Kelsey squealed with laughter.

"You hit like a *girl*."

That *really* got her going. "That's it! You're going *down!*" she yelled, nearly in tears from laughing so hard. Raising her fists in front of my face, she bobbed and weaved back and forth like a boxer. When she jabbed one fist forward in the air, I grabbed it. Then, the other. Then, I held both fists firmly down by her sides.

"You're utterly defenseless now," I said, all traces of amusement suddenly gone. My breathing became all fucked up as I watched her chest heaving from all the laughter. Without letting go of her hands, I leaned in closer to stare at her lips, waiting for her to give me the go-ahead. Kelsey went in for the kill, attacking my mouth with hers, sending us into a mash-up of lips, teeth, and tongues—kissing, biting, and licking like we couldn't get enough.

"Do you have any idea how much I want you?" I murmured against her lips.

"Bedroom. *Now*," she moaned into my mouth.

All the encouragement I needed. Swiftly picking her up from the island, I carried her into my bedroom.

~ ~ ~

My stomach somersaulted when I heard the train approaching the station. *This was it.* I would have to get by for two whole days without her. I'd had my arms wrapped around her so tightly, she could hardly breathe. "Easy, Mark," she cautioned, pushing gently against my chest.

I loosened my grip a little to peer down at her sweet, gorgeous face. "Sorry about that."

Her brows furrowed as she peeked up at me through her lashes. "Hey, I don't have to go. Why don't I just stay here with you?"

I shook my head. "No, I *want* you to go." Releasing my hold, I stepped back to take one last look at her. "You deserve to have fun with your friends, Kelsey. Besides, it's only for the weekend. I'll be here waiting when you get back." Her hair was swept high off her face in a ponytail, making her look younger than her twenty-one years. She took my breath away.

When the train pulled in, she hesitated to move, holding onto my hand for dear life. "Go, Kelsey," I encouraged. "I'll be fine." In truth, I wasn't really even sure if I believed my own words.

"Will you promise to call if you need me?" she asked.

"Yes, I promise."

Kelsey started toward the train, arm outstretched behind her, hand lingering in mine until we became too far apart for our fingertips to touch.

"I'll miss you," she whispered over her shoulder.

"Not as much as I'll miss you."

I watched her board the train and take a seat at a window near the front. She flashed me the most radiant smile before mouthing the words *"I love you"* through the glass. I caught one last glimpse at her angelic face before the train pulled away to take her out of my sight.

Kelsey had become my sanctuary, my buffer against all the shit that constantly threatened to infiltrate my recovery. I just hoped that without her, I would be strong enough to ward off my demons.

NINETEEN

Kelsey

IT WAS A FOUR-HOUR train ride that seemed to go on for days. The passenger beside me slept like a log the entire trip, snoring loudly in my ear while using my shoulder as his own personal headrest. By the time the train pulled into New York City's Penn Station, I was more than ready to disembark and reclaim my personal space. As I stepped out onto 7th Avenue and into the semi-fresh air, I tried to shove down the anxiety that had been festering since I left Massachusetts. But it was a lost cause.

Hailing a cab in zero-time flat, I slid across the backseat and fastened my seatbelt, progressively weary of my decision to participate in this girls' weekend. As much as I'd longed to re-connect with my dear friends, a part of me felt selfish for taking this time for myself when Mark was still so vulnerable. *What if he needed me?* With each passing minute, I became more riddled with guilt and fear. I prayed that Mark was okay. I prayed that he was sober. I prayed that he was safe. But most of all, I prayed that leaving him back home to fend for himself wasn't a humongous misstep I'd live to regret.

I bit out, "Cyprus Hotel," to the cab driver, too tired and cranky to care how bitchy I sounded. Not even the slightest bit deterred by my rudeness, the cabbie chattered nonstop, enlightening me on the personal details of his life, tipping the TMI scale to the point of making me squirm in my seat. As he launched into an intimate account of his recent case of the gout, I silently cursed the gridlock traffic and wished I could fast-forward to Monday.

When the cab finally stopped in front of my hotel, I pressed my face up to the window, my eyes bulging out of their sockets. To say that the place was a dump would be the understatement of the century. Standing before me was a box-shaped structure made of dirty pink stucco, with black iron bars across its windows, and a large neon sign welded to the flat-top roof. The words "Cyprus Hotel" intermittently flashed in a partially illuminated fluorescent pink, but with some of the bulbs out, the sign read more like a random sampling of letters: "Cy—us H—el."

The place looked like a Miami Beach reject, sticking out like a sore thumb among the taller, more sophisticated, red brick buildings that surrounded it. Handing my cab fare over and thanking the driver, I jumped out, bracing myself for what I might find inside.

Even worse than I thought.

Stepping into the lobby sent me through a time warp, instantly transporting me back to the decade of Free Love. With giant, mustard-yellow, pinwheel-like flowers on the wallpaper and threadbare, burnt orange carpeting revealing spots of floor, evidently, none of the original décor had been touched since the owners went to Woodstock. And I didn't even want to *consider* the history of the visible stains.

After checking in at the front desk, I followed the attendant up a narrow stairwell to my room on the second floor. The walls of the dark hallway were painted olive green, and my feet plodded over the same burnt orange carpeting as in the lobby. When the faint odor of what could only be described as old gym sneakers assaulted my nose, it became clear: This was without a doubt the worst, *worst* hotel I'd ever, *ever* been in.

I didn't have to enter my room to know that my friends had already gotten the party started—the paper-thin walls gave that away. Sliding my key into the lock, I twisted it and swung open the door.

Before I could even blink, Cali rushed me in a linebacker-tackle. "Kelsey! You're here!" she shrieked.

"In the flesh," I quipped, dropping my duffel bag to throw my arms around her in a tight embrace.

Looking over Cali's shoulder, I spotted Debra and Maia, both wearing huge smiles as they sat on one of the room's double beds. It felt like I hadn't seen them in years, which made me unexpectedly emotional. "Come here," I said, gesturing toward myself while blinking back tears.

They sprang from the bed to join in on the reunion, our eight arms all entwined in a quadruple hug. When we finally managed to pry ourselves apart, Cali let out a hearty chuckle while tipping her chin toward the room's solitary window. "Kels, before you do anything else, you *have* to check out the view."

Eyeing her suspiciously, I walked to the window, peeling back the rust-colored linen curtain to take in the view: *A brick wall.* A brick wall, partially obstructed by iron bars. Hearing the girls sniggering behind me, I twirled around and handed them some snark. "It's too bad I forgot to pack my ball and chain." At that, they erupted into fits and giggles.

"God, I know! Seriously, could this place be any more of a shit hole?" Cali blathered, slicing the air in front of her with her hands. "It seemed so trendy and retro when I checked it out online."

"You mean this place actually has a website?" Debra asked in disbelief.

"Oh, it's not *that* bad," Maia commented, ever the optimist. The rest of us looked at her like she was a crazy person.

Cali pointed to one of the beds, which was covered with a dingy, multi-stained quilt threaded in red and brown psychedelic patterns. *"Not that bad?* Maia, when do you suppose was the last time anyone washed the bedding in here? I'm gonna guess that I was probably still in diapers."

Debra piped up, defending Maia's glass half-full attitude. "Okay, so the place is a little unkempt, but who cares! We are in *New York!* We're gonna take this city by the balls!"

Cali's lips curved up into a face-splitting grin. "You know what? You're absolutely right. We're gonna have the time of *our lives!*" she yelled, her enthusiasm back in full force.

"So what's the plan for tonight anyway?" I lugged my duffel bag over to the bed I assumed I'd be sharing with Cali.

Cali held up her index and second fingers. "Two words," she said. "Club Cosmos."

I tried not to wince as I met Cali's hopeful gaze. "What kind of club is it?"

Debra answered on Cali's behalf. "It is *the* place to *see* and *be seen* in New York City."

Facing Debra, I watched with both fascination and repulsion as she downed an entire can of beer in two large gulps. "How do you know that?" I asked.

"I have my sources," she stated curtly, pretending to be insulted by my question.

Out of nowhere, an unexpected proclamation echoed from the corner of the room. "I am soooo ready to get my party on!"

I whipped my head in Maia's direction, stunned by what I'd just heard. "Excuse me?"

Maia's red curls bounced like springs against her shoulders as she fetched a can of beer from an antique-looking minifridge. "Weird, right? I know I'm not usually gung-ho on parties, but after barely surviving my midterms from hell, I'm ready to throw caution to the wind for a change."

"No crime in that. You should follow her lead," Cali said, staring me down with her head cocked and an arched brow.

"Yeah. Yeah. Well, I'm here, aren't I?" I reasoned, unzipping my bag to pull out my clothes.

An evil smile tugged at Cali's lips. "In that case, let's get this girl a beer!"

Hands on my hips, I shook my head at her relentlessness. "You never give up, do you?"

"It is my mission in life to make sure you have a good time," Cali's profession was matter of fact.

I turned my attention back to my heap of clothes, color-sorting my socks and unmentionables, when out of the corner of my eye, I saw someone peek his head into the room. "You girls mind if I join you?"

It took a moment for me to process that it was Tracy who had just spoken, and now, he was standing in our hotel room, slowly scanning the length of me as my face flushed ten shades of discomfort.

What the hell was he doing here?

I shot Cali a look that conveyed my complete and utter disapproval, and that feeling quickly morphed into anger. Apparently, our so called *"girls' weekend"* was, in actuality, not a girls' weekend at all. I should have known Cali would have an ulterior motive. Being lured unsuspectingly into a vacation with male counterparts was underhanded and sneaky. *And a deal-breaker.*

I started grabbing fistfuls of clothes, channeling my rage by shoving them forcefully back into my duffel bag. When done,

I harshly zipped up the bag, yanked it off the bed, and headed to the door. My eyes burned into Cali's. "You are *unbelievable!*" I stomped out of the room.

"Ugh!" I groaned as I tramped down the hallway. When I reached the stairwell, I sat myself down on the top step. As I fished my phone out of the front pocket of my windbreaker, I muttered, "I should've stayed the hell home." The still-cracked faceplate stared back at me, reminding me of the man I loved, the man I wish I'd never left behind. I held my breath as my finger landed on his number.

"Hi baby," Mark answered. "How's New York?"

I sighed heavily into the phone, a combination of *relief* that he sounded okay and *frustration* at myself for being so far away from him. "Well—" I started to say.

"What is it, Kelsey?" Mark immediately sensed my displeasure. "Did something happen?"

"I should never have agreed to this trip. I feel so stupid, Mark." I had to fight to contain the emotions swelling up in my voice.

"What's got you so upset?" he urged.

"I just hate that I'm so naïve. I continually get sucked into these ridiculous situations, when I should know better," I lamented.

A slight pause. "What kind of situations?"

"Well, let's take tonight, for example. Guess where Cali's dragging me?"

"Where?" his voice pitched down a notch.

"Club Cosmos!" I scoffed. "Tell me that isn't the cheesiest name on the planet."

Dead silence.

"Uh…Mark?"

When he finally spoke, his voice was laced with concern. "Kelsey…I don't think that's a good place for you to be."

"Why not?"

"Just take my word for it. Some crazy shit goes on in there."

"Have…*you* been there before?" I couldn't help but ask.

"Yes," Mark admitted. "But I wish I could forget."

"Well, everyone seems pretty dead set on going," I explained.

"Kelsey, I *really* don't want you going there. Someone like you would get eaten alive in a place like that," he warned.

"Don't worry, I promise I'll be caref—" My voice caught at the sight of Cali standing behind me, arms crossed over her chest.

"I'm sorry…I…I gotta go," I stammered, bringing the call to an abrupt end.

"Who were you talking to?" Joining me on the top step, the accusation in Cali's voice was clear.

I considered my options, mentally running through a list of viable excuses. But knowing that I couldn't avoid the situation forever, I decided to put on a brave face and come out with it. "I was talking to Mark," I answered, wondering how long before she registered the name.

"As in *THE* Mark? But I thought he was out of the picture." Cali scrunched up her face like she had just sucked on a lemon. "He's not right for you…I thought we agreed."

"I agreed to no such thing," I defended, meeting Cali's disapproving gaze. "He's a good guy."

"Come on, Kels!" she scolded. "Don't you remember how much he hurt you?"

How could I forget? But things were different now, and I needed to make Cali understand that. After a deep breath, I presented my case, delivering the SparkNotes edition of the progression of my relationship with Mark. By the conclusion of my impassioned narrative, Cali's frown had inverted, and I knew I was in the clear.

"Okay." Cali squeezed my hand. "If you're *truly* happy with Mark, then I'm happy for you. But I sure as hell hope you know what you're doing."

"I don't know what I'm doing *exactly*," I admitted. "But I *do* know that I love him."

~ ~ ~

Arm in arm, Cali and I walked back to our room to find Tracy hovering in the doorway. He scrubbed his hands through his reddish-brown hair, which had grown out from its crew cut into half inch, teased-up spikes. "Listen, I didn't mean to cause any problems. The guys and I can get a room on a different floor. It'll be like we're not even here," he offered.

Tracy's tone and expression revealed complete sincerity. *Jeez.* I had forgotten what a nice guy he was. Suddenly, I felt like a real shit for having reacted so poorly to his presence.

"Tracy, I was incredibly rude to you back there." I tilted my head toward the room. "It was uncalled for, and I'm sorry."

"That's okay, Kelsey. I didn't mean to catch you off-guard by coming here. I thought that Cali would have filled you in."

I glanced at Cali, guilt-ridden and eyes on the carpet, a lock of long blond hair twirling around her finger. She was a real pain in the ass sometimes, but deep down, she had a heart of gold. "It's all good," I assured him. "No harm done."

Suddenly, Debra appeared in the doorway, her black bob pinned up on the sides with sequined bobby pins. Obviously, she had already begun primping for our night out on the town. "Are you people gonna congregate out here in the hallway all night, or are we finally gonna kick-off this weekend the right way?"

Cali leaned toward Debra with a raised hand, earning her a high-five. "You know what this moment calls for? A toast!" she exclaimed. "Tracy, did you and the boys bring the champagne?"

"Yup. I'll go get it." As Tracy headed to his room—the one adjacent to ours—I shot him a sideways glance. When our eyes met, he rewarded me with his ever-enthusiastic double thumbs-up. I couldn't help but laugh at his signature move, which was dorky, yet slightly adorable.

Maia, who sounded like she had consumed several cocktails in the short span of time I had been gone, bellowed at Tracy from inside the room. "And make sure you bring those sexy-as-fuck friends of yours over here!"

My jaw practically hit the floor, shocked to hear such vulgarity spilling from Maia's typically prim-and-proper mouth. When I walked back into the room to find her sprawled out on her bed—a half-dozen empty beer cans strewn around her—I knew I was going to be in for a long night.

Hoisting my duffel bag back onto the bed, I unzipped it, ready to unpack once and for all, but a resonant ping inside my jacket halted my efforts. When I pulled my phone from my pocket to glance at the screen, the sight of Mark's text made my stomach drop:

I'm on my way.

"Shit."

TWENTY

Mark

A VISIT TO CLUB COSMOS was like passing through the gates of Heaven, only to inevitably plummet to the depths of Hell a few hours later. Flashbacks of my last club experience permeated my thoughts, reminding me of the dire consequences that awaited if I overstayed my welcome. The place had an allure that could not be denied. Everything—from the strobe lights, to the thumping techno music, to the sleek furnishings, to the unnaturally beautiful people, to the 100 proof concoctions, to the assortment of "club drugs" handed out like candy—was deliberately and strategically planted to attract and ensnare party-seekers, promising them unimaginable pleasure by bringing them to a level of fuckeduppedness never before experienced. But once the club hit closing time, patrons would be thoughtlessly tossed out onto the curb like heaps of garbage, leaving them cold and alone and in search of their dignity.

My eyes began to sweep the expansive dance floor, trying to spot Kelsey amidst the sweaty, gyrating crowd. I knew she was here, especially since she had texted me numerous times begging me not to come. She doubted my ability to keep it together in this kind of atmosphere, fearful that my willpower would turn to dust under the pressure. Yes, she was rightfully concerned for my welfare, and I loved her for that, but it would be a cold day in hell before I let this place drag her over to the dark side. I just needed to stay focused and keep my wits about me. *I could do this.*

I trudged toward the long mahogany bar to get a different vantage point, and that's when I saw her—dressed to turn heads in a little black number that hugged her curves like a second skin. The outfit obviously wasn't her idea since she kept pulling at the hem of her minidress as if wishing it would grow longer. I wasn't used to seeing Kelsey dressed so provocatively and I had to admit she looked radiant. Gorgeous. Sexy. She was with Cali and two other friends whom I immediately recognized as Maia and Debra based on Kelsey's numerous descriptions of them during our conversations. They were all equally dressed to impress, dancing together in a circle as girls often do. Actually, her friends were dancing, but I doubted that what Kelsey was doing would fall under the same category.

I had never before witnessed her footwork, and bless her heart, the girl couldn't dance worth a shit. She had two left feet, busting out one atrocious dance move after another. I watched her in awe, her rhythm-challenged body moving completely against the beat of the music. Yet somehow it worked for her, making her awkwardly adorable and all the more appealing. Apparently, I wasn't the only one who felt that way, as several men in her vicinity openly ogled her like a piece of merchandise. I needed to get her the hell out of here, fast.

The place was besieged with clubbers, and I elbowed my way through the mob, desperate to get Kelsey out of this predatory environment before the whole scene turned into a shit show. I was half-way across the dance floor, when a leggy blonde tapped me on the back. "Hey, handsome, you wanna try a Mind-Bender? First one's on the house," she purred.

My eyes expanded to saucers, skimming across the tray of shot glasses balanced on her hand. A beautiful assortment of rainbow-colored liquids beckoned to my parched lips. "No, I'm all set. Thanks," I said, bringing my focus back to the dance floor. Kelsey was no longer anywhere in sight.

Blondie ran a red manicured nail down the front of my Oxford shirt, letting it catch along one of the buttons. Batting her fake lashes at me, she pursed her lips. "Come on. Just one? It's my job to get rid of all these drinks. You wouldn't want me to get in trouble, would you?"

I didn't give a rat's ass about this girl's job, but those drinks looked damned tasty. Maybe I could have just one. It would help me calm my nerves.

No, wait. What the fuck was I thinking? I was here for Kelsey. I needed to find her.

"I *said* I'm all set," I asserted. "Now, if you'll excuse me…" Turning to once again survey the dance floor, my eyes landed on Kelsey, now holding a fruity-looking drink in her hand. *Dammit, where did she get that?* I began to move in her direction.

A bony hand squeezed my shoulder, catching me off-guard. "Just one little drink won't hurt, will it?" Blondie whispered in my ear.

Jesus, this girl didn't know when to quit. She followed so closely, I could feel her breath on my neck, her overbearing perfume wafting in my face and assaulting my sinuses. The sensory overload of this woman was making me claustrophobic. "Go find yourself another guinea pig," I spat. "I'm *not interested.*"

Finally taking the hint, she backed away. "Okay, fine. Have it your way. But if you change your mind, I'll be here all night," she said with a wink.

"Don't hold your breath," I said as I walked away.

It was taking an eternity to push my way through the crowd that had grown so large, people were now shoulder to shoulder as they danced. I started shouting Kelsey's name, hoping she'd notice me coming for her, but the music had increased to an ear-splitting volume, drowning out my voice. As I gradually inched my way closer, I noticed that one of Kelsey's male admirers was dancing all up in her personal space. Eyes following her every movement, he continuously checked out her ass as if it were on display just for him. Grabbing her hips from behind, his hands remained glued to her body as they swayed out of sync with the music. Kelsey appeared to be quite enjoying herself, throwing her head back and laughing while she sipped her fruity drink through a straw.

I could feel myself starting to lose it.

Who the fuck was this jackass and what made him think he could put his hands on my girlfriend?

Desperate to get her attention, I called out Kelsey's name again while pushing more forcefully through the swarms of party people. Completely oblivious to my presence, she turned around to face her dance partner, now resting her hands on his shoulders. *What the fuck?* Why did it look like she was really *into* this guy?

A girl in tight leather pants and a tube top flounced in front of me, momentarily blocking my view. "Hi-ya, cutie. Wanna dance?"

"No thanks. I'm looking for my girlfriend," I answered with annoyance.

Reaching up, she brazenly put a finger across my lips. *"Shhh.* It'll be our little secret."

One good look into her half-mast eyes was all it took to realize she was completely obliterated. And she was young—sixteen, tops. It surprised me she'd even been allowed into the club at all. Gently, I pushed her aside. "Do yourself a favor and go home," I advised.

"Whatever," she mumbled as she moved on to a more willing candidate.

When I brought my eyes back to the spot where Kelsey and her very willing dance partner had been, I quickly discovered they had disappeared. "Fuck!" I groaned out loud, knowing full well that nobody would hear me.

I scanned the entire dance floor, turning myself a full 360 degrees until every space had been accounted for. Still no sign of Kelsey or the jackass. *Where the hell did they run off to?* My heart began thumping hard against my chest. I was afraid to consider the possibilities.

Maybe that drink wouldn't be such a bad idea after all.

She must have sensed I was about to cave, because as soon as the thought flashed through my head, the same cocktail waitress that'd been up my ass earlier, suddenly appeared, offering up those shots with do-or-die devotion. It was almost as if she'd been tailing me the entire night. It didn't matter. I wanted that free drink. *Just one.* I could handle just one.

I swiped a glass from the tray and downed it in half a second. "I knew you'd come around," she gloated.

"Congratulations," I sarcastically muttered.

She lifted a glass off the tray and held it out to me. "How about another?"

I nervously ran a hand through my hair. "I don't think I should."

"You don't even have to pay me now," she offered with sickening sweetness. "We can put everything on your tab so you can be free to enjoy yourself."

Fortunately, I knew damn well what she was doing, and I wasn't going to be stupid enough to fall for it this time. This club had been employing the Bait-N-Switch for years, keeping the drinks flowing all night before leaving customers dirt broke by dawn when they were asked to pay up. "Thanks anyway, but I'm gonna have to pass," I replied.

With a nonchalant shrug, Blondie said, "Suit yourself." Setting the glass back on the tray, she allowed her index finger to dip into the crystal blue liquid. She then sucked invitingly on her finger and moaned, *Mmmm…You don't know what you're missing."*

As the effects of my free shot took hold, an icy hot ooze entered my hair follicles and traveled to the ends of my toes, making me feel nice and relaxed. I supposed one more shot wouldn't hurt. *Just one.*

"Okay, one more," I conceded.

A huge smile spread across Blondie's face as she graciously handed me the glass of blue. I stared longingly at the liquid before downing it in one swift gulp.

"And another for good luck?" she suggested, this time handing me a glass full of emerald green.

"Okay, but three's my limit," I rationalized.

"Whatever you say, handsome," she hummed.

~ ~ ~

I wasn't sure what time it was or how long I had been here. I was too busy trying to control my elastic limbs to concentrate on much else. As I took a long drink from my pint glass, I smiled inwardly, feeling completely relaxed and at peace.

My eyes tried in vain to adjust to the flashes of light that ricocheted off the mirrored walls. I blurrily watched people as they danced, their bodies seeming to billow and then recede in a manner I had never before experienced. It was a beautiful thing to behold.

I was miles beyond wrecked. Glancing around the establishment, it was plain to see that pretty much everyone was just as far gone as me. It was like being part of some secret society where like-minded people could go and be free without judgment or ridicule. I felt accepted, invincible, victorious.

My gaze landed on a section of the club where rows of plush leather booths jutted out from the wall. My feet steered me there while the rest of my body struggled to keep up, my legs buckling with each step. Some chick with jet black hair suddenly appeared in my path, pulling at my shirt and dragging me onto the dance floor. She shimmied skillfully in a low-cut blouse, showcasing her impressive cleavage. When she caught me staring, a seductive smile spread across her face. She brought a hand up and brushed her dainty little fingers along her chest before reaching inside her cleavage and pulling out a tiny, clear vial.

She handed it to me, then reached around my lower waist to pull me right up against her scantily clad body. I opened the vial and did a bump, feeling the instantaneous hallucinatory effects.

"Hey, save some for me," she teased. I passed her the vial, and she did a bump before putting it back into her cleavage.

Smiling widely, she closed her eyes as the effects took hold, her head plopping onto my chest. Her hands, still around my waist, dipped down to squeeze my ass. "Whoa," I murmured, pushing her away as I tried to steady myself. She was cute and had a smoking hot body, but she felt all wrong. She wasn't Kelsey.

Kelsey.

Fuck! Ohgodohgodohgod.

My memory, though fuzzy, returned in chunks: I was supposed to be saving Kelsey from this hell hole.

What the fuck have I done?

Adrenaline pumped through my veins in record speed, propelling me forward. I hoped I wasn't too late.

With a tug at the back of my shirt, a squeaky voice rang out, "Where do you think you're going?"

Spinning around, I shoved at the girl's hand and slurred, "Don't *fuuucking* touch me."

"What the fuck's your problem? You were all over me a minute ago," she whined.

Ignoring her, I darted full speed ahead, leaving her to scream obscenities at my back. Heading toward the leather booths, I willed myself to walk properly, but instead, I stumbled over my own two feet, each of them now magnetized to the floor. I noticed that the crowd had thinned out considerably. My breathing accelerated as I became consumed with fear.

Kelsey.

A familiar-looking form materialized, then multiplied in front of me, and I fluttered my eyelids in an effort to make her regain singular status. When I reached for her, she playfully swatted my hand away. "Mark, you are a naughty, *naughty* boy." At that, she laughed hysterically. Tapping teasing fingers on my chest, she continued, "I *told* you to stay home." Then, like a sex-crazed nympho, she attacked.

Grabbing my face, she slammed her lips against mine, pulling the shit out of my hair while rubbing the front of her body all over me. And…as good as it felt, I knew she wasn't in her right mind. "Kelsey, don't," I pleaded, staggering backwards.

"Come on, baby, don't make me beg," she sassed, sliding into an empty booth beside us. She crooked her finger, indicating for me to join her as she laid down flat on her back.

I was torn. I wanted her, but this was a public place. Plus, she was drunk, and quite possibly strung out. But my mind was still too fucked up to process my conflicting thoughts, all logic having long since vanished beneath the chemical haze. Climbing into the booth, I slid on top of her, grinding myself down into her body. She locked her arms around my neck, kissing me ravenously in response. "That's better," she moaned against my lips.

"Fuuuuck," I groaned, furiously returning her kisses.

Suddenly, a strong arm pulled me off Kelsey by the back of my collar, yanking out some of my hair in the process. "Get the fuck off of her, asshole!"

I spun to face my attacker, and it was *him*—the jackass from the dance floor. As I remembered his hands on Kelsey's body, anger curdled in my gut, my heart beating so hard, I could feel the blood rising. *"Aaaahhhh!* Get yer *fuuucking* hands off *meeeee!"*

Suddenly, Kelsey was at the jackass's side, and he put a steadying arm around her. "It's okay, Tracy," she said to him. "This is Mark."

Tracy? What the fuck kind of "guy name" was that?

"You can do so much better," Tracy muttered to Kelsey under his breath.

I snapped.

And pandemonium ensued.

Vaguely, I remember sucker punching Tracy in the face and sinking my teeth into his arm. His friends descended on me like flies on shit, pummeling me to the floor. Kelsey screamed hysterically at them all to stop. I, however, kept right on ticking—working out my anger through haphazardly-directed swings at anyone who came within arm's length. Tracy delivered a couple of lucky punches, landing a shiner on me that closed up my left eye. Blood began to spill from my mouth...

"Oh my God, somebody HELP HER!" a female voice shrieked from nearby.

Suspending our boxing match, we all turned our heads in the direction of the screams. I could see Kelsey, now sitting at a booth with her head slumped on the table. She appeared to be out cold. Cali sat beside her, trying to shake her best friend back into consciousness. Maia and Debra paced frantically as they barked into their phones.

"Kelseeeey!" I screamed, stumbling toward her.

"Somebody must have roofied her drink," Cali speculated to no one in particular. "God, why won't she wake up?"

"Oh God," I croaked, feeling sick to my stomach.

Cali's eyes hardened when they found mine. *"You!"* she yelled. *"You* did this!"

"Noooo!" I vehemently denied. "Kelseeeeeeey!" As I reached a hand up to brush the hair out of Kelsey's face, I saw her eyes roll back into her head.

With a ferociously protective grab of my hand, Cali pulled my fingers back. *"GO AWAY!!!"* she screamed wildly. Eyes fixed on "the jackass" now, Cali gave him an icy order. "Tracy, get Mark the fuck out of here."

At this point, I was sobering up fast. "I just want to help her," I said. Backing away from the table, I put my face in my hands, feeling completely powerless.

"Don't you think you've done enough already?" Cali's voice spewed with venom.

Just then, two Emergency Medical Technicians entered the space, promptly laying Kelsey down onto a stretcher. They quickly checked her vital signs while hooking her arm up to an IV-drip. As they wheeled Kelsey out, Cali closely shadowed the medical team, and I started to follow suit.

Sensing my presence, Cali whipped around, jabbing her finger harshly into my chest. "Don't you *dare* follow us."

"I wanna be with her," I pleaded.

"Well, if you would have *been with her* instead of going and getting tanked off your ass, none of this would have happened." Her blame was completely irrational—but I was her scapegoat.

"That's not fair, Cali." Maia put a hand on her shoulder. "We *all* should have been keeping an eye on her."

"Shut up, Maia," Cali spat. "Don't you defend him!" At that, she fell back into stride with the emergency personnel as they wheeled Kelsey out of the building.

I watched in horror, the stretcher becoming a squall of white through my misty eyes. Looking to my left, I saw Tracy consoling a distraught Debra, now sobbing uncontrollably into his cable-knit sweater. As the world spun around me, all I wanted was to spin the clock back and start the night all over.

Rushing to the exit, I got there just in time to see the ambulance pull away from the curb. This propelled me to throw myself into the back of one of the numerous available cabs lined up at the sidewalk, barking orders to the driver to floor it to the nearest hospital. As I slumped back into the pleather upholstery, I had to continue swallowing past the vomit rising up in my throat.

TWENTY-ONE

Kelsey

I CRACKED OPEN MY EYES, lids so heavy, I could barely hold them up. The fuzzy and distorted scenery refused to snap into focus. I was on a gurney, whizzing through a labyrinth of icy hallways, intense bands of light assaulting me from above. The brightness was blinding, the movement nausea-inducing.

Voices buzzed and hummed around me, but all I could hear was gibberish, the sounds mangled, as if spoken underwater.

And then it all went dark.

"Kelsey, I need you to open your eyes," said a man in an authoritative but calming voice. He'd repeated himself over and over again until I could fully grasp the words.

My eyes opened infinitesimally, peering into an assemblage of heads and shoulders bearing down on me. Blank shapes stood in for faces, lacking in any distinguishable features. The one closest to me spoke. "You were drugged with a high dose of Rohypnol. Can you tell me what happened?"

Now focused on the pumpkin-shaped face hunched over me, I pulled at my memory, hoping to knock loose any nuggets of information that might help me recall what had happened. Unfortunately, my brain seemed to have gone on strike. Squeezing my eyes shut, I tried to push back the waves of nausea rippling through my core, but they continued to swell, building into a crescendo that could not be contained. When I lurched forward, a faceless woman in blue knew to shove a bedpan under my chin—and not a moment too soon. The vomiting episode literally turned me inside out. In the aftermath, the amount of time I gagged and heaved, trying to evacuate all the contents from my stomach, seemed endless. When finished, I collapsed back onto the gurney, completely spent.

I must have started to drift off again because the man's voice grew louder and more forceful. "Kelsey, my name is Dr. Morris. I'm here to help you, but you must open your eyes and stay with me," he urged.

I couldn't move.

"Kelsey? Kelsey, can you hear me?" Dr. Morris asked, and I could detect his fear.

I couldn't speak.

There was total commotion. Feet shuffling, shouting, and then…the bellow of a familiar voice nearby. "Kelsey!"

"Sir, this is a restricted area," a female voice asserted.

They must have placed me in a room because I no longer sensed the motion of being in-transit. The beeping and blipping of machines now surrounded me.

"But that's my girlfriend in there! I need to see her!" The familiar voice had become frantic and close.

"Step back, sir! You need to calm down and let the doctors help her."

"Just tell me if she's alright," he demanded. *Tell me!* he repeated, the words a boomerang inside sterile walls.

The voice finally registered with my brain, and I whimpered, "Mark," but nothing audible came out of my mouth.

Suddenly, cold fingers pried open my eyelids, an unbearably bright dot of light flickering across my line of vision. Spikes of pain shot to my head through my eye sockets. It felt like holes were being burned into my skull. I moaned in discomfort.

"Kelsey, it is very important that you stay awake. Do you understand?" Dr. Morris implored.

I barely nodded in response, groaning as the movement intensified the pain—my whole head was going to explode at any given moment, I was sure of it.

Next, a burning sensation flooded my left arm. Managing a glance to the side, I noticed the faceless woman in blue administering medicine into an IV that had at some point been inserted into my hand. The pain in my head quickly subsided.

When I heard more incoherent voices mumbling out in the distance, I turned my head toward the door. Large silhouettes with flailing arms appeared to be acting out a dramatic scene in the hallway. I wondered what play they were rehearsing. Then, the shadows breezed into the room, drifting all around me as I dozed off once again.

Random pieces of conversation filtered into my subconscious as I slept:

"This is all my fault," a familiar female voice sounded. "She wouldn't be in this mess if I hadn't dragged her to New York in the first place."

Cali.

"We need to call her mother," stated a female voice of reason.

Maia.

"*I* fucking let this happen. *Oh God.* She's going to be okay, right? She just *has* to."

Mark.

"*No, baby, it's not your fault! You warned me! I should have listened to you!*" I screamed, wanting to reassure him, but my body refused to wake up, trapping the words in my head instead.

"You need to get better, Kelsey. I can't live without you. *Do you hear me?!*" Mark's voice cracked as he yelled.

"Sir, I am telling you for the last time that you can't be in here. We're doing all we can for her. Let us do our job."

Faceless woman in blue.

I needed to tell Mark how much I loved him. *That I was going to be fine. That I would never leave him.* Nothing was more important to me in that moment. I prayed for the strength to carry out my mission.

Finally, my soupy eyes found his tall, dark figure pacing frantically by the door. "Mark," I whispered through the muddle.

He froze upon hearing my voice. "Kelsey." He rushed to my side.

"I'm afraid I'm going to have to ask you to leave," Dr. Morris demanded.

He took my hand, ignoring the doctor's orders. "I love you, Kelsey," he said through kisses on my fingers. *"I love you,"* he restressed—over and over and over again. "I'll never stop loving you. You're a part of me now."

Reaching up with my hand, I managed to touch his face before my arm fell limply back to my side. When I felt my fingers wet with Mark's tears, my heartbeat quickened, and the beeps of the nearby machine raced to assert my distress. As the muscles in my chest tightened and constricted, I could barely breathe, but I fought through the pain. I *needed* to speak my piece. "I love you, Mark. Always."

And that…did me in. I took several deep breaths, but the pressure in my chest kept building and building, leaving me no choice but to succumb to the suffering.

"Code Blue! *STAT!*"

"What's happening? *WHAT'S HAPPENING TO HER?!*"

"Sir, you need to leave *NOW*," Dr. Morris shouted.

"No! Kelsey, don't you dare leave me!" Mark shrieked. *"DON'T FUCKING LEAVE ME!"* Any remaining shred of composure had now abandoned him.

I could sense a swarm of medical staff working on me as I struggled to hang on to my last breaths of air. Defibrillator paddles pressed against my sternum, my body bouncing up and down with each shock like a fish out of water.

"Kelsey, I need you. Don't let go. *PLEASE*."

"Somebody get security!" an irate Dr. Morris commanded.

"No. No. *NO!*" Mark cried. He sobbed. He shrieked uncivil diction.

With a blink, my eyes registered the contours of everything around me before all of it just…bled—shape upon shape and shade upon shade all seeping into one another. Then…*nothing*.

TWENTY-TWO

Mark

I'D ALWAYS HATED hospitals. In my experience, they were nothing but breeding grounds for misery and death. Desolation seemed to spill from every orifice, mixing with the tang of disinfectant. My entire world hung in the balance as I kept vigil at Kelsey's bedside. I sat. I prayed. I wished. And I waited.

So much waiting.

The erratic gait of high-heeled angst bounced off the synthetic rubber floor in the hall, stopping as the door swung forward to reveal Cali with two cups of coffee in hand. She stepped inside, her noise-making footwear an exaggerated *clack-clack* within the small space. The sound got under my skin like nails on a chalkboard. It was all I could do to refrain from ripping her shoes off and stuffing them in the trash. But it wasn't her fault. She was still wearing her nightclub getup, refusing to leave the hospital to shower or change clothes. I understood because I, too, had no intention of walking out of here unless Kelsey was walking out with me.

Cali handed me a cup of coffee before roosting on the lumpy upholstered armchair that no doubt was about as comfortable as a bag of rocks. She wrapped her hands tightly around her own cuppa Joe, as if to absorb its warmth. Shifting her attention to the bed, Cali's expression ran from observant to forlorn. "She doesn't look good, Mark. It's like she's fading right in front of us."

Turning my gaze toward the bed, my eyes ran over Kelsey's unmoving form. "She just needs time," I offered, though in truth, I agreed with Cali's assessment. Despite Kelsey being alive, I was hard-pressed to detect any signs of actual *life*. She was so frighteningly pale, her lips dry and cracked. My eyes landed on the machine now pushing air through her lungs. She looked anything but improved, or even inclined to head in that direction. However, with Calista, I decided to keep my opinion to myself.

No matter how bleak the outlook, I was still indebted to Dr. Morris and his team, who'd been heroic in their efforts to revive Kelsey when she'd gone into cardiac arrest. They were the reason her heart had begun pumping again. But then, her mind had given up—she'd wound up slipping into a coma.

And that was two days ago.

Two days spent hoping and waiting.

Two days spent in my own personal hell.

The perpetual whooshing of the ventilator was a constant reminder that it was the only thing keeping Kelsey alive. Hearing it made my heart sink. But I held on to a glimmer of hope. And I prayed for a miracle.

Glancing back at Cali, I asked, "Any luck reaching Mrs. O'Reilly?"

Cali frowned as she finished taking a sip of her coffee. "No. She's not answering her home or cell phone. And she hasn't been to work since Friday."

I panicked. "Cali, we need to get in touch with her somehow. Kelsey needs her mother more than ever right now."

"I'm well aware of that," she snapped. She pushed a tuft of blond tangles off her forehead before continuing, "Debra and Maia are heading back to Quincy to see if they can track her down."

I brought my coffee to my lips and tilted the cup back. The warmth of the liquid calmed me down and softened my voice. "That's a good idea. I'm sure they'll find her."

"I hope so. There's just no telling with Mrs. O'Reilly these days." With a heavy exhale, Cali placed her Styrofoam cup on the rolling tray beside her. "She's been a bit of a head case."

My mind drifted back to my first and only encounter with Mrs. O'Reilly. "Oh," I said, recalling how emotionally unstable she'd appeared that day. "What about her dad?"

"Her father is dead," Cali bit out through clenched teeth.

I cringed, feeling like a real dick for not knowing that already. Kelsey and I still had so much to learn about each other. I prayed we'd get that chance. "I'm sorry. I had no idea," I muttered.

Cali looked down at her lap while smoothing out the wrinkles in her red satin dress. "It's a long story." With a weary sigh, she concluded, "We'll just leave it at that."

"Okay." I didn't want to push the issue.

Nothing seemed to be working in Kelsey's favor. Here she was in the ICU, just barely hanging on by a thread, and nobody could reach the only family she had left. The thought of it made me so sad I wanted to curl up into myself, bury my face in my own chest, and weep. But I had to be strong. *Strong for Kelsey.* And strong for her best friend, who appeared as if she was just barely hanging on herself.

I studied Cali for a long moment. She looked like complete shit, and truth be told, I was worried about her. Her eyes were sunken and had lost their luster. On her head sat a rat's nest of golden straw. But most concerning was the blanket of guilt that lay across her features. It was a look I was all too familiar with. I wore it like a uniform.

"You look exhausted. Why don't you go back to the hotel and get some rest?" I suggested.

She scoffed at me with a flick of her manicured hand. "I can sleep here."

"Taking cat naps with one eye open isn't the same, and you know it. Kelsey wouldn't want you to make yourself sick," I countered.

"I'm not leaving, Mark. I just can't, okay?" she protested, rising to her feet.

"Okay," I relented, knowing it was pointless arguing with her when she was just as stubborn as I.

Setting my coffee down on the windowsill, I watched as Cali approached the bed, her eyes watering as she tucked the blanket up snugly under Kelsey's chin. My heart panged at the sight of it.

Then her next questions took me off-guard. "What if this is it? What if she doesn't come back to us?"

"You shouldn't talk like that," I said through a clenched jaw. "She might hear you."

"She can't hear anything. She's a vegetable, Mark."

As my blood boiled at the insensitivity of her words, my left hand curled into a fist. Never, in my life, had I been so tempted to hit a woman. "Watch your fucking mouth! That's your best friend you're talking about!" I shouted, making her flinch.

With narrowed eyes, Cali got right into my face. "*That* is *not* my best friend," she shot back. "It's just a body with no person attached to it! Can't you *see* that?" she screamed, her arm jutting out to point at the bed from behind. "Kelsey is *gone!*" Throwing her face into her hands, Cali started to cry.

Seeing her fall apart was so gut wrenching, I had to blink back my own tears, try my damnedest to maintain composure. With a gentle squeeze on Cali's shoulders, I said, "She'll get better, Cali. She *will*."

She lowered her hands to peek up at me, her blue eyes caked with two days' worth of smeared mascara. "You don't know that."

"She'll get better," I repeated, gripping her shoulders a little tighter. "Kelsey isn't a quitter."

Cali's lips quivered. "But you heard the doctors. We need to prepare ourselves for…"

Cutting her off, I blurted, "Yes, I know what the doctors said, but Kelsey's a fighter. She'll beat this."

Cali wiped her runny nose on the sleeve of her dress. "Maybe you're right." At that, she offered me a hint of a smile.

"I *know* I'm right," I assured, wondering who I was trying to convince more.

~ ~ ~

That night, Cali and I retired to our respective chairs—hers in the corner of the room, mine right beside the bed. Cali dozed off in restless bursts of sleep. Doctors and nurses floated in and out every so often, checking Kelsey's vital signs, writing things down on their little clipboards. But there was never any news. Never any answers.

My optimism was waning.

Cali's choppy snoring kept me awake most of the night, not that I would have slept anyway. I dragged my chair as close to Kelsey's bed as possible. Lowering the bedrail to take her hand in mine, I stroked her fingers with the pad of my thumb. "I love you, Kelsey," I croaked, no longer able to contain my emotions.

While softly crying, I kept trying to rub some life into Kelsey's cold, limp hand. "I'm so sorry, baby," I whispered, bringing her hand to my lips. I kissed each of her fingers one by one. "Please come back to me."

Watching her chest rise and fall, I wondered if Kelsey would ever be able to breathe on her own again. I was fraught by the knowledge that her consciousness, if regained, might come with a price: physical and cognitive impairments that could be substantial—possibly *irreversible*. There was no way I'd be able to live with myself if that happened.

She may have sustained severe brain damage.

As Dr. Morris's words seeped into my thoughts, I suddenly felt sick. Carefully placing Kelsey's hand back down at her side, I had to leave and head for the bathroom. The moment I hit the stall, I threw up bile, coffee grounds, and the one bite of corn muffin I'd managed to force down for breakfast. Once done, I turned on the faucet, trying my best to gargle and spit away the regurgitated aftertaste.

When I caught my reflection in the mirror, I froze.

"Grotesque" didn't even begin to describe me. My left eye still had residual swelling and bruising over it—evidence of Tracy's lucky punch. My lip was busted up, and my Oxford shirt showed the dirty red splotches of set-in blood. It truly looked like I'd spent a night at *Fight Club*. Removing my shirt, I tossed it into the garbage can. Some of the blood had soaked through to the T-shirt underneath, but at least I looked marginally better than before. I ran my hands through my hair, trying to tame it into some semblance of order. If Kelsey were to wake up, the least I could do was try not to appear like something out of a horror movie.

I crept quietly back into the room, careful not to wake up Cali. Resuming my position in my chair by the bed, I clutched Kelsey's hand, interlocking her fingers with mine.

"You need to get better, Kelsey. If you do, I promise I'll spend the rest of my life making you happy." As I began to cry again, I could hear my voice cracking while I spoke. "Oh God, what am I going to do? I'm *sorry*. I'm so fucking sorry." Now at a full sob, I could no longer see Kelsey through my tears.

"It's not your fault," Cali broke in from her corner of the room. "I shouldn't have blamed you."

I shifted in my chair, watching as Cali wiped at her own tears. "No, you were right, Cali. She's here because of me," I panted, trying to catch my breath between sobs.

"No," she sputtered. "I threw you under the bus. I couldn't face what I had done."

"You didn't do anything," I sniffed, drying my eyes with the back of my hand.

Tears cascaded down Cali's cheeks. "Yes, I did. I brought Kels here to New York under false pretenses. I talked her into going to that club, when deep down I knew she didn't want to."

I shook my head at her irrational thought process. "What happened was an accident. I may not know much about you, but I *do* know that you'd never hurt Kelsey intentionally."

"But she got hurt anyway, Mark. I was selfish when I should have been paying attention. This is all on *me*."

"Cali, blaming yourself isn't going to do Kelsey any good. She needs you to be strong for her right now."

She seemed to consider that for a moment, before reluctantly nodding her head in agreement. Forcing a weak smile, she gestured at me with her hands. "Maybe you should take your own advice."

"Fair enough," I said. Our gazes locked in an exchange of mutual understanding.

At that, I twisted back around to focus all my attention on Kelsey. Leaning over and out of my chair, I kissed her eyelids, her forehead, her nose, her chin. Again and again I kissed her—I couldn't stop. I wanted her to feel that I was with her, to feel how much I loved her. Taking her hand, I pressed it against my cheek. As the touch of her skin against mine brought back memories of the first time we made love, I wondered if we'd ever be together like that again.

"No matter what, I'll always love you," I whispered. Taking my seat, I kept Kelsey's hand firmly in mine—and I held on for dear life. "I love you," I echoed over and over until my eyelids grew heavy, my head dropping to rest on the edge of the bed.

~ ~ ~

A tingling sensation woke me from my fitful slumber as cool fingertips caressed the side of my face, traveling a path up to my bad eye, tracing softly along my brow. As I came to, I lifted my head to find myself looking into a pair of dazzling hazel eyes. I rubbed my palms into my eye sockets, convinced I was dreaming. I looked again. Her eyes were wide open, staring back at me, unmoving. *Great, now I was hallucinating.* It was official: I was losing my fucking mind.

Then Kelsey blinked.

I nearly hit the ceiling, causing her hand to fall away. She continued to survey me, her gaze huge and full of questions. The same hand that was just touching me began to shake, and I took it in mine. Feeling the delicate squeeze of her fingers, I broke down, my words finally finding their way through the deluge of emotion.

"Welcome back, baby."

TWENTY-THREE

Kelsey

BLURRED FACES LOOMED over me, moving in and then away as they conversed in strange tongues. Hands hoisted and shifted my body around on a bed, but I had no idea where I was or how I'd gotten here. Blanketed in a harsh light, the room intermittently faded to darkness whenever I tried to focus in on my surroundings. Each time I woke up, I felt a thick haze clouding my vision—the world seen through fog-colored glasses.

What was wrong with me?

A familiar voice rang close to my ear, but I couldn't follow the dialect. *Was somebody speaking to me?* I glanced at the talking head but couldn't make out the image through the glowing mist.

And just like that, the room went dark again.

Next thing I knew, I was lying on a park bench with a man on top of me. We were going at it in front of a crowd of willing spectators, goaded into action by their cheers and raunchy words of encouragement. I caught a glimpse of the man's face above me. *I knew that face.*

Then my eyes opened, bringing back the blurred images and strange voices. Was *this* a dream? Or had I been dreaming *before?* Too many conflicting thoughts took up residency in my head. I tried in vain to separate what was real from what wasn't. Delirium had overthrown me, and I was petrified.

The familiar voice was in my ear again and this time, when I studied the corresponding face, recognition shone through the smog of my muddled and confused mind. Even out of focus, I would know that face anywhere: *Mark.*

Oh, thank God. He'd have the answers.

As I tried to speak, an obstruction in my throat pressed painfully on my vocal cords, and I groaned and cringed and gasped for air. This made me lose my shit completely. Thrashing wildly, I pulled at cords, desperate to get out of bed. Suddenly, people scurried all around me, binding my hands and feet in restraints until they rendered me completely helpless, at the total mercy of strangers. It seemed my little stunt had caused a rather big stir. Now, as if punished, all I could do was lie there like a corpse while trying to comprehend what was going on.

"She's afraid," I heard someone say.

And once again, it all went black.

The next minute, I was in a forest with tall pine trees encircling me—branches filled with thousands of beady-eyed, hungry black and white magpies. They descended upon me in droves, pecking at my arms until I bled. I flailed violently, anxious to get them off me, but they were relentless, becoming more and more aggressive until my flesh was gone and I was nothing but bones…

"Can you tell me your name?"

I blinked in confusion. Were the birds talking to me now? And why was it so difficult for me to remember my name?

"Kelsey," I finally answered, but the sound that came out was too high-pitched, resembling the squeal of an injured animal. Was that *my* voice?

The talking magpie morphed into the shape of a man in a white lab coat, the name, "Dr. Morris" spelled out on a tag in red lettering. He didn't look like a doctor to me, though. More like the character "McLovin" from *Superbad*. He wrote something down on what I assumed was a medical chart. *My* medical chart.

I was in a hospital.

A stout nurse in blue scrubs checked my IVs, which seemed to be stuck into every vein I had. Grinning when she caught me staring, she declared, "You're one lucky young lady."

"What happened to me?" Getting the question out was a huge strain. The obstruction in my throat had disappeared, but the lingering aftereffects were ruthless.

"You were in a coma for nearly three days," Dr. Morris replied.

I didn't understand. "How?" I asked.

"You overdosed on a date rape drug that you ingested without your knowledge. Do you remember anything about the nightclub, Kelsey?"

I tried to get the gears turning in my mind to formulate a credible memory. But all my thoughts were loose, fragmented nuts and bolts just clanging around in my head, refusing to operate like the well-oiled machine it once was. I was tempted to ask about the park bench and the magpies, but I was afraid I'd be put in a strait jacket and committed to the nearest asylum.

"No," I answered through a throat of sand.

"How about telling me your last name?" Dr. "McLovin" asked. "Can you do that for me, Kelsey?" He obsessively clicked his ballpoint pen.

As I opened my mouth, I realized that I couldn't for the life of me recall what the correct answer was. I fought back my emotion, but it was too much to handle. Tears spilled down my cheeks as I sputtered, "I...I can't remember."

With an upward push of his wire-rimmed glasses, the doctor studied me for a moment before making more notes in my chart. "It may take some time for your memory to return fully, but that's *not* unusual," he reassured.

"Don't worry. It'll be okay, baby," a masculine voice said from beside me. It was the most welcome sound I'd heard in forever.

As soon as I turned toward the voice, my breath hitched. Somehow, mercifully, the fog had dissipated, and I could see the man's face as clear as day. "Mark?" I choked.

Upon hearing his name fall from my lips, he beamed. Warm caramel eyes laced with saltwater stared into mine. "God, I love you," he said as he stroked my cheek.

I pressed my face into his hand, reveling in his touch. "Me too."

Another hand touched me, stroking my hair from the other side of the bed. I rolled my head to the left to see a stunningly beautiful blond eyeing me with adoration. "You gave us quite a scare," she said, smiling warmly as she wiped away her tears with the other hand. Although her face and voice were familiar, I couldn't place her name or exactly how I knew her. At the sight of my blank stare, her smile fell, the hurt swimming visibly in her crystal eyes.

Feeling terrible that I'd obviously upset her, I said softly, "I'm sorry."

She leaned over and kissed the top of my head. "Don't be silly. It'll all come back to you in no time. You just concentrate on getting better."

"Okay." Giving in to her words, I hoped along with her that she was right.

~ ~ ~

Gradually, I experienced longer periods of lucidity, and after one week in the hospital, I was finally discharged. Sorting through the aftermath of what had happened was frustrating. I felt disoriented, my memory still quite fuzzy, but Dr. Morris had said this was to be expected under the circumstances. Although my road to recovery would be a long one, he was thoroughly pleased with my progress. Thankfully, he expected me to make a complete turnaround.

I'd almost died.

What a difficult concept to fathom. It all felt more like a weird and twisted dream. But still, every day, I felt so grateful. Grateful to be *alive*.

Although I'd been released, I was under strict orders to remain on bed rest for the next month. Mark, who hadn't left my side for more than five minutes, insisted on staying with me at my house until I could get around on my own. That meant four solid weeks of together time…*in my bed*. I wondered how my mom would feel about that.

Mark played chauffeur, driving me and the stunning blond I'd been told was my best friend—*Cali*—back to Quincy in his oversized shit box. The muffler was even noisier than I'd remembered—and I loved it. With an inward smile, I laid down in the backseat, melting into the vintage upholstery, pleased that at least some of my memories remained intact.

Cali was noticeably quiet in the front passenger seat, the tension between us palpable. She faced her own battle of wills, repressing her resentment and anger while offering encouragement and support to a best friend who couldn't remember her.

I decided to break the ice. "Why didn't Mom come to visit me in the hospital?" Finally, I gave a voice to the question that had been floating around in my head all day.

Mark and Cali visibly tensed before Cali twisted around in her seat, plastering on a saccharine smile as she responded, "Your mom's been busy at home getting everything ready for your arrival. She can't wait to see you, Kels."

That felt more like a lame excuse than a plausible answer, but I decided to let her off the hook, as exhaustion had gotten the better of me. My body then succumbed to the sleep it could never seem to get enough of.

~ ~ ~

I stirred at the sound of someone's muffled weeping. Night had fallen, wrapping the car in darkness. I laid completely still as alertness slowly crept into my senses, homing in on the conversation taking place in the front seat.

"You just need to give her time," Mark said.

He was talking about me.

"Deep down, I know you're right. And I'm *trying*," Cali replied, her voice wavering. "But we've been best friends since we were in first grade. I just don't understand this, Mark. Maybe…maybe I'm just not worth remembering." Then she completely let go—full sobs. I could practically feel the entire vehicle shaking along with her shoulders.

The car swerved and came to an abrupt stop. I stiffened as my eyes popped completely open, riveted to the front seat.

"Look at me, Cali," Mark commanded.

"No."

"You are so goddamned stubborn. Look. At. Me," he ordered, grabbing her chin between his thumb and forefinger.

With an exasperated breath, she obeyed. "Fine."

"Listen to me. Kelsey loves you. You just have to be patient with her. She'll come around."

Fresh tears sprang from Cali's eyes. "How can you be so sure?"

Mark leaned in to wipe her tears away with his thumbs. "Because you're a terrific girl…and a wonderful friend."

"You really think so?" Cali peeked up at him through her unnaturally long lashes.

"I know so," he said, placing his right hand on her left shoulder. My pulse began to race as I zoomed in on it, illuminated perfectly by the headlights of a passing car. My eyes widened in astonishment as my *boyfriend's* fingers glided, squeezing and releasing, massaging the spot between Cali's neck and collar bone. Then, in response to Mark's ministrations, my *best friend* placed her hands on top of his, their faces moving in closer together…

As my stomach twisted into a knot, I slammed my eyes shut, wishing I could just fade back into oblivion.

TWENTY-FOUR

Mark

CAMPING OUT AT THE O'Reilly household wasn't all that it was cracked up to be. A bizarre shift in Kelsey's demeanor overrode any opportunities for intimacy. The romantic scenes I had envisioned were replaced with harsh stares, cold shoulders, and emotional distance. After four days spent in psychological combat, things had only gotten worse.

Kelsey's memory was still sketchy at best. Bits and pieces came to her at random with an intense sadness attached to them, resulting in severe and frequent bouts of crying. When she wasn't crying, anger consumed her. Anger at herself for not recovering faster. Anger at her mother for being neglectful. Anger at Cali for simply existing. And anger at me for reasons unknown.

With Kelsey sound asleep in her room, I ventured downstairs to see if Mrs. O'Reilly needed any help in the kitchen. The woman was a machine, baking, sautéing, and frying in constant rotation, usually with a glass of wine to accompany her. She was a bundle of nervous energy, an emotional basket case, busying herself like a fiend so she wouldn't have to face the turmoil upstairs. Any breaks from cooking she spent cleaning—scouring sinks, wiping down countertops, mopping floors. Even washing the windows seemed to take precedence over spending time with her own daughter. Although I was tempted to voice my concerns, I chose to hold my tongue. To me it wasn't worth overstepping my bounds at the risk of wearing out my welcome.

Sauntering into the kitchen, I caught Mrs. O'Reilly in the midst of one of her crying jags. Standing over the sink, her hands trembled as they held a large sauté pan under a heavy stream of steaming water. Short rapid breaths escaped her mouth, teetering on the cusp of hyperventilation. Feeling intrusive, I reversed my steps, moving briskly back out into the hall, thankful for having avoided that awkward encounter. But this just made me wind up running into Cali as she entered the front door.

"Hey," she mumbled. "Kels awake?"

"Nah. Sleeping like a log as usual," I chuckled softly. "Whatcha got there?" I asked, gesturing toward the leather-bound binder tucked under her arm.

She pulled it out, casting it a loving look while running her fingers delicately along the word "Memories" embossed on the front. "Just an old photo album. Pictures of me, my family, my friends. Me and Kels…" she trailed off, keeping her emotions in check. With a shrug, she cocked her head to the side and continued, "…thought maybe they'd help her remember."

"I bet they will," I said. Then, cracking a smile, I queried, "Am *I* allowed to see them?"

"Sure. Why not?" she replied, walking toward the staircase. Perching on the bottom step, Cali crossed her denim covered legs in front of her. She opened the album up on her lap.

Taking a seat beside her, I watched as she flipped through the pages. Immediately, my attention snagged on a photo of Kelsey and Cali posing in togas. Kelsey's expression was priceless, screaming, *"How the hell did I get myself into this?"*

I laughed as my finger landed on the page. "There *must* be a story behind this picture," I taunted, nudging Cali with my shoulder.

Cali smiled for a moment before it quickly fell away. Sadness washed across her features as she spoke. "One of the frat houses on campus threw a huge toga party my sophomore year. Everyone who was anyone was going to be there. I really wanted to go. Kelsey didn't, but I somehow talked her into it." She slumped her shoulders and hung her head, allowing her mass of blond waves to cover the page. "I was always doing that…making her do things she didn't want to do. Some friend I am, huh?"

"Did she end up having a good time at the party?" I asked hopefully.

Lifting her head just a fraction, Cali tucked her hair behind her ears. She peeked at me out of the corner of her eye, a small smile tugging at her lips. "Actually, she did. She played beer pong for the first time…and kicked everyone's ass," she giggled.

"I would have paid good money to see that," I joked, putting my arm around Cali in support. "See? You're a good friend. Stop beating yourself up."

"Well, isn't this *cozy?*" Kelsey snarled from behind.

Cali and I spun around in surprise, my arm falling away from her shoulders. Clutching the rail, Kelsey attempted to navigate the stairs, the hem of her terrycloth robe dusting dangerously along the tops of her feet. After just a few steps, her legs began to quake. Groaning in frustration, she sank to a sitting position, eyeing Cali with a deadly glare. "By all means, please continue your snuggle fest. Far be it for me to interrupt," Kelsey spat.

Pushing to my feet, I peered up at Kelsey, my eyes trying to assess what the hell had gotten into her. When she avoided my gaze, I knew I had been banished to the doghouse. "Come on, baby. You know it wasn't like that," I pleaded. As I started up the stairs, Kelsey thrust her hand out in a stopping gesture, fixing me with a cold stare. At that, all I could do was crawl back down with my tail between my legs, wondering when my punishment would be over.

Cali put on a brave face, climbing the stairs to her inevitable doom. She grabbed Kelsey by the elbow, assisting her as she rose to stand. "We were just looking at some old pictures I brought over to show you. Why don't I take you back upstairs?" she suggested. "I think you'll get a big kick out of seeing them."

"Don't touch me." Kelsey jerked her arm away. "I can do it *myself.*" She left Cali's hand hanging in the dust.

Her best friend's face fell. "I'm sorry, Kels. I was just trying to help."

"Well, I don't need your help." Kelsey held onto the rail with a vice-like grip, glowering over her shoulder while cautiously beginning her ascent. "And I don't need your stupid pictures either."

Although I knew the move would bite me in the ass, I jumped to Cali's defense. "How about laying off a little, alright? She just wants you to remember—"

"—Remember *what* exactly?" Kelsey's foot had frozen mid-step as she chewed me out. "That she's a *backstabber* who's trying to steal my *boyfriend?*"

"Kelsey! That's enough!" Mrs. O'Reilly roared as she emerged from the kitchen.

Kelsey dropped her foot while gripping the railing with both hands, turning to face the woman who had barely acknowledged her presence since her return. "Gee, thanks so much for the support *Mom*," she sniped. "Why don't you do me a favor and go back to hibernating in the kitchen?"

As Mrs. O'Reilly wiped her hands on her apron, her expression was unreadable. "I know you're upset, sweetheart, but we're all just trying to help you."

"Help me? Like you could give a shit," Kelsey seethed.

"You're my daughter, Kelsey. I love you."

"Whatever."

The beeping of the oven timer reverberated into the hall, snapping Mrs. O'Reilly to attention. She eyed the kitchen door longingly. "Well, I should probably get back to the lasagna before it burns." And with that, Kelsey's mom disappeared into her culinary abyss.

Taking her cue from Mrs. O'Reilly's departure, Cali tucked the photo album back under her arm and headed toward the front door. "I can see you're not in the mood for my company, so I think I'll get going. I'll be back tomorrow, okay?" Still, her voice was filled with hope.

"Don't bother," Kelsey snapped.

Cali opened the door, hesitating as she stood under the threshold. "I *will* be back tomorrow. And the day after that. And the day after *that*." A single tear slid down her cheek as she met Kelsey's icy stare. "Somewhere inside you is my best friend. I'm not giving up until I find her." At that, she walked out into the afternoon haze.

Kelsey looked at me, wide-eyed. "How about you?" she asked, her posture sagging as exhaustion took its toll. She sat down and hung her head between her knees. "You gonna leave too?"

"Of course not," I assured her, rushing up the stairs.

"Why not?" she demanded. "Don't you want to be with Cali?"

Gently pulling Kelsey to her feet, I shook my head. "Why would you even ask me something like that?"

"I'm not stupid, Mark. I know there's something going on!" she wailed, breaking down into hysterics.

Scooping Kelsey into my arms, I carried her the rest of the way up the stairs and into her bedroom. I lowered her onto the bed, pulling the comforter up to her shoulders, but she just faced away from me to sob into her pillow. Deciding to bite the bullet, I stripped down to my boxers and got in beside her. When I tried to spoon her, she shrank away.

I let out a heavy sigh. "You want to tell me what this is all about?"

She curled into a ball, her sobs diminishing into muffled cries. "That night…in the car…I saw you touch her."

"Kelsey, *no.* I was just trying to help her—as her friend."

"I see the way she looks at you, Mark. And she's so pretty." Her voice dropped, barely audible. "I can't compete with that," she whispered, accepting defeat.

I reached out, tentatively stroking her soft chestnut hair. "First of all, she may be pretty, but you are *beautiful.* And secondly, I can assure you that she only views me as a friend. We sort of bonded while you were in the hospital."

"Maybe you don't see it, Mark, but I do. She wants you. I wouldn't blame you if you wanted her too."

"Please stop this, Kelsey. *I love you.* You're the only one I want."

Her body relaxed, uncurling and stretching across the length of the bed. "You don't want her?"

"*No.* Cali and I are *friends.* Nothing more. She's been having a hard time with all this. She loves you too, baby."

Kelsey stiffened in offense. *"She's* having a hard time?"

"Listen, I know this has been a nightmare for you. I'd give anything to take away your pain, to erase what happened to you. It's been hard…hard for *you*…hard for *all of us*."

I risked moving in closer, pressing myself into her back. Pulling down her robe slightly, I exposed one shoulder so I could plant a soft kiss there. "I thought I'd lost you, Kelsey. When you went into a coma, I thought my life was over. I didn't know how to go on without you."

She rolled over and faced me, placing her small, delicate hands on my chest. "You don't have to. I'm right here," she said through her tears.

I reached for one of her hands, placing it over my heart. "Don't ever doubt how much I love you. Not even for a minute." Our eyes locked, and I knew I was finally getting through to her. "I am *yours*. I don't want to be anyone else's."

She pulled her hand out from under mine, dragging her fingers down my naked torso. They skated along the waistband of my cotton boxer briefs. "Show me."

TWENTY-FIVE

Kelsey

QUIET AS A MOUSE, I tiptoe toward the living room, stopping just shy of the threshold. I peer around the corner, careful to remain unnoticed. He's lounging on the loveseat, World's Greatest Dad mug cradled in his large hands. Steam billows up from the hot liquid inside. I watch as he skims a cooling breath over the mug's lip, takes a sip, and places it down on the coffee table in front of him. The morning newspaper is splayed across his lap. He resumes his reading, picking it up and shaking it out loosely until it completely unfolds. Getting comfortable, he lifts one foot until his ankle rests on the other knee. He holds the paper wide open at eye level, face blocked from view, presenting me with the perfect opportunity to enter the room unseen.

I make my move, prowling with cat-like agility as I near my tar-get. I stifle the laughter bubbling up from inside my belly. It's our ritual. We do this each and every Sunday morning. But this time, I'm determined to come out victorious. As my feet come to a stop, I hold my breath for a few seconds, poised to strike. Slowly, carefully, I reach for the newspaper, preparing to yank it away and scare Daddy sense-less.

Suddenly, the top corner folds down, revealing his amused face.

"Gotcha!" he bellows, tossing the paper aside to pull me into his lap. His hands begin tickling me mercilessly, causing me to laugh so hard I gasp for air.

"Daddy, stop! No more! No more!" I scream through panting breaths, loving every minute of the torture.

"Are you sure about that, baby girl?" he taunts, a devious grin spreading across his face. "I don't think the Tickle Monster is finished with you yet."

I furiously shake my head, pigtails slapping me in the face as I play right into his little game. His fingers alternate between poking and grazing, unrelenting as they hit the money spot beneath my rib-cage. I twitch and jerk convulsively while cackling with delight, a high-pitched resonance that could shatter glass. "Go away, Tickle Monster! Go away!" I squeal, not meaning a word of it.

Allowing me time to catch my breath, Daddy slows down his movements, looking down at me in a way I don't understand. His carefree mood has slipped away in the blink of an eye. I reach up to cup his cheek, stroking my thumb along the stubble at his jaw line—I always love how it tickles me. I smile at him with all the love in my heart, yet his face grows more serious, his features setting in a grim expression. He turns away from me while holding his hand to his mouth. *"What's the matter, Daddy?" I ask, scrambling further onto his lap, turning his face back toward me with my small hands.*

I study his handsomely rugged face, noticing the tears dancing along his lower lids. They spill over when he blinks, dribbling down his cheeks and wetting my thumbs. "Why are you crying? Did I do something wrong?"

He wipes at the wetness with the back of his hand, shaking his head as he speaks. "Daddy's just being silly. Don't you worry about me, okay?"

Feeling uneasy, I stretch out the bottom of my pink frilly nightgown, tenting my knees up inside of it. "But I wanna know why you're sad. Please tell me, Daddy."

He kisses my forehead before pulling me in for an all-consuming hug. "Have you ever felt sad, but you don't why?" he asks, to which I nod my head in understanding. "And you want to make it go away but you don't know how?"

My brows pull together, as I cannot fully grasp the severity of his words. I snuggle into his plaid flannel bathrobe, absorbing its softness while I find a solution for him. "What if I promise to be extra good from now on?" I offer, thinking it is a most brilliant plan. "Then you won't have to be sad anymore."

"Oh, Kelsey. No, sweetheart. My being sad is not your fault. Don't ever think like that. Promise me."

"Okay, I promise."

"Daddy loves you more than anything in the whole world. No matter what happens, I want you to always remember that." His face reddens, prominently outlining the "V" of his receding hairline. Tears fall silently, fast and plentiful as he fights to stifle a full-on outburst. I swallow hard as a lump forms in my throat.

"I love you, Daddy. Please don't cry," I beg, wrapping my arms tightly around his neck.

"I'm really going to miss you, baby girl," he whispers softly into my hair.

"Where are you going, Daddy?" I ask, suddenly panic stricken.

He doesn't answer. Instead, he sobs harder, clutching at me as if I might disappear...

~ ~ ~

"Kelsey...." The sound of my name echoed in the corners of my mind. "Kelsey..." the voice continued to chant, faintly and muffled at first—before quickly progressing into a trumpeting blast. It felt like someone had just pulled the cotton out from my ears and the onslaught of sound made me frantic. My eyes flew open in alarm, landing on Mark, who was leaning over me, shaking my shoulders.

"Wake up, baby. You were having one of your dreams again."

I looked up at the ceiling, feeling slightly embarrassed. "Did I say anything this time?" I asked, leery.

"No. But you were really thrashing around. I was afraid you were going to hurt yourself," he replied, planting a soft kiss to my lips. "You wanna talk about it?"

A shudder rippled down my spine as I began to recall the dream. Only I knew it wasn't just a dream, but a memory as well. Gradually, my memories were returning home, but still just in fragments, leaving me with more questions than answers. And rarely were they pleasant, carrying with them an undertone of constant sorrow. Rather than face them head on,

I preferred sticking my head in the sand, pretending they didn't exist. It was less painful that way.

"Talking is overrated," I hummed, biting my lower lip. I sat up, pulling my Boston Red Sox nightshirt over my head and tossing it on the floor beside the bed. "I have a much better idea," I teased, reaching for Mark's boxers with greedy, needy hands.

Mark pulled back, catching my hands before they had a chance to make contact. "No, Kelsey. You can't keep stalling like this. You need to start dealing with things."

Flopping down onto my back again, I folded my arms over my chest. "You don't *want* me," I whined, knowing I was being unreasonable, but feeling rejected, nonetheless.

Mark leaned in closer, stopping inches from my face. "You *know* that's not true," he countered, dipping his head to press his lips to mine. He coaxed my lips apart with his tongue, rewarding me with a kiss so sensual and deliciously wet, it made my toes curl.

Breaking the kiss, we both panted while coming up for air. I smiled as I touched my fingers to my lips, still throbbing from the intensity of it. Peeking up at Mark, I said, "Okay, you've made your point. I'm sorry."

"Don't get me wrong. The constant sex has been *amazing*, better than I ever imagined. But we can't keep living in our own little bubble, as tempting as that may be. You need to get back to living your life."

"I *am* living my life, with *you*. That's all that matters."

"Kelsey, I love you, and I'm not going anywhere. But you have school to think about. Your family. Your friends."

"I don't care about any of that anymore," I huffed, angling my body toward the wall.

He rubbed my bare back, making large circular motions with his palm. "You say that now, but believe me, you *will* care. I think deep down, you already do."

Rolling back over, I searched Mark's face, completely lost in those caramel orbs, which were now eyeing me with overwhelming concern. "Maybe you're right," I relented.

"Talk to your mom, Kelsey. *Really* talk to her. Go to her and tell her you need her help."

When I felt my face turning sour at the mention of my mom, I broke eye contact. "She doesn't care about me."

He tilted up my chin, his expression softening. "Yes she does. She's just having a hard time dealing."

"I don't know. I'm just not ready to talk to her yet."

"Okay, what about Cali, then? I know she'd love to talk to you."

My bottom lip stuck out in a childish pout. "I don't want to talk to Cali. I don't feel comfortable around her," I confessed.

"I know it's confusing because you don't remember much about her, but I think if you give her a chance, she could really help you."

"I can't explain it, Mark. I always feel myself getting agitated around her. It's like she's trying too hard or something. It just seems so put on...so fake."

"I agree that she may be overdoing it a little, but she's just overcompensating. She never knows how you're going to react to her."

As Mark's words sank in, I slowly nodded my head, acknowledging my own shortcomings. "Yeah, I guess that makes sense," I concurred. "Tell me something: was I always such a bitch?"

"You could *never* be a bitch. You're just frustrated…everyone understands that, baby," Mark said, crawling to his side of the bed to lie on his back. "Come here."

I slid over to settle onto his chest. For quite some time, we held each other as I tried to sort through my jumbled thoughts. Mark's heartbeat at my ear lulled me back into dreamland.

~ ~ ~

Later I awoke to a dark room and an empty bed. Still unable to manage the concept of time, I glanced at the clock on the nightstand. It read 9:03 PM, but that didn't hold much significance when I couldn't keep track of what day it was.

Evidence of yet another unsettled slumber appeared in the form of me in a tangled mess of yellow and white. Shaking my legs vigorously, I freed myself from the confines of my striped comforter. It was a relief to find that my body was healing quickly, my muscle strength having returned by leaps and bounds. If only the same could be said of my mental state.

Sitting back up, I swung my legs over the side of the bed, spotting my nightshirt on the floor. Leaning over, I picked it up, smiling to myself in recollection of Mark's searing hot kiss. I pushed to my feet, slipping the shirt over my head while making my way out into the hall and down the stairs. My hope was to entice one very sexy boyfriend back to my room to pick up where we'd left off.

Conversation emanated from the kitchen as I reached the bottom of the staircase. Padding in that direction, I slowed my pace as the volume skyrocketed. I stood at the door, pushing it slightly forward to peer through the opening.

Mark shoved his hands through his hair and pulled at the ends, a clear sign of distress. He paced the room while passing looks between Cali and my mom, a man caught in the middle of a conversation in which he wanted no part. "Ladies, *please.* Let's just try to calm down for a minute—"

"—Calm *down?!*" Cali shot him a killing look. "Are you serious, Mark? *She* needs to start acting like a *grownup!!*" she squealed, with a red, acrylic-tipped finger jabbing in Mom's direction.

"I *aaam* a grownup," my mom slurred. Slouching against the granite countertop, she held a red wine bottle firmly in her grasp.

"Oh yeah? Well, you could have fooled me! It's time you start acting like a mother. Kelsey needs you," Cali scolded.

"What bout what *I* need, huh?" Mom spat, facing Cali with a glazed-over expression. The bottle teetered in her fist as she attempted to lift it to her mouth. Some of the wine made its way into her throat while the rest spilled down the side of her face, marking red streaks on her skin before continuing a path to her baby blue polo shirt. "You think I like being a widow?

Do you?!" she thundered before dissolving into a mound of loose limbs.

"I'm sorry for your loss," Mark whispered. Approaching her cautiously, he slowly pulled her to her feet. "You must miss Mr. O'Reilly very much."

"*Heeey.* You're a real *sweethaaart,*" she crooned, patting his cheek roughly while leaning her dead weight against him. "She looks just like him ya know."

"What?" he asked, his eyes squinting in confusion.

"Like her father. Every time I look at her…all I see is him," she groaned.

"Would you like to talk to me about it?" Mark offered, leading her to a vinyl-padded stool.

"Let her sober up first, Mark," Cali warned.

At that, Mom boisterously objected, *"Nooooo,"* before stammering, "I wanna talk *nowww.*" Sitting half-assed on the stool, she leaned with both elbows on the counter. "He blew his fuckin' brains out," Mom sputtered. "Can you believe that shittt?" A burst of her insane, hysterical laughter ensued.

"Jesus," Mark muttered.

That ear-piercing, blood-curdling, horrific cackle awakened something inside of me—I practically felt the flick of a switch in my brain. All the memories—*all of them*—flooded back in a current until they overtook me in tsunami-like waves. Bursting into the kitchen, I crossed the floor until I reached the basement door. I stood there, paralyzed, staring a hole through the oak paneling. Images flashed before my eyes, fast and furious and ruthlessly, with no consideration for any repercussions.

His lifeless body.
The hole in his temple.
The blood-soaked floor.
The 9mm pistol.
The funeral.
The endless tears.
Mom's depression.
The pitiful stares.
The loose, gossiping lips.
Feeling too much.
Feeling nothing.

I turned around to face my audience in the kitchen, who had now gone silent. My eyes cut to the one person who had always been my constant. My unwavering support. My bright spot through all the cloudy days.

"Cali!" I screamed.

At that, my legs gave out, and I fell to my knees, breathless.

TWENTY-SIX

Mark

THE ANGUISHED LOOK on Kelsey's face as she recalled the horrific details of her father's death would remain imprinted in my memory forever. Agony, despair, sorrow, desolation—a whirlwind of distressing emotions erupted from her core, a demonic force taking over her body. Desperate to soothe her pain, I rushed to her side, but Cali had beaten me to the punch.

"DADDY!!" Kelsey wailed, pulling Cali down to the floor with trembling hands, clutching her fiercely. "I want my *daddy* back!"

Cali sat huddled with her best friend, her own tears falling silently. She wrapped her arms tightly around Kelsey's waist. "I know you do, hon. I know," she said softly, kissing the top of her head. "I'm so sorry, Kels."

A bemused chortle escaped Mrs. O'Reilly's loose lips. "You always *did* love *him* more," she chirped drunkenly from her stool.

Cali shot me a pleading look. "Can you get her out of here?"

With a nod, I crouched down, turning Kelsey's tear-soaked face toward mine. "Baby, I'm just gonna bring your mom upstairs, but I'll be right back in case you need me, okay?"

"Don't worry. I got this," Cali retorted before Kelsey could respond.

I was taken aback by Cali's dismissive tone but tried not to take it personally. She had been so patient with Kelsey during her recovery; I supposed she'd earned this time to coddle her best friend without the overprotective boyfriend watching over her shoulder.

Pushing to my feet, I approached the stool where Mrs. O'Reilly sat slumped over like a question mark. I carefully raised her arm, supporting her elbow while hoisting her up. "Let's get you upstairs so you can get some rest, okay?"

"Pffft," she protested, barely able to keep her eyes open.

"You can lean on me," I assured her, pulling her to a stand. "I won't let you fall."

Even with my support, Mrs. O'Reilly was really unstable. So I just focused on the door, taking one step at a time as we passed through it, continuing down the hall at a snail's pace. Then she was all over me like a cheap suit as we navigated the stairs, taking what seemed like an eternity to reach the top. The smell of her wine-soaked shirt wafted into my nostrils, making my mouth water. Despite the pungent odor, it ignited a craving in me that had been dormant for weeks. I shuddered internally, knowing I needed to get a handle on myself.

After steering Mrs. O'Reilly into her room, her body met the bed with a ragdoll wallop. She was motionless as I slipped her shoes off and covered her with a quilt. I then waited, listening quietly until the wet razz of her gargled breathing told me it was safe to leave her alone to "sleep it off." I shut the door behind me to head back down to the kitchen.

Kelsey and Cali sat together on matching stools, deep in conversation, their intertwined hands on the countertop, a box of tissues nearby. "Daddy always thought you were crazy, you know," Kelsey remarked, chuckling softly at the memory.

"Yeah, I know," Cali responded with a giggle of her own. "He was right, though. I *was* crazy…still am."

"I have to agree with you there," Kelsey joked, patting her friend on the wrist. "I *do* remember the time you set me up with that guy, *Blade,* who took me bungee jumping on our first date! I wanted to kill you!"

"Just admit it, Kels. It totally turned you on," Cali teased, with a suggestive eyebrow-wiggle. "Plus, Blade was totally hot!"

"Oh yes," Kelsey chuckled, turning red with embarrassment. "He most definitely was," she admitted.

Cali smiled wide, victorious. "Ha! I knew you had the hots for him! What a sexy mother…"

Before subjecting myself to further talk of *Blade's* hotness factor, I cleared my throat, immediately silencing the two of them. "Uh…how long have you been standing there?" Kelsey asked, clearly horrified by my eavesdropping.

"Not long. Just a couple minutes," I answered, with an awkward scratch of my head.

"*Jeez.* How embarrassing," she moaned, throwing her head in her hands.

"Hey, it's no big deal. We were just reminiscing, right Kels?" Cali defended.

"Yeah, I know but *still…*" she trailed off, looking as uncomfortable as I felt.

I shuffled my feet, feeling guilty for having intruded on their BFF reunion…and even a bit unwelcome. But I knew this wasn't about me; it was about encouraging Kelsey to ride the wave of her breakthrough. "Why don't I give you some privacy?" I offered, crossing the room to rest my hands on Kelsey's shoulders. "I'm sure you two have a lot of catching up to do."

Kelsey sagged with relief. "You don't mind?"

I squeezed my hands, working my fingers in rhythmic patterns along her pressure points. "Of course not. I have some unfinished business to take care of anyway."

She scrunched up her nose, perplexed. "Unfinished business?"

"Don't worry, baby. I'll tell you all about it when I get back," I promised, giving her a peck on the lips.

~ ~ ~

My eyes traveled the height of the beige triple-decker, a dwelling that once deceived me with its affordability and cheerful exterior. When I moved in months ago, it was with high hopes for a fresh start and a suitable home. But it hadn't lived up to the hype. Nope. Rather than providing a safe haven, it had only served as a place to cultivate temptation while feeding off my addictive tendencies. If I never passed through its gaudy mahogany doors again, it would be too soon.

The structure now stood tall and ominous, casting a dark shadow onto the sidewalk and over me, chilling me to the bone. A tinge of nervousness crept into my gut as I anticipated the confrontation awaiting me inside. Just as my mind started to run away with itself, I took a deep breath to settle my jitters. Refocused, I cast all negative thoughts aside, steadfast and determined to accomplish what I had set out to do. I was here for one reason and one reason only.

To get my shit and then get the hell out.

I jogged up the stairs to the third floor, my heart thumping loudly in my ears. Turning my key in the lock, the door opened to a stale apartment. I closed it quietly behind me, blinking rapidly as my eyes adjusted to the dry, stagnant air. I marched swiftly down the hall toward what used to be my bedroom. All I needed was five minutes to pack up my stuff and another five to drag my mattress out to the car and tie it to the roof. Then I'd seize the opportunity to leave this snake pit for good and never look back.

As I entered the room, my jaw dropped to the floor. Except for a few dust bunnies and a rusty cast-iron radiator, it was completely barren. I whipped my head in the direction of the closet, discovering its door wide open, now revealing nothing but a row of lonely, bare wire hangers.

All my shit was gone.

Fuming, I barreled down the hall toward Brett's room. Flinging open the door, I stopped dead in my tracks, then wished like hell I'd taken the time to knock first. The sight before me rendered me frozen, powerless to divert my bulging eyes from the two bodies moving together on the bed. Lena was underneath Brett, her platinum blond hair fanned out wildly behind her, eyes closed as she gripped his bare ass, her long, purple nails biting sharply into his peachy flesh. Her pale, vein-exposed legs were locked around his lower back. Moans escaped Brett as his movements quickened, paying absolutely no mind to the fact that I was standing there, watching. Lena's nauseating screams of ecstasy released me from my paralysis. Slamming the door behind me, the announcement of my presence stopped Brett mid-thrust.

"Where's all my shit?!" I demanded, pointlessly shielding my eyes from the pornographic display when the damage had already been done.

Lena snickered, slapping Brett on the ass before rolling out from under him, unabashedly exposing her naked body. Facing me, she leaned on her side to prop up on one elbow, providing me with an unwelcome view of her overused lady bits. "You didn't expect us to hold on to your useless shit forever, did you?" she asked, narrowing her eyes at me.

"That stuff was *mine!*" I emphasized, eyeing her with contempt. "What gives you the right—?"

"—We haven't heard a goddamned word from you in weeks, Mark," Brett interjected, leaning over the bed to fish around for his underwear on the floor. "What the hell did you expect us to do?"

"I don't have time for this, Brett. Just tell me where my stuff is," I insisted.

Brett pulled a pair of tighty-whities out from inside a pair of discarded jeans at the foot of the bed. Standing up, he pulled them on, securing his "junk" away from my bleeding eyes. "We *sold* your shit, dumbass. Consider it payback for leaving the business without our consent."

I met Brett's smug expression, entitlement oozing from his every pore. "Are you fucking kidding me?!" I roared, rushing him until I had his body pinned against the wall. "I don't need your goddamned consent to do anything!"

"Get your fucking hands off of him!" Lena screamed, leaping at me from the bed, attaching herself to my back like a monkey.

The feel of her naked breasts pressing through the thin fabric of my T-shirt made my skin crawl. I made quick work of moving her back to the bed and shaking her loose. The vision of her saggy breasts, smacking and flapping against her abdomen as she landed on the mattress, was a sight I wished could be unseen. She licked her lips, oblivious to her own repulsiveness as she slithered across the bed to retrieve a small plastic Ziploc bag from the side table drawer. Opening the bag, she stuck her hand inside, scooping up a nailful of white powder with her pinky finger. When she lifted the finger to her nose, I averted my gaze and headed for the door as a confusing combination of disgust and yearning warred within my senses.

Brett remained against the wall, supporting his overexerted body as he continued to recover from my assault. He panted and sniffed continuously, a distracting sound that broke my stride. I paused at the door, shooting an annoyed glance in his direction. Blood now trickled from his nose—the unmistakable result of his frequent cocaine use.

My eyes flitted from Brett to Lena, then back to Brett again. "You know what? You deserve each other," I said, reaching for the door.

As I turned the knob, Brett staggered toward me, wiping his nose with one hand while clutching his heaving chest with the other. "You think because you've been clean for a minute you're better than us now? Cut the shit, you self-righteous prick," he exclaimed, pushing the sand-colored, sweat-dampened hair off his forehead. "Just one hit and you'll be crawling back here on your hands and knees."

"I'm done listening to your bullshit," I informed, opening the door and passing through.

"Not so fast, sweetie" Lena goaded, hurling her small plastic bag with all its remaining contents at me. "Here's a little going away gift."

The bag deflected off my hip, landing on the hallway floor by my Chuck-Taylored feet. When the white powdery softness revealed itself through the clear plastic, I stepped back, running my hands nervously through my overgrown hair. "I don't want this shit. Take it back," I ordered.

Brett joined me in the hallway, picking up the bag and dangling it in front of me. "I saw the look in your eyes, Mark. You want this. You *need* this," he rationalized, moving in so close, the bag nearly touched my nose. "Take it…on the house."

Of its own free will, my arm shot up, waiting for my hand to make its move. Working in cahoots with one another, my fingers locked tightly around the bag's enclosure, my arm ripping it away from Brett's grasp. The self-satisfied smile with which he awarded me made my hair stand on end.

"I *own* you," he sneered. "Remember that."

Right then, I hated Brett with a passion. I hated him for preying on my weakness. I hated him for seeing right through me. I hated him for knowing I was just as much of a lowlife as he was.

But I hated myself even more.

TWENTY-SEVEN

Kelsey

RECLAIMING MY STATUS as a college student left me feeling unprepared and overwhelmed. I'd barely been back a week, but the sheer magnitude of my course load was already daunting. A month's worth of back-logged papers to write, tests to take, and concepts to master was proving to be more than I'd bargained for. It felt like I was swimming against the tide, forging full speed ahead while going nowhere fast. Add Mark's erratic behavior to the mix and I was about ready to have myself a full-blown panic attack.

Apprehension swelled in my gut as I arrived back in Quincy. As *The T* pulled into the station with a loud groan, I closed my eyes, bracing myself for whatever awaited me at home. *Would Mark even be there?* Lately, he came and went like the wind, offering no apologies or excuses for his unpredictability. I suspected he was using again, but it remained a closeted, unspoken truth. And although a confrontation was inevitable, I'd held it at bay, turning a blind eye so as not to rock the boat. I just wanted this bump to smooth out so that things could get back to normal. But it was always there, growing and casting its cloud over our relationship. It remained the proverbial elephant in the room.

Walking the few blocks from the station to my home, my anxiety level rose with every step. I stopped at the end of my driveway, eyes fixating on Mark's car for a moment before traveling a path to the charming red house that had been my sanctuary since birth. As a new, unwelcome realization hit me, I sucked in a shaky breath: what had once been my refuge, my heartbeat, my great escape…had unwittingly transformed into a constant emotional battleground.

Begrudgingly, I plodded up the pathway to my house, my feet replaced by cinderblocks of worry weighing me down. When the front door opened, my mom appeared, dressed to the nines in a tailored cream work suit, an apron tied around her waist. "You're late. I was starting to worry," she scolded softly, brows pulled together in concern.

"My ride never showed up," I bit out. Brushing past Mom into the house, I marched straight for the living room. And there he was—Mark, stretched across the sofa in the same sweatpants and T-shirt from the day before. His eyes were vacant as they watched the TV. My first instinct was to withdraw, to slip away to my bedroom until dinner was ready. A few deep breaths later, I thought better of the idea, shrugging the backpack off my shoulders to lean it against the wall.

I strode to the sofa and sat down, wedging myself between Mark's lounging feet and the armrest. "Hey," I muttered, keeping my voice even.

"Hey," he replied, tilting his head slightly in acknowledgement.

As soon as he opened his mouth, I could smell the wine on his breath. My heart took a nosedive, landing somewhere down by my feet. "I waited for you at school."

"Oh yeah?" he grunted, eyes still glued to the tube. "I must have lost track of the time. Sorry, baby."

His flippant response struck a nerve, and my heart jackhammered inside my chest. "Are you drunk?" I asked—but it was more of an accusation than a question.

He sprang to his feet to face me, finally giving in to eye contact. "Jesus, Kelsey! I had *one* drink," he defended, holding one finger in front of me for emphasis.

I stood, raising my hands in surrender. "Okay. Okay."

"You don't believe me?" he asked.

"I never said that."

"You don't have to. It's written all over your face."

Frustrated, I paced the room while Mark faced the large picture window, staring out at the rose bushes. Several minutes passed without a word spoken. Unable to take anymore, I closed the distance, sliding my arms around his waist, pressing my cheek to his back. "I believe you, Mark. I *do*," I lied, hoping to diffuse the situation.

He twisted around to stare into my eyes. As I stared back into overly dilated pupils, the reality of this moment wrung out my insides. The elephant in the room was not only alive and well, but it had just trampled my sternum. I expected Mark to continue his string of denial, maybe debate me some more, but instead, he gave me a slight nod—like he understood. He made his best effort at a smile, but it was pained, pathetic even. Leaning in, he rested his chin on the top of my head. "I love you, Kelsey." His declaration broke the silence. "No matter what happens, that will never change."

"Hey," I said, jerking back. "We're in this together. *You and me*."

"Yeah," he sighed, unconvinced.

My hand moved to his cheek, tracing it gently. "I mean it, Mark."

He took one long look at me before his eyes fell away, his hands sliding to my waist. Gently, he pushed me back. "I need to go out for a bit," he announced, releasing me to head into the hall.

I felt like a lost puppy as I followed closely behind him. "Where are you go—?" The front door closing behind Mark abruptly cut me off.

Dumbfounded, I stood there, staring at the door for several long minutes. Succumbing once again to panic, I spun around, seeking out a target. Anger soon threaded its way through the anxiety as I darted down the hall and into the kitchen—Mom's neutral zone. As expected, she was slaving away over the stove, three pots going at once. A wine bottle, overturned and empty, lay gingerly on top of the overflowing garbage pail. On the countertop sat a second one, uncorked and well on its way to securing the same fate.

"How could you let Mark drink like that?!" I practically shouted. Mom's back stiffened at the sound.

With a free hand, she cranked the burners down to a low heat, then she twisted around to face me. The other hand held a wine glass filled to the brim with merlot—her poison of choice. She brought the glass to her lips, taking a long, languorous sip before addressing me. "Mark is an adult, Kelsey. If he wants to have a drink or two, who am I to stop him?"

"He has a problem. You're just enabling him."

"Oh, so now this is *my* fault?"

"God, Mom! Will you stop making everything about *you* for one goddamned minute and listen to me?!"

"You know what? I really don't need this shit," she snapped, tearing off her apron and flinging it aside. She slid her wine glass onto the countertop, trading it for the even fuller bottle. I blocked her path as she made a beeline for the door. Nerves coated her exterior as I moved closer, invading her personal space.

"I need my *mother*," I pleaded.

"I'm right here," she answered dryly.

"No you're not," I replied bitterly. "You checked out on me months ago."

"That's ridiculous," she snorted as she tried to push by me.

Refusing to let her pass, I yanked the wine bottle from her hand, my emotions getting the better of me. "What happened to you, Mom?" At that, a tear leaked from my eye to dribble down my cheek. "You used to love me."

She stood still, her face dripping in shame. Staring at the floor, Mom just fidgeted with her hands. When she didn't answer my question, I couldn't contain my anger anymore. "You can't even look at me!" I barked, swiping my tears away. Defeated, I finally moved aside to let her pass. As she pushed her way through the kitchen door, I called out after her, "That's it. I am *done* giving a shit about you."

~ ~ ~

I pulled into my driveway at 2 AM, feeling empty, despondent. I had driven around half the night looking for him, but he was nowhere. Not at the old apartment. Not at any of the local bars. Not at the all-night greasy spoon known for its inebriated clientele. *Nowhere.*

With my heart in my throat, I schlepped into the house to stand guard in the living room by the front window. I remained there for a long while, waiting. Waiting and thinking. I should've gone after him as soon as he walked out the door. *Why didn't I?* Squeezing my eyes shut, I mentally berated myself for being so stupid.

Each time a pair of headlights came into view, I felt a glimmer of hope surge through me. But it was dashed just as quickly when each vehicle passed by without fanfare. Mark's black jalopy remained at large.

Every five minutes I dialed his number, but all attempts at communication were pointless. He had obviously turned his phone off, which further fueled my agony. Drunk, sober, or high as a kite, it didn't matter. I just wanted him back home, safe. Not knowing his whereabouts was the worst kind of torture. My chest hurt and my head was splitting from the strain.

Eventually too tired to stand up anymore, I removed my hoodie, pulled out my ponytail holder and curled up on the sofa in jeans and a T-shirt. With eyes closed, I thought back to all the weeks I spent recuperating from the coma. I had been so focused on my own set of challenges, I'd allowed Mark's problems to take a back seat. He had loved me unconditionally, sacrificing so much of himself, and all I did was take, take, take. Guilt and regret hung in the air as I tossed and turned. Slowly, I drifted off.

I don't know how long I'd been sleeping when I felt someone shaking my shoulder. I jerked up and glanced around, momentarily forgetting where I was. A beam of moonlight streamed in through the window, illuminating the face of the man I'd been waiting to see. As soon as we made eye contact, he started to cry. "I'm really sorry, baby," he gurgled.

Relief washed over me, and I lunged at him, pulling his head against my chest. "Oh, thank God you're okay!" I blurted into his overgrown hair.

Mark pulled back to scan my face. His was drenched in tears and streaks of dirt. "Please forgive me."

TWENTY-EIGHT

Mark

SURPRISING KELSEY AT school the next day was my way of extending an olive branch, an act of vulnerability that I hoped would prove my heart was still in this thing. Even a small gesture was still a first step—the first step to a path of righting all that I'd wronged. I was determined to set myself straight, to pave my way through the hunger, the craving, the *need* that had completely taken over my body and my life. Continuing to deny the ugly truth was not only stupid, but pointless. The cat was already out of the bag, ripping my life to shreds while tearing into the souls of anyone who dared to love me. My dependence had managed to claw its way up to the top of my priority list, branding itself as an absolute necessity. Kelsey had been demoted, settling in at number two. *She* knew it and *I* knew it. But my heart wanted her back at the top, sitting high on the pedestal where she had once been revered. It was her rightful place.

I really couldn't fathom how Kelsey still loved me after all that I'd put her through. Yet, she did, and I wasn't worthy of it—never really had been worthy of it to begin with. The smart thing…*the right thing* would have been to set her free before dragging her even further down into the black hole of my madness. But I couldn't let her go. I was too selfish. *And I needed her.*

Exiting my car, I launched myself in her direction the moment she appeared through the double doors of the university's Business and Finance Center. She jogged down the expansive concrete steps, at first, oblivious to my presence. When her head snapped up and our eyes connected, her lips spread into a dazzling, ear-to-ear smile that stole my breath. Dressed for the unseasonably warm weather, her denim cut-off shorts showcased her long, slender legs. Her hair was worn in a high ponytail that danced along her shoulders as she moved. Just the sight of her set my pulse racing.

With both surprise and visible relief washing over her, she barreled toward me, dropping her backpack to the ground and slinging her arms around my neck. "You came," she sighed through uneven breaths.

"I missed you—" I'd barely spoken the words when Kelsey's mouth closed over mine with a kiss so passionate, I suddenly wished we could have some private time.

Then all too soon, she tore away her lips. Softly brushing the fallen hairs from my eyes, she fixed me with a steady stare and whispered, "Thank you."

I cupped her face in my hands. "I love you."

Sliding her hands up under my T-shirt, she placed them flat on my back. A smile broke over her features. "I know. I love you too…more than anything."

The sparks her simple touch ignited traveled a path up my spine. Coiling my arms around her, I formed my own cocoon to absorb her warmth. As she melted into me, I could feel the connection between us—the depth of her feelings for me. Finally, the tension that had been curled up in both of us for so long was unwinding. I dared to think that maybe, just maybe…we were going to be okay.

The intrusive sound of Kelsey's phone jolted me out of my thoughts. She wriggled out of my embrace, bursting our happy, protective bubble. Crouching down, she dug the phone out of her backpack. "Shit! I was supposed to meet Cali five minutes ago," she said as her thumbs got busy texting.

"Oh?" I replied, trying to hide the annoyance in my voice.

"Yeah. We're meeting at Beefy Burger for a late lunch. You'll join us, won't you?"

I scratched at my chin, confused and a little put off. "Shouldn't Cali be at school?"

"She only had one class today, first thing in the morning."

"So she drove all the way here?"

"Yup. She's spending the weekend with us!" Kelsey beamed.

My face flushed with the disappointment I could no longer contain. "I wish you had told me."

Fiddling with the zipper of her backpack, Kelsey glanced at the ground then back up at me. "I *did* tell you," she mumbled. "Two days ago."

Of course she did. Only I had probably been too fucked up to notice. The realization caused a crushing pressure in my chest, amplifying the mistakes I'd made, all the ways I'd wronged her. *I was such a fool.* "Kelsey, why do you put up with me?"

"Because you're the most important person in my life." Not even a hint of hesitation before that response.

At the sight of the sincerity in her eyes, the impression of it in her words, pleasure ran all through me. I didn't deserve to hold the top spot on her priority list, but I had to admit, it felt damn good. Offering up my hand, I pulled Kelsey to her feet. "Come on. We've kept Cali waiting long enough."

~ ~ ~

By the time we arrived at Beefy Burger just a short while later, all my good vibrations had petered out, making me suddenly feel off kilter. Walking into the air-conditioned establishment offered at least some relief to my hairline which had grown slick with sweat. The earlier determination I'd been holding onto so tightly was slipping away, making me feel twitchy and agitated. And my mind was all over the place.

We settled into a corner booth, Kelsey and Cali already waist deep in animated conversation as they sat huddled across from me. Feeling very much like a third wheel, irritation flared through me. I slumped against the wall, flipping mindlessly through the song selections on the retro table-top jukebox. My reaction was childish and irrational, I knew that, and I bore no ill will toward Cali. But I just wanted Kelsey all to myself, and Cali's arrival had thrown a big wrench into plans to spend the weekend romancing my girlfriend into satiated bliss.

The waitress handed us menus and took our beverage orders. Cali blathered on about her latest frat house conquest and by the time our drinks were served, she had barely taken a breath. Still sweating profusely, I gulped down my soda, then proceeded to chew the ice cubes. Suddenly, I felt two pairs of eyes on me, my obnoxious crunching a deterrent to their ongoing conversation.

Cali cleared her throat. "I guess I've monopolized the conversation long enough. Sorry about that." Her crystal blues were probing as they assessed my current state. "So, how have *you* been, Mark?" she asked, raising her glass and tipping it back.

Feeling a full-fledged inquisition coming on, I summoned a fake smile, hoping to head her off at the pass. "Oh, you know how it is. Same shit…different day." I threw in a lighthearted chuckle to complete the joke.

"Actually, Mark, you don't look so good," Kelsey observed. She reached for my hand, but I pulled it back—I didn't want her to feel how clammy it had gotten. With widened eyes, she asked, "What's wrong? Are you sick?"

"Jesus. What's with all the damn questions?" I blurted a little louder than intended, earning a few curious stares from the customers in the next booth.

Kelsey's gaze dropped to the table, her fingers tracing along the squares of the red and white checkered tablecloth. "Nothing. I was just worried, that's all."

"Well, stop fucking worrying. I'm fine," I snapped, unable to rein in my dickish behavior.

"Okay," was all Kelsey could muster in response, her eyes never leaving the table.

Cali offered up a diversion, launching into a tirade about the injustice of the 11 PM curfew her college had recently implemented for all its dormitory residents. At that, we all tried our best to chip in and keep the conversation going, but it felt noticeably forced and uncomfortable. Finally, the waitress took our lunch orders—and that's when Cali made her move.

Rifling through her purse, Cali said, "Dammit, I forgot to put money in the parking meter!" She pulled out a handful of quarters. "Kelsey, would you mind running out real quick and plopping these in for me before I get towed?" For added effect, she batted her thickly coated lashes.

"Sure thing. I'll be right back." Grabbing the change, Kelsey slid out of the booth.

She was no sooner out the door when Cali's red-acrylic claws dug into my arm, hard. "What the hell do you think you're doing?" she pressed, glaring at me with anger and disapproval.

I let my head fall against the back of the booth. "This is none of your goddamned business, Cali." I willed myself to hold in the obscenities just dying to spill out.

She pushed up, leaning fully over the table, long hair curtaining both sides of her face, casting dark shadows along her cheekbones which accented her infuriation. "You better damn well believe it's my fucking business!" With a shove of her finger, Cali finished, "Kelsey deserves better from you!"

The combination of her finger in the face and my intensifying lightheadedness was the straw that broke the camel's back. *You think I don't fucking know that?!!"* I screamed, slamming my hands down on the table, which made Cali jerk back into her seat. "I love her!" I continued, hot tears filling my eyes. Nausea swirling through me, I clutched my stomach, leaning over until my forehead hit the table. "Just stay the fuck out of it, Cali," I mumbled into the checkered cloth.

"Look at you, Mark. You're a fucking disaster. If you really love her like you say you do, then get your shit together."

TWENTY-NINE

Kelsey

DESPITE THE SUB-ZERO air conditioning, the atmosphere at Beefy Burger had become stifling, swirling with a tension so thick we could cut it with a knife. Cali and I barely picked at our meals while Mark shoved his plate aside in protest, his body language revealing a hankering for something else entirely. Eager to put an end to our sub-par dining experience, we threw a wad of cash on the table and left the establishment with our hunger pangs still intact.

Cali and I paused on the sidewalk as she informed me of her plans to make a quick pit stop for some toiletries before heading over to my place. Mark cursed under his breath, obviously annoyed. He went to his car ahead of me, slamming the door before revving up the engine, and for a moment, I thought he might leave without me. Feeling slighted and a bit miffed, I schlepped over to the black sedan. I tried the passenger side door, half expecting it to be intentionally locked, but felt grateful when it opened. However, the relief at being "welcomed" into the car became short lived when Mark refused to acknowledge me. Blowing out a deep breath, I slid into my seat, bracing myself for a bad attitude and a hairy ride.

Mark shifted the car into drive, gunning the gas pedal and jolting us into traffic before I could finish fastening my seatbelt. He drove like a complete lunatic, impervious to my fear and our joint danger. My stomach somersaulted and I pressed my foot down hard, as if willing my own brake to materialize from the rubber floor mat. It was all I could do to keep the few morsels of beef I had ingested from making a repeat appearance. Mark veered onto the expressway, staring bleakly at the open road, gripping the steering wheel until his bones visibly jutted through the tightly drawn skin of his hands.

"Why don't I drive?" I offered softly, touching his shoulder.

"I'm fine!" he barked, taking a hand off the wheel just long enough to wipe the sweat from his brow.

But one look at him told me he was anything but fine. With the labored breaths I could see him struggling to take, I knew he was deteriorating quickly. The reality of the situation crawled through my body, eating at my insides with a parasite sickness. I remained silent for the rest of the ride home, lost in my own thoughts, trying to wrap my brain around what the hell I was supposed to do.

By the time we walked through the front door, I was one giant ball of knotted emotion. Mark caught me off-guard, pulling me into his arms until my backpack slipped off my shoulders. I ran my fingers through his dark, dampened hair, searching his face for any signs of residual strength. The twitch of his jaw and the shiftiness of his eyes confirmed my fears: he was buttering me up so he could get the hell out of Dodge.

"I'm sorry I snapped at you before," he said, with a longing look at the door.

"It's okay," I sighed.

He released me then, plotting his escape. "I need to go—"

"—*Wait*," I pleaded, sounding as urgent as I felt. Desperate for him to stay, I quickly formulated a game plan. Pulling out my wild card, I reached up, removing my ponytail holder to shake out my hair until it framed my face. My fingers slid down to make quick work of unfastening the top button to my shorts. As Mark's eyes grew wide, I knew I'd gotten his attention.

"What are you doing?" he mumbled with a slackening jaw.

Biting my bottom lip, I said, "I want you to come upstairs." At that, I skimmed my index finger along the waistband of my shorts.

Visibly torn, Mark glanced at the door, then back at me. "I really have to go."

Fuck that, I thought to myself. Unzipping my shorts, I shoved them past my hips. "Come upstairs with me," I murmured.

Zeroing in on my thighs now, Mark took a step forward. He reached out, his fingertips grazing my arm. "Why are you doing this?"

Self-conscious, yet determined to see this through, I stepped back, grabbing the hem of my T-shirt to whip it over my head and toss it onto the floor. "Don't you see, Mark? I *need* you."

He stepped forward again, but then hesitated, peering over his shoulder at the door that seemed intent on continuing its beckoning call. And I understood its pull on him: through it was the world of illusion he craved, and in that world, I held no power. But as long as I could keep him on *this* side, my influence still carried some weight.

Burying whatever modesty I had left, I reached behind me to unhook my bra. Peeling the straps down, I let the satin fabric fall to my feet. I stood utterly bare before him—exposed and completely vulnerable. "Take me upstairs, Mark," I ordered.

He tore his eyes from the door, trading one desire for another as his gaze ran the length of my body. Slowly nodding in compliance, he took my hand to lead me up the stairs.

I had won this round.

~ ~ ~

Moonlight streamed through the window and hit me square in the eye. Yawning, I reached across a chasm of empty mattress space, flicking on the bedside lamp.

Wait. Mark?

Sitting upright like a shot, I scurried to the side of the bed where I'd urgently removed and deposited Mark's clothes mere hours ago. *Nothing.* Rising fully up, I moved briskly to the window, eyes frantically scanning the pavement below. A cluster of cars sat colorfully in the driveway—Mom's blue hatchback, Cali's red jeep, and my green coupe. But a certain black sedan was noticeably absent.

Feeling used and discarded, I hugged myself in a brief gesture of forlorn comfort. With a sigh, I fetched a nightshirt from the top shelf of the closet. Padding to the bathroom, I turned on the faucet, splashing my face with cold water and a harsh dose of reality.

As I treaded down the stairs in my nightshirt, now in search of my best friend, I spotted my backpack in the front hall, lying in the same place where it had fallen, undisturbed. Mysteriously, all evidence of my earlier strip tease had vanished. I flushed scarlet at the realization that either Cali or my mom had removed it all from the scene.

Regaining my composure, I pulled my phone out of the front compartment of my backpack and punched in a text to Mark:

Where are you? Please come home.

I wondered how long it would be before he noticed it.

Tucking the phone into my shirt's front pocket, I found Cali asleep on the couch in the living room. I didn't want to disturb her, so I continued on to the kitchen to put on a pot of coffee. As the aroma encompassed the room, it blissfully awakened my dull and groggy senses. Filling up my mug, I savored that first heavenly sip, but nearly lost it when Cali appeared as if out of nowhere at the far end of the counter.

"Jesus, you scared me," I sputtered, clutching my chest at the surprise and from nearly choking on the hot liquid.

"Sorry, hon—the smell woke me up," she grinned widely. "I never could resist a good jolt of caffeine." With that, she helped herself to a mug from the cabinet.

I rolled my eyes at her but couldn't stifle my smile. "I thought you were trying to cut down on all the java?"

"I tried," she shrugged. "But I couldn't handle the withdrawals. I guess I'm too addicted." Her tone was light and playful.

Although made in jest, her comment hit a little too close to home. Setting down my mug, I braced myself against the counter as my knotted ball of emotion began to unravel. Tears burned my eyes, a sob slipping from my throat.

Cali's gaze flicked to mine, awareness of her unwitting faux pas covering her features. Grabbing a tissue from a box on the counter, she rushed to my side. "Oh, Kelsey. I'm sorry. I wasn't thinking."

As she dabbed at my dampened cheeks, I asked her the one question I knew she couldn't answer. "Where is he, Cali?"

"I don't know," Cali responded with an anger not directed at me. She tipped up my chin to look me right in the eyes. "Believe me, if I did, I would go kick his ass."

Cali's expression softened as a laugh broke through my tears. "Oh, I *bet* you would," I snickered.

Just then, a text alert echoed through the fabric of my shirt, surprising us both. Pulling the phone from my front pocket, I looked down to see a message from Mark:

crashinng at a frends.. see yoo tomorrpw,

I stared at his thumb-slurred words in horror as panic rose in my throat, threatening to choke me. That's when I realized my "wait and see" approach to Mark's addiction had been grossly ineffective. The situation was dire, and I knew I had to do something, and fast. No more woulda shoulda coulda.

Blinking back the tears, I swallowed hard, a new resolve setting itself in steel. Glancing up from my phone, I met Cali's questioning eyes. "I need your help."

THIRTY

Mark

MY EYES JERKED open, fixating on the ceiling fan above me. Slightly askew, it spun in an alternating pattern of wobble and evenness that consequentially matched the ebb and flow of my nausea-ridden stomach. When I shifted on the mattress, one of the springs sent a pistol-like shot in my back. Leaning over the side of the bed, I spewed the remnants of last night's overindulgence onto the floor.

"You better clean that up," a girl said from beside me.

I rolled over to meet a pair of hard eyes, cold and black with dilation. "Who the hell are you?" I scowled.

Laughing while flipping onto her stomach, she allowed the sheet to fall from her body. Now lounging spread-eagle over the other side of the bed, she bared her back and ass to me in shameless display. "Don't tell me you don't remember, baby," she crowed.

Shit.

I looked down at myself, horrified to discover my own nakedness. As the memories poured in, I couldn't filter through the haze—nothing seemed absolute. Suddenly up and off the bed, I searched the unfamiliar room for my jeans and T-shirt, but they were nowhere to be found. "Where the *fuck* are *my clothes?*" My voice sounded as panicked as I now felt.

"How the fuck should I know?" she spat, fingering her short, red, spiky hair. When she sat up, I could see a large python tattoo inked across her midriff. "What do you need your clothes for anyway?" A smile slowly spread across her face and her voice softened. "Come back to bed, baby."

The sound of my pet name for Kelsey, *"baby,"* from this…*person's* plumped lips made me sick. "Don't call me that. I'm not your baby. I'm not your anything."

Rising from the bed, she sauntered toward me, zeroing in on my nether regions. "Oh, believe me, you are everything and then some."

Motherfucker.

Like a punch to the gut, shame and guilt hit me swiftly and hard. I turned and staggered out of the room, trying to recall exactly where I was and how I ended up here. All I knew was that I needed to escape this place along with the nightmare from which I couldn't seem to awake.

Searching for a way out, I rounded a corner, stumbling upon a scene so repulsive I wished the floor would open up, swallow me whole, and put me out of my misery. So many bodies. All displayed in varying degrees of undress, a mess of tangled limbs and skin that I couldn't quite process. The hordes of uninhibited individuals were all strangers to me, some passed out, and some, semi-conscious—all draped over one another in an orgiastic display of gender combinations.

Moving further into the room, I stepped over used condoms and empty wrappers. Finally, I spotted my clothes in a heap by a card table scattered with white dust. As I quickly dressed, visions from the previous night's lunacy swamped my brain. I squeezed my eyes shut—a pathetic attempt to make it all disappear.

"This isn't real," I said, whirling around to take another look at the mass display of skin-on-skin. *There's no way...*

"Who ya talkin' to, baby?" The nasally voice echoing off the nicotine-stained walls sent a shudder through me. I glanced behind to where the tattooed redhead stood, now dressed in her underwear. My mind instantly registered her black push-up bra and panties, and with the realization of what I'd done, my whole world crumbled around me.

I threw my head back. "FUUUUCK!!!" I screamed.

"Oh yes, please," the girl said, biting her lip.

As I flew past her, I started to wretch, bursting through the front door of the building just in time to vomit all over the sidewalk. Glancing up from the ground, I wiped my mouth with the back of my hand, eyes landing on my car, straight ahead and parked, one wheel up on the curb. I bolted for it and got inside. The keys were still in the ignition but at least I'd been coherent enough last night to turn off the engine. My head fell to the steering wheel as I tried to focus.

Kelsey deserved better than me. I'd known that from day one. And nothing proved that more than my inexcusable behavior over the last twenty-four hours. The pain of what I'd done was too much, and I didn't know how I'd ever be able to face her. I reached into the back pocket of my jeans to pull out my phone, sliding my thumb across the lock. Tears filled my eyes as I read the text that had arrived sometime during the course of my indiscretion:

Please come home. I love you.

"What have I done?" I gurgled, slamming my forehead back down against the steering wheel in punishment. Suddenly, an impulse that had become all too familiar took over, compelling me to scour through my glove box out of desperation to extract my pain and replace it with complete numbness. When my fingers grazed the plastic, I clutched the bottle of pills, pulling it out and popping the lid without bothering to read the label. Pouring the contents into my mouth, I swallowed them whole, feeling the tablets scrape harshly along the walls of my esophagus on the way down. I tossed the empty bottle to the floor and leaned back against the head rest, waiting for the nothingness to envelop me.

Before long, my head swam with an altered perspective and a feeling of peace. I picked the phone off my lap, hitting Kelsey's number before giving myself a chance to rethink my bravery.

"Mark," she breathed. Her voice was raw. She had been crying.

The concern in her tone eradicated all hallucinatory effects of the pills, and a hard lump formed in my throat. "Kelsey," my voice cracked on her name.

"Shhh. It's okay. Please come home," she whispered hoarsely.

My eyes grew wet, the truth flying out of my mouth before I could stop it. "I fucked up, baby," I choked. "I fucked up real bad."

At the sound of Kelsey's sobs into the phone, my heart broke into a million pieces. I was speechless, disgusted with myself while I listened to her struggle to catch her breath and pull herself back together. "We can talk about it later, okay?" she panted. *"Please.* Just *come home."*

I hesitated, thinking it would probably be best if she never saw me again.

"Mark? Are you there? Mark!" she croaked.

Sighing heavily, I knew I couldn't leave it like this. "Okay. I'll be home soon." At that, I ended the call.

I pressed my fists into my eyes, dreading the devastation that was sure to follow once the truth was out—that I was an asshole and Kelsey had made an enormous mistake in loving me.

"Fuck." I said it once. I said it a million times. I couldn't take any more of this.

Shoving my hands inside my pockets, I searched frantically for something—*anything*—that would erase the pain. That's when I hit the mother lode, a plastic baggy with enough white fluff to keep me in utopia for hours. I couldn't remember where I'd gotten the stuff or who'd given it to me, but I didn't much care. Pulling out the bag with fervor, I dumped the contents onto the dashboard and went to work.

THIRTY-ONE

Kelsey

ALL THE VALUABLE players were accounted for, congregating in the living room while trading handshakes and flashing courteous smiles. Their gestures felt stiff and forced—a fruitless attempt to distract from the discomfort lurking beneath the surface. We had come together in solidarity for the sake of Mark's welfare, but apprehension seeped from our pores, converting to palpable fear as it hit the air.

Mr. and Mrs. Hudson sat across from me, fidgety and awkward and looking as though they could hardly stand to be in the same room together. A quick Google search had made tracking them down easy, but convincing them to participate in their son's intervention was another matter entirely. Fortunately, with Cali as my accomplice, her handy persuasion tactics and undeniable charm eventually wore them down. But now, as I watched them avoid eye contact with each other as well as anyone else within a ten-foot radius, I wondered if their presence would be more of a hindrance than a help.

Debra assumed her position by the large picture window, delegated to keeping a lookout for the guest of honor. Maia breezed to the center of the room and assumed an authoritative stance. Summoned to act as a moderator, her impartial and level-headed personality stood in stark contrast to the emotional minefield surrounding her. As I watched her stern expression—all business—I once again knew she would be perfect for the job.

With a quick wink in my direction, she cleared her throat loudly to command the room's attention. "Thank you all for coming," she said, flipping back her red curls. "I think it would be a good idea to lay down some ground rules before Mark gets here, so that everything runs as smoothly as possible."

Mrs. Hudson's objection was immediate as she raised a bony finger in the air. "With all due respect, young lady, I say to hell with the ground rules." She released a heavy breath, blowing a tuft of gray hair off her forehead. "I *know* my son. What he needs is some tough love, plain and simple. No more pussyfooting around like you've all been doing these past few months."

True to form, Cali sprang from her seat, temper flaring. *"Excuse* me, but where in the hell have *you* been all this time?" she demanded, getting her own finger in on the action.

"Ladies. Ladies," Maia interjected, holding her palms out in front of her. "Let's not play the blame game, okay? It's counterproductive and it certainly isn't going to get Mark clean. I think we can all agree that we have his best interests at heart."

Sitting back down, Cali seemed to register for the first time the agonized expression of a mother at the end of her rope. "You're right. I overreacted. I'm sorry."

Mrs. Hudson allowed the slightest of smiles to filter through the cracks in her stoic features. "I was out of line, too." She glanced over at her husband, who'd remained silent and appeared wary of the whole setup. "It's just that we've been dealing with this problem for nearly two years and it's gotten to the point where we've almost given up."

Unable to sit still, I pushed up from the loveseat to circle the room. I stopped directly in front of Mrs. Hudson, compelled to speak up on behalf of the one person who wasn't here to defend himself. "We *can't* give up on him," I urged. "He needs our help." Clenching my jaw, I swallowed past the lump that had formed in the back of my throat. "No matter what he's done, he deserves to have the people in his life care enough to help him through this."

"We *all* care, hon. That's why we're here," Cali uttered at my back.

I turned to address my best friend, but stopped in my tracks as I noticed Debra's abrupt change in body language. She fingered her black bob nervously, peering through the window-pane with eyes narrowed. Her gaze jerked to mine. "He's here."

The room grew so quiet, the only sound to be heard was that of my thundering heart. Approaching the window, I stood off to the side so as to remain inconspicuous. As I spotted the black sedan, my pulse raced and I struggled to draw air into my lungs. I watched in horror as Mark stumbled out of the driver's side and rounded the trunk, looking rumpled and in need of a cold shower. Wobbling across the front lawn, he tripped over his own feet as he neared the house. Making his grand entrance, he thrust the door open with such force, we all jumped in unison when it smacked against the wall. Then, we could hear him mumbling obscenities as he continued shuffling noisily around in the front hall.

I felt sick.

Paralyzed by anxiety, I remained stock-still, waiting with bated breath for Mark's entry into the room, my eyes glued to the threshold. Finally, he revealed himself, a disheveled heap of chemically altered chaos. His body swayed so severely, he had to stick out his hand to brace himself against the white-painted molding. I peered into his face, seeking the comfort of his warm brown eyes, but all I could find was an over-dilated, icy cold stare.

With great effort, I put one foot in front of the other, call-ing on my bravery to make a much-needed appearance. I wanted Mark to know that I was here for him, that I still loved him in spite of his errors in judgment. Reaching out, I touched his shoulder, but he shrugged my hand away, flipping me off in the process. His eyes burned into mine, branding me with their dead expression. I'd seen Mark under the influence on many occasions, but this time was eerily different. He had gone rigid, devoid of remorse or empathy. He was in a real bad way, the likes of which I had never seen. My fear increased tenfold, rushing over me and balling into a tight knot at the pit of my stomach.

Mark turned away from me, staggering before his waiting crowd of spectators. As he registered their faces, light slowly dawned through the fog of his obliteration. He whirled back around, locking his abysmal stare on my face. "You set me up," he spat.

"No," I murmured, hugging myself.

Maia took over, giving me a moment to regain my composure. "Mark, why don't you sit down?" she offered, gesturing toward an empty spot on the sofa. "We'd like to have a talk with you."

His face burned red hot with anger. "Fuuuck off," he sputtered.

Mr. Hudson bolted out of his seat, eyes bulging. The perspiring baldness of his misshapen head glistened in the sunlight beaming in from the window. "Apologize to her right now!" he screamed in unrestrained fury at his son.

Mark poked his father in the chest as he eyed him with disgust. "Fuuuuuuccckkkk yoooouuuuuu!" he yelled, drawing out each slurring syllable.

In an effort to rein in the emotional upheaval that had taken center stage, Maia calmly inserted herself between the father and son. "Gentlemen, please sit down so we can discuss this rationally."

Giving in to reason, Mr. Hudson backed off, his hands held up in surrender. He resumed his position on the sofa beside his wife, who dabbed at her eyes with the sleeve of her polyester shirt. Mark, on the other hand, refused to comply as he stood teetering in the same spot, fists clenched. Obviously, he wasn't about to go down without a fight.

I inhaled deeply, trying in vain to calm my escalating nerves. "We're all here because we love you," I whispered.

He looked at me for a moment before shifting his gaze to the surrounding audience. They showered him with heartfelt smiles and nods of agreement, but he wasn't buying into their brand of support. Instead, he vigorously shook his head in protest as paranoia won over reason.

"You wanna get ridda me!" he stammered. Pushing the overgrown hair out of his eyes, he probed the faces that had suddenly gone blank with despair. He grew increasingly agitated, scratching at his mottled complexion while leaving behind further traces of irritation. "You wanna send me away," he claimed, his head jerking back to mine.

My eyes filled as I heard the tinge of emotion etched deep within his words. I quickly looked away to conceal my tears. "We just want to help you."

Sensing my weakening stability, Cali piped up on my behalf. "All we're asking is that you hear us out, Mark. What happens after that is entirely up to you."

I could tell that the effects of whatever drugs he had taken were starting to wear off because he suddenly couldn't tear his eyes away from me. Some of the warmth in them had returned, but there was also that look, that desperation I had come to know all too well. "Baby," he choked.

Fighting back more tears, I tentatively approached him. "Let's sit down and talk, okay?" Finally, he allowed me to lace my fingers through his.

"We just want a few minutes of your time. That's all," Maia concurred. "Why don't you sit down and get comfortable." She gestured once again toward the sofa.

Mark paused for a moment as he seemed to consider the idea. But then, just as quickly, he withdrew his hand from mine to retreat. "I can't."

"You *can* do this! You *WILL* do this!" Mrs. Hudson hollered, squinting at him through eyelids now red and swollen with grief. She looked like she had been through the wringer. *We all did.*

"It's too late," he lamented.

"It's never too late," Debra chimed in. The look on her face spoke volumes—*she knew this from experience.*

Mark spun around to face me, but his imbalanced equilibrium sent him stumbling into the coffee table. I jumped to his side, but he refused my help. As he scrambled to right himself, I could see the levee of his inner turmoil just…break.

When he returned his gaze to mine, it was that of a ghost. Shivers ran down my spine as I watched his eyes roam over my body in an awkward perusal that left me feeling extremely vulnerable and confused.

Sitting on the edge of the coffee table, he dropped his head into his hands. "I slept with someone last night." The confession shot mindlessly out of his mouth like a bullet.

The entire room let out a collective gasp, and despite the fact that he had already alluded to the transgression over the phone, my legs still buckled in the aftermath of his words. Overwhelmed by it all, I began to bawl as my thoughts surged through a rollercoaster ride of mixed emotions.

Cali rushed to where I'd doubled over in anguish. Clutching her to me, I sobbed into her blouse. She peered over her shoulder at Mark, eyes flashing violently. "How could you?!" she snarled.

Lifting his face, a single tear slid down Mark's cheek. "I love you, Kelsey. I'll always love you. You'll never know how *sorry* I am."

Sorry.

He had spoken the word with emphasis, and my head jerked up at the sound of it. *Sorry.* It was a word he threw around too easily, one I'd come to associate with empty promises and sleepless nights. He had abused it time and time again, stripping it of all meaning. And deep down, I knew that if we continued on this path, I'd be setting myself up for even more of his heartache.

Pulling away from Cali, I swiped the wetness from my cheeks. I studied Mark's features, visibly contoured in deep-seated regret. My heart clenched with the love I had for this man, but I knew now that it wasn't enough. I squeezed my eyes shut, remembering something his mother had said. It was a call to action, a necessary means to an end. And as much as I hated to admit it, she had been right on the money.

What he needs is some tough love.

The breath I was holding escaped in bursts as I struggled to get the words out. "I can't be with you anymore. It's over."

THIRTY-TWO

Mark

PAIN. SO MUCH fucking pain. Excruciating, unrelenting, debilitating, knock-the-wind-right-out-of-you
pain. And I couldn't escape it, couldn't ignore it...
couldn't drown it in bourbon or barbiturates. That was no
longer an option.

This place, this rehab, this prison—I hated it with a mad
passion. I'd been fed to the lions, stripped of my dignity, and
robbed of my soul. Deemed "unfit for the real world," I'd become a specimen under a microscope, a lab rat poked and prod-
ded through the bars of its cage. Confined to a room the size
of a shoebox, I was guarded like a criminal—forced to share
limited, precious air with a cokehead whose incessant under-

breathed mumbling was the only sound to fill the silent void of my existence.

And then there were the group therapy sessions, where fellow junkies and I were expected to sit arm in arm in a "Kumbaya" circle, pretending to give a shit about each other's problems. But I wasn't interested in forming connections or embracing my fuckups in front of virtual strangers. Instead, I avoided their intrusive stares, cowering in corners, childlike and fearful as the in-your-face addiction counselors picked apart and analyzed my life until I felt reduced into near nothingness.

No, this wasn't the celebrity method of treatment with its posh Malibu digs and ocean view vistas. This was a state-funded, no-nonsense facility that didn't give a fuck about cheerful décor, sea breezes, or bedside manner. Stark and merciless, there was no sympathy to be found here. After two weeks spent incarcerated with the derelicts and heathens only a mother could love, I was clinging to my sanity by the skin of my teeth.

The detox portion of my treatment was a cakewalk compared to the agony I now had to suffer at the hands of my own sobriety. With a mind free of dope and a conscience full of guilt, the pain persisted unabashedly, bringing with it a steady stream of haunting memories and recurring nightmares. The ramifications of my deplorable actions leeched the life right out of me, sucking me dry while leaving me wounded and scarred—constant, fatal reminders of all I had lost.

I never fully appreciated what I'd had until it had all been taken away. Gone were my independence, my family, my friends, my pride. *Kelsey.*

I missed her.

Thoughts of her consumed every minute of every hour of every day. And although my addiction, my compulsion to self-medicate continued to gnaw at me, it paled in comparison to the overwhelming need I had to see her again. I needed it more than air.

Today, she would graduate from Bay Colony University. I longed to be there with her, to show my support, for her to know how fucking proud I was. To pull her into my arms and tell her how much I loved and missed her. To admit what a fool I'd been and that I couldn't breathe without her—God, I wanted that so damn much. But more than anything else, I wished to beg her forgiveness while searching her hazel eyes, to recognize the love they still held for me. But I feared that ship had already sailed. My well of apologies had run dry, my allotment spent. I would forever be branded a heartless prick and a hopeless cause.

Or was there still time?

I wished I could retrace my steps back to all the mistakes I'd made so I could wipe them away, creating a clear path and a fresh start. But life didn't work that way. It was near impossible to accept what I'd done—to myself, to my family…to Kelsey. Still, I was desperate to find a way to make peace with it, to latch on to the notion that it *wasn't* too late for me, that maybe I hadn't yet run out of chances. People were often given second chances, even third, fourth and fifth chances. God knows, I'd been given more chances than I probably deserved.

But maybe, just maybe, I had one left.

Pulling a semi-clean T-shirt from the heap of random clothes on my bed, I threw it over my head while shuffling past my state-appointed roommate. He suspended his psychobabble just long enough to acknowledge me with a parting nod, as if he understood what I was about to do. Stepping out of the room, I walked purposefully down the corridor.

Frantic footsteps smacked the linoleum behind me, growing louder with each passing second. I ignored them, quickening my pace as I strode toward the lobby. A pear-shaped, grandmotherly woman wearing a tight, snow-white hair bun poked her head out from behind a computer monitor. Her sharp gaze swept over me as she sprang from her chair. "Young man! Where do you think you're going?!"

"I'm outta here," I grumbled, busting through the double doors.

~ ~ ~

As I tentatively exited the cab outside my parents' dilapidated bungalow, I heaved a huge sigh of relief. In an unbelievable stroke of luck, my car was parked in the driveway, as if it had been anticipating my arrival. The fact that it hadn't been impounded or sold off to the nearest junkyard was a surprise I welcomed with open arms.

I held up a finger, alerting the driver to sit tight while I collected his cab fare. I then moved carefully, tracing a familiar path toward the front steps as my sneakers delicately pressed into the gravel beneath them. But my plan to slip into the house undetected was foiled by the squeaking of the rusty-hinged door. Cringing at the obnoxiousness of the noise, I forced myself to push ahead, maintaining a determined stride until reaching the kitchen. It was there that I spotted my car keys, dangling invitingly from a magnetic hook that clung to the refrigerator. Knowing I didn't have much time, I snatched them up while breaking into a half-sprint and booking it back out of the house.

I headed straight for my car, shoving my key into the lock and flinging the door open in a race against the clock. Leaning over the driver's seat, I opened the glove box to retrieve a small wad of cash that I'd kept stashed away for emergencies. I jogged over to the cab driver, now wearing an impatient expression as he waited for me to settle up. Once paid and on his way, I retreated back to my car, but noticed movement out of the corner of my eye. My gaze shifted, zeroing in on my mother who had emerged through the front door, her mouth dropping open.

Adrenaline coursed through my veins as I threw myself into the driver's seat. My mother stood there like a statue as I turned the key in the ignition and stuffed it out of the driveway, barreling down the street with only one destination in mind: *Bay Colony University.*

~ ~ ~

My heart tried to pound its way out of my chest as I watched the clusters of soon-to-be graduates migrate toward their designated folding chairs. *She was here…somewhere.* The seats filled quickly and before long, I was staring into a sea of burgundy caps and gowns, mentally begging my eyes not to fail me as they darted anxiously around the space. They widened as they came to rest upon a familiar veil of chestnut brown hair. The head it was attached to angled itself slightly, revealing the stunning profile of the woman who held all the answers for me. Without her, it was a struggle to simply exist. My pulse lurched and my eyes refused to budge.

I stood there staring for several long minutes and by the time I fell out of my Kelsey-induced trance, the crowd had thickened considerably. I subtly scanned the area before sinking into one of the last remaining seats along the outskirts, hunching my shoulders and trying my best to blend in.

As the ceremony got underway, my mind began to drift, replaying scenes from my most-cherished moments with Kelsey. I missed the taste of her lips, the smell of her hair, and the feel of her skin. Her smile, her voice…the way her eyes crinkled when she laughed...

I missed every bit of her.

But I was quickly sucked back into reality as I looked around at the crowd, noticing Kelsey's cheering section a few rows in front of me. Cali was beaming, obviously elated for her friend as she bounced enthusiastically in her seat. Maia and Debra sat to her left, engrossed in conversation. To her right, sat Mrs. O'Reilly, who appeared put-together, relaxed and happy. It was a look I hadn't seen on her before, and I had to admit, she wore it well.

My eyes followed the group's movements—so jubilant and animated as they all shared in the excitement of Kelsey's big day. Every flail of hands, every nod, every smile…filled me with immense pride and…*something else* I couldn't quite put my finger on.

As prestigious alumni and members of the university faculty delivered speeches designed to inspire the masses, I couldn't help but reflect on the fact that I'd let my own college education fall by the wayside. If only I'd allowed Kelsey's ambition and strong work ethic to rub off on me, even just a little, maybe I would have had the gumption to stick out the semester and actually make something of myself. But in the scheme of things, I knew that being a college dropout was the least of my problems.

The scene continued to unfold around me, and I couldn't help but bear witness to the absolute adoration shared among the graduates and their families. The immense pride. The tremendous sense of community. In that moment, I realized I was present without being a part of things, a filament lost amidst the multitude. And as I sat there, wedged between walls of achievers and happy people, I had never felt more completely and utterly alone.

Tears bit at my eyes, but I forced them back angrily, wanting only to focus my full attention on the graduates, who were finally being called up to the podium one by one. As soon as Kelsey's name thundered from the loudspeakers, my chest ached and I swore my heart stopped beating. All smiles and oozing grace, she was utterly confident as she approached the stage. She made her way down the assembly line of faculty members, shaking hands and taking in their congratulatory remarks. Turning to face the crowd, she clutched her degree proudly to her chest while absorbing all the accolades. I could see her reveling in the moment—*her* moment—waving and blowing kisses in the direction of her boisterous cheering section, whose antics had reached the point of teetering on obnoxious. I was so damn proud of her, it was all I could do to keep from rushing the stage, scooping her up in my arms and never letting go.

Then somehow, her eyes cut to where I was sitting, and she was looking...*right at me.* I held my breath, waiting for some sort of acknowledgement...a nod, a special smile, a glimmer of recognition. But she looked straight through me, as if I were a ghost. I wanted to throw up.

I watched her exit the stage, eager to rejoin her family and friends, and my nausea intensified. The pride I had just been swimming in plunged down my throat until I choked on it. I had no choice but to face the fact that Kelsey could still function...maintain her sense of purpose. She could share in the give and take of normal conversation. She could smile, laugh, receive and reciprocate affection. She had moved on without me. Two weeks was all it took. Two fucking weeks.

At least, now I knew.

My chances had run out.

EPILOGUE

Twelve months later…

Kelsey

SOMETHING INSIDE of me still screamed for him. No matter how I tried to forget, no matter how I pleaded with myself to make it stop, the separation festered in my gut like a slow burn. Letting him go was the right thing to do. I knew that. He was broken and I couldn't fix him. But I was broken too. The crack in my heart ran deep, siphoning the fear that pooled beneath it.

But all I could do was press on. What other choice did I have? Each morning, I got out of bed and simply put one foot in front of the other. I approached life second by second, minute by minute, moment by moment. That's all I could handle. Stretching myself beyond the "now" only caused my mind to become disjointed. Because as much as I couldn't envision a future *with* Mark, I could neither imagine one *without* him. And that alone carried with it, its own brand of torture.

The sudden blast of a car horn jarred me loose from my thoughts. My mood lifted marginally, and I cracked a hint of a smile despite myself. I peered out my bedroom window down at the driveway below, narrowing my eyes at the silver buggy that had come to represent a different kind of reality…something comfortable, something safe. The man behind the wheel had become my only saving grace in an otherwise meager existence. Pleasant and easy to be around, he never pressured me to think too hard or feel too much. And all he ever asked of me was a chance to spend some time in my company. I knew it wasn't love—at least, not for me…nor would it ever be. But it sure beat the alternative of spending my days folded into the fetal position, wallowing in self-pity.

He got out of his car, maneuvering around a wheelbarrow steeped in gardening mulch that had been neglected on the side of the driveway. I fussed with my hair, picking at the split ends while my eyes were drawn to his biker boots, which completely clashed with his boy-next-door image. He lifted his chin and caught me staring, acknowledging me with a double thumbs-up. He moved toward the house, and I panicked as his long strides mimicked the urgency I suddenly felt. I launched myself out of the bedroom and down the stairs, remembering that my mom was home and fearing the condition I'd find her in.

I plowed down the hall, skidding on my heels as I entered the kitchen. Mom was standing at the sink, still in her work clothes, sipping coffee. She looked clean and unrumpled, which I took as an encouraging sign. Sucking in a few deep breaths, I calmed myself as I assessed her mental faculties. The doorbell rang and she set her mug down on the counter, smiling.

"It's nice to see you in love again," she said.

I winced, not wanting to have this conversation.

"It's not like that," I replied, brushing the lint off my black chemise. "We're just friends."

She approached me then, pressing a kiss to my forehead. "Give it time, honey. He could be just what you need."

The coffee she had consumed did a poor job of masking the very distinct odor of Chablis that encased my personal space, suffocating me. I took a step back, disgusted. My blood boiled as the doorbell rang again. Sensing my irritation, Mom rolled her eyes, firing off her usual string of excuses.

"It was just two glasses, Kelsey. Am I not entitled to unwind after working like a dog all day?"

The doorbell rang again and I wanted out of the house immediately.

"Yeah. I guess so," I muttered bleakly, giving up the argument.

As I turned to leave, she grabbed my arm, gently squeezing my bicep.

"I'm perfectly fine, Kelsey. I promise. You don't need to worry about me anymore."

The desperation in her voice made me crumble. I offered her a weak smile, but deep down, I knew she was just kidding herself. She had her moments of clarity, but by and large, she was still a mess. It was becoming increasingly difficult to be around her. I loved her ridiculously, but it wasn't enough to thaw the frigid emotional temperatures that had crystalized my resentment.

Reaching across my chest, I gave her a pat on the hand as the doorbell rang again. "I gotta go, Mom."

"Sure, sweetheart. Have fun."

I jogged down the hall, feeling guilty for having kept Tracy waiting. I had my hand on the doorknob when the phone rang from back in the kitchen. An unsettling feeling washed over me like a merciless wind. I spun around, rushing back to my mom who stood bracing herself against the wall with one hand, the phone frozen in the other. The expression she wore was so distinct I could practically hear her thoughts.

I wished I could have ignored it. I didn't want to move another inch, but I couldn't stop and I didn't know why. Steeling myself for impact, I pried the phone out of Mom's hand and held it up to my ear.

"Hello?"

"Kelsey? This is Mrs. Hudson."

Those were the last words I remembered before stumbling over myself in the hollow that had suddenly enveloped me. I fell against the wall, sliding down to the floor as I tried to make sense of what had just happened. But nothing made sense anymore.

The doorbell continued to wail. *Tolling. Tolling.* As if on cue, rain pelted the window over the kitchen sink and I looked at my mom, who stood clutching her stomach like she had just been shot. My eyes fell closed as my insides eroded.

I had become a shell. Gutted. Depleted.

Emptied out.

The story continues in book two:

FILL ME IN

ABOUT THE AUTHOR

S. A. Healey (aka "Sue) is a coastal New Englander, a married mother of two, and an award-winning author of novels that typically fall into the College and New Adult contemporary romance categories. She creates compelling stories with complex characters that leave readers guessing until the very last chapter. Her books are emotional, angst-infused, heart-first dives into relationship dynamics influenced by deeper themes. Serious moments are often balanced with humor.

Her first book, *Empty Me Out (The Liquid Series Book 1)*, is an Amazon Bestseller and Summer Indie Book Awards Top Three Winner in New Adult Fiction.

When her pen is at rest, Sue enjoys an active family life and can also often be found with her feet in the sand, a Dunks in hand, her nose in a book, and a song in her head. Or…streaming the latest bingeable TV series while curled up on the sofa with her beloved dog Sammi and a pint of Ben & Jerry's New York Super Fudge Chunk.

Word-of-mouth is crucial to an author's success. If you enjoyed this story, please consider leaving a review at the site where you made your purchase and/or Goodreads and Book-Bub. It would be more than appreciated.

Sue loves connecting with readers and invites you to stay in touch with her on social media and through her biweekly newsletter. Visit **sahealey.com** for more.

ACKNOWLEDGEMENTS

First and foremost, I'd like to thank my wonderful husband, whose unwavering love, encouragement, and support has carried me through all the ups and downs along this incredible journey. Michael, I love you more than words can ever express. You are my light and my life.

Thank you to my amazing daughters—my treasures beyond measure and biggest cheerleaders. Elizabeth and Maddie, I love you so much that some days I have to pinch myself because I can't believe how lucky I am.

A ginormous thank you to my fabulous editor and cover designer, Jeannine Rochon, whose incredible talent, creativity, and sharp eye for detail have been invaluable. Jaye, thank you from the bottom of my heart for your professionalism, honesty, and friendship. I couldn't have done this without you.

I can't forget to say a very special thank you to my mom, Wanda, who has been my ultimate confidante, sounding board, and one of my most devoted readers; my dad, Robert; my brother, Bobby; and my stepmom, Susan; as well as all my family and friends for being there and inspiring me to chase my dream. I love each and every one of you to the moon and back.

And finally, another HUGE thank you to my readers for taking a chance on my stories, lifting me up, motivating me, and building my confidence as a novelist. It means the absolute world to me.